DANIELLE MARCUS

JACK GIRLZ

BLACK ODYSSEY MEDIA

WWW.BLACKODYSSEY.NET

Published by
BLACK ODYSSEY MEDIA

www.blackodyssey.net
Email: info@blackodyssey.net

Library of Congress Control Number: 2023900481

First Trade Paperback Printing: December 2023
ISBN: 978-1-957950-05-1
ISBN: 978-1-957950-06-8 (e-book)

Cover Design by Ashlee Nassar of Designs With Sass
To the extent that the image or images on the cover of this book depict a person or persons, such person or persons are merely models and are not intended to portray any character in the book.

10 9 8 7 6 5 4 3 2 1

Manufactured in the United States of America

Distributed by Kensington Publishing Corp.

Dear Reader,

I want to thank you immensely for supporting Black Odyssey Media authors, and our ongoing efforts to spotlight more minority storytellers. The scariest and most challenging task for many writers is getting the story, or characters, out of our heads and onto the page. Having admitted that, with every manuscript that Kreceda and I acquire, we believe that it took talent, discipline, and remarkable courage to construct that story, flesh out those characters, and prepare it for the world. Debut or seasoned, our authors are the real heroes and heroines in *OUR* story. And for them, we are eternally grateful.

Whether you are new to Danielle Marcus or Black Odyssey Media, we hope that you are here to stay. We also welcome your feedback and kindly ask that you leave a review. For upcoming releases, announcements, submission guidelines, etc., please be sure to visit our website at www.blackodyssey.net or scan the QR code below. We can also be found on social media using @iamblackodyssey. Until next time, take care and enjoy the journey!

Joyfully,

Shawanda Williams

Shawanda "N'Tyse" Williams
Founder/Publisher

CHAPTER ONE

"GOTDAMN, MA. WHAT'CHU doing to me?"

Loud grunts and the sound of skin slapping echoed throughout the hotel room as Angel stood in the bathroom's smudged mirror, applying a fresh coat of lipstick. She admired the short red dress that accentuated her thick curves before pulling the chrome .357 from her purse and clutching it tightly. She closed her eyes for just a second, inhaling deeply, relieving the nervous energy from her being. Tonight, she had to be on her A-game. One false move could cost her life, and just the thought had her adrenaline on a thousand.

"Like that, daddy?" Shanell, her homegirl, purred from the other side of the door as the headboard squeaked. She was giving Domo the business. Two cups past tipsy, shame was long gone.

"Just like that. Where your girl at? Tell her to hurry up." Domo growled, his breathing growing heavy.

Angel paused for a second, shaking her head. Sex wasn't in the equation for her. She had never slept with any of her victims and didn't plan on starting now.

Domo was in for a big surprise. When Shanell gave her the signal, Angel would emerge from the bathroom and relieve him of all his cash and jewels. Then the two of them would be gone like a thief in the night, hitting I-75 on their way back to Detroit, never to be heard from again.

1

Boom!

As if on cue, a loud thud, followed by a deep and shrewd scream, alerted Angel that playtime was over. She pulled the bathroom door open, brandishing the chrome .357 and pointing it at Domo's head while Shanell pointed her own metal over him.

"He put all his money and jewelry in the safe, boo," Shanell called out, pulling her naked, corn-bread-fed frame from the bed. Shanell's body was sick. She had the type of shape that would have grown women questioning their sexuality.

"What's the code to the safe?" Angel smiled innocently at the raging bull.

"Mannn, y'all can't be for real right now. Put that shit away so I can get my nut off." Domo chuckled in disbelief. He'd been in the game a long time, and his family's connection to the underworld was even deeper. Their name alone made the toughest nigga think twice about trying him. Certainly, these two females weren't the exception.

Angel's heels clinking against the hotel room floor was the only sound heard before her gun crashed into Domo's head. She cocked it, pressing the metal into his temple.

"What's the fucking code, nigga?" Angel gritted.

"I ain't telling y'all shit."

"OK, I see we gon' have to do this the hard way," she smirked, grabbing the pillow from behind Domo and putting it to his head. She pressed the metal into the pillow with her fingers on the trigger.

"Whoa, wait. Wait!" Domo's eyes grew wide with shock. "The combination is three-five-seven-two. Take all that shit but leave that chain."

Shanell ran over to the safe, unlocking it instantly as Angel kept her gun trained on Domo. Inside sat about ten thousand in cash and an unknown value in jewelry. Her face lit up in greed as she slid all his belongings into her duffle bag.

"Y'all hoes couldn't have done y'all research. I promise, this won't be going down like this," Domo fumed, nostrils flaring as he helplessly watched his belongings being taken. He attempted to sit up, but Angel cocked her pistol, squeezing tighter on the handle. Pussy had clouded his better judgment, and now, he was cursing himself for not being smarter...something his father always scolded him about.

"I wish you *would* get up. I guess you trying to have a closed casket funeral, nigga," Angel threatened.

"I swear, if y'all let me walk away, I'm going to take my last breath finding you," he threatened, causing a chill to run up Angel's spine. She held her poker face, but the threat was menacing...loud.

"I think I got everything." Shanell held up the Gucci duffle bag that she had thrown his belongings in. Her eyes scanned the hotel room for any other valuables before making her way to the door and turning to point her gun at Domo so that Angel could make her exit without being attacked.

"I'm telling y'all, leave that chain." Domo gave one last plea, eyeing the bag with all his belongings. He thought about rushing them. He thought about his gun in the drawer just a few feet away. However, he had to think about his life and his family. The wrong heat would stir up more confusion than it was worth. They were all the way out in west bubble fuck with rich white folks who would have the laws beating down that hotel room door in seconds.

Angel and Shanell ran to their rented Charger and zoomed out of the parking lot. Angel's heart raced. The adrenaline and power of taking someone's shit always got her off. Money is what excited her. It never switched up, hurt her, or left her hanging.

"That was too easy, but that nigga was big mad. We bet not ever cross his path again. I believe his fine, big-dick ass will take our heads off," Shanell chuckled, lighting a fat blunt filled with the weed she had stolen from Domo.

Angel looked over to Shanell. "Where did your cousin say she knew him from again? She bet not had of put us on nobody that's gon' come back to bite us. He was talking real saucy back there."

Shanell frowned over at Angel. "From the way. She said his people doing their thing down here in the A, they got big money, and he a trick."

"From the way, how, Shanell?"

"She used to mess with his cousin or something like that. I know you not sitting up here having a conscience now."

"No, I'm not. Something just not sitting right, though."

"Stop tripping. We good," Shanell tried assuring her.

"Anyways, on the real, Nell, you got to slow down on the pills. We need to be on our A-game." Her lips turned into a frown. "You sloppy, and you was really fucking him, moaning and shit."

Shanell smirked. "Did you see how big that nigga dick was? Besides, I don't need you schooling me. I taught you the game. I got this."

"If you say so, girl. Yo' coochie gon' fall off." Angel turned her nose up. She was growing impatient with Shanell's lack of self-control. They were playing a dangerous game, and being on point was necessary.

"No, my coochie is going to come, and it came harder knowing that after I finished, I'm sitting on a few stacks. We hit a big lick with this one. He had some nice jewels. I can't wait to get to Pooh 'nem to see how much they hitting for."

"Well, do you, boo." Angel turned up the music, taking a hard toke from the blunt and passing it back to Shanell. They were two different types of chicks. Angel was all about the money, and Shanell was...different.

The next day...

Loud music blared through the speakers of Ice nightclub as naked women slid down poles, and horny men watched in amazement. Dollar bills fell from the sky like a snow blizzard in a Michigan winter, and thick clouds of potent weed filled the air. The party was in full swing.

Angel's eyes slanted toward the VIP section, where the crowd was going nuts. One table in particular, Mello...fine, chocolate, and paid, he was *that* nigga, and he stood out amongst everyone in his circle; despite his efforts to stay low-key.

"They cutting up tonight, huh?" Shanell slurred as she leaned up against the bar next to Angel. "Passion said the one in the blue done threw five thousand, and they just got here. I'm about to hit his ass where it hurt since he want to show off."

Angel rolled her eyes. The music was so loud that she felt her chest vibrate. "Go ahead. I ain't messing with them niggas. What's up on that lick? Did Pooh get back to you about that money for the jewelry?"

Shanell frowned. "Eww, you killing my little buzz. Why you keep asking about that money? When he give it to me, you know I got you. Have I ever played you?"

"Gir—" Angel's sentence was cut short as a big, stocky man came stalking toward them.

"Where the fuck my money at?" His voice was cold and calculating. Angel's heart instantly began to race...until the angry bull walked right past her and snatched up Shanell. "Ol' pill-poppin'-ass hoe." He continued as he wrapped his meaty hands around her neck.

"Let me go!" Shanell began to claw at his hands. "Somebody get this big nigga off of me!"

"Uh-uhh. Let her go!" Angel offered, attempting to pull at his arms. The duo had gotten down on so many unsuspecting men that she couldn't recall if he was one of their victims. Then again, Shanell was always into some shit, and Angel made a mental note to start distancing herself from the girl.

Things escalated fast. The man grabbed Shanell, the bouncers were pulling him off and kicking his ass in the next instance, and the smug look on Shanell's face after it all unfolded caused Angel to shake her head.

"Dumb-ass nigga," Shanell spat, rubbing her neck. "Yeah, that's right. Get his broke ass out of here," she continued, the slur in her voice giving away just how intoxicated she actually was.

"Chill out before that nigga be waiting outside to stuff yo' ass in the car. What did you do to him?" Angel frowned.

Shanell adjusted her thong before attempting to smooth her hair down. "You know how I do. Nigga was slipping, and I got him. Now he want to act butt hurt," she snarled at the angry man as the bouncers began to throw him out of the club. "Weak-ass nigga."

"Aye, yo, let me holla at y'all right quick." It wasn't a request. It was a demand, and Angel was surprised to hear his voice. Mello wasn't the type that spoke often. He was a man of very few words.

Before either of the ladies could reply, they were whisked off to the back of the club by two strong hands and taken through a set of doors. It was forceful yet gentle, and when they finally settled, Angel's hand rested on her hip as her brow rose.

"I could have walked. Don't be grabbing on me like that," she sneered at Mello's security, then over at Mello. "I didn't have nothing to do with whatever just happened. Ol' boy walked up on a thousand and snatched her up. I just helped."

"But what did *she* do?" Mello's head tilted toward Shanell. He shook it. "I been peeped the way y'all get down. It's cool. Get money. But let this be my first and last warning. Don't bring that shit to my establishment." He frowned at Shanell. "As a matter of fact, go home. You need to lay off whatever shit you on, and you," he pointed at Angel, "pick better company."

Mello didn't wait for a response. He nodded at his security and smoothly left the room. Angel was pissed. Shanell's bullshit always found a way to wind her into the mix. She had to figure out how to get money without her.

CHAPTER TWO

A N HOUR LATER, the night was back to its regular rhythm, and Kenneth "Mello" Davis watched as his guest entered the club. He was escorted through a set of double doors, and Mello's eyes never left the silver-haired man until he disappeared. That was his cue.

Tapping his right-hand man, Rock, on the shoulder, Mello signaled for him to follow. Every other week, they met at the same spot, made their exchange, and Mello was out of the club without a second thought. Purchasing Ice was solely a business move. Clubbing just wasn't his thing. Mello had worn himself out in his early twenties. He'd partied so much that many nights went without sleep, he'd fucked too many women to count, and traveled all over the world.

Mello climbed the ranks of poverty and anguish to get to a life of luxury. He sold crack on the corners of Detroit's ghetto until he was able to sit on the throne as one of Detroit's most ambitious and calculated..."*businessmen.*" Many men respected and feared him. He'd lost soldiers and was the cause of many RIP pictures on T-shirts.

Now, at twenty-eight, Mello craved simplicity. He had done the work and was ready to sit on a yacht, smoking a cigar and enjoying the fruits of his labor. Having a wife by his side and a few shorties running around wouldn't hurt. However, he wasn't pressed for that either. It was a cold world, and he knew that putting his trust in a woman was a critical mistake. His own mother never gave a damn about him, so he knew a random woman wouldn't give two shits. They all had motives.

"When we gon' dead that nigga? I'm tired of having to look at his cocky ass." Rock grimaced, referring to the man of the hour, Commander Gerome Robinson...a dirty cop with enough connections and clout within the police force to keep Mello's "*businesses*" afloat without interference from the law. Mello never responded. He heard that complaint twice a month.

Rock continued. "I mean, for real, my nigga. Dude be in the way, and I'm tired of him squeezing our balls for paper."

Just as they reached their destination, Mello stopped, facing Rock. "Look, don't say—"

"Yeah, yeah, I know. Don't say nothing and leave my strap on my hip. You tell me that every time, my nigga," Rock scoffed, pushing the office door open and stepping in.

Rock and Mello had known each other since they were young, broke, and on the come-up in the gritty streets of Detroit's Westside. Their bond was created by the struggle, but loyalty made them brothers. It didn't take much for them to climb the food chain and blossom into get-money niggas. They were both hungry and down to grind. Once they came up, they brought their people with them, which made them well respected in the streets. Some called them an underworld mafia with the way the operation had grown. However, Mello didn't consider them that. They were just a group of niggas getting to a bag, whether it was weed, crack, cocaine, pills, businesses, or selling real estate. Wherever there was a dollar to be made, they would grab it.

A braless exotic dancer was planted on the desk in front of Robinson. She immediately sauntered out of the room when she saw Mello. Everyone knew the drill. Don't disturb them when they are conducting "business."

"Damn, you couldn't wait just ten more minutes? Mess up a wet dream," Robinson smirked, shaking his head.

Mello's face remained expressionless. "So, what was so important we had to meet tonight?" He got straight to business.

"Always serious." Robinson pointed at Mello. "We're in a club full of beautiful women, and you—"

"Fuck these hoes. Now, what's up?" Mello cut him off.

"I have a problem that's potentially *your* problem if it's not handled."

"I'm listening."

"Santiago. He's been causing a lot of confusion. He's stepping on toes and acting recklessly. Raising the attention of people we don't need in the mix."

Mello frowned. "Santiago? Dude that run CBF?"

Robinson nodded.

"And you coming to me for what? I don't deal with them. They do their thing, and I do mine. Don't I pay you to take care of shit like this?"

"No. You pay me to keep the law off your ass, and I've done a damn good job of doing that. This shit right here is personal. Don't you think I would have handled it if it was a simple fix? The fucker has receipts on me that lead to you, and him trying to bust my balls isn't good for nobody. I need more muscle to make him go away. He needs to feel us."

Mello tugged at the hair on his beard. "Us? So, what you saying is, you being a greedy motherfucker got you into some bullshit, and now, you need me and my people to start a war that we don't need to fix your mess?"

"No, we eliminate a problem, you gain more territory, and we all make more money. A win for everybody." Robinson shrugged nonchalantly.

"Here you go with yo' bullshit."

"There's an event this weekend. It will be a big trade-off, and I've convinced Santiago to have a sit-down with us. A friend of mine is catering, and we're looking for a few beautiful women to work the crowd, pass out a few drinks, or whatever." Robinson emphasized the word *whatever*. "And I do mean *whatever else* we need. I'll handle the rest."

"You tripping. You know that, right?" Mello scoffed. He wasn't the one for bullshit, and Robinson was on some straight bullshit.

Robinson shrugged, grabbing his hat and placing it back on his head. "It's all a part of the game. If it was supposed to be easy, everybody would be pushing dope. I'll contact you again soon."

Mello found himself stretched out on the satin sheets of a California king-sized bed in the comfort of his home, smoking a blunt with trap music lightly blasting in his background. Sleep never really seemed to find him in the wee hours of the morning. He used that time to meditate, think, and plan. In his world, he didn't get quiet time, so he took advantage of those treasured moments.

The conversation with Robinson was heavy on his mind. He wondered what kind of trouble the man was trying to weave him into. There was never any real beef in the streets.

Mello and Robinson crossed paths five years before on a traffic stop gone wrong. Mello was pulled over with a hundred thousand dollars in money and drugs. Instead of taking him in, the arresting officer called his commander. To Mello's surprise, jail never came. Instead, he gained a "business partner" that was proving to be beneficial...until recently.

This some straight bullshit, Mello thought as he looked over to the side and watched his company for the night's light snore. Tiffany wasn't his girl, but she wasn't a stranger either—the daughter of the infamous Graham Parker, one of the retired founders of CBF.

The City Boyz Family was a well-known gang notorious around Detroit for guns, drugs, and violence. They had been around a long time and gained the city's respect. Mello had his own relationship with certain members of the crew, and beefing with them wasn't something he was too fond of doing.

That's where the plot got intricate. Mello and CBF had ties that no one knew about. Graham was like a second father to Mello. He respected the man. He couldn't beef with Santiago without beefing with Graham.

Mello blew out another thick cloud of smoke, tossing his head back. Life had been good to him. He jumped into the game feetfirst when he was fifteen years old. He and Rock were foot soldiers. After working his way up from being a corner boy, he was now the owner of nightclubs and weed dispensaries, and he still had his hands in the streets heavy. Mello had men that moved on his command. One word, and he could have whoever he wanted touched. That kind of power was addictive...yet, tiring. The cost of staying on top wasn't worth the risk at times. He was tired of constantly having to be three steps ahead because he never knew when the jack boys were ready to get at him or the Feds were coming to bust down his door.

"Dang, that weed loud." Tiffany's groggy voice interrupted his thoughts. "I must ain't do my job right. Why are you still up?" Her petite, thick frame curled beside him as her hand slid across his chest. "I like waking up with you next to me," she added with a smile.

"Oh yeah?" That was all that Mello offered. He wanted to tell her not to get used to it. After he got what he needed out of her, he'd be sending her on her way and getting his day started. He didn't have room in his life for a girlfriend...well, at least not for Tiffany. Outside of good sex and occasional company, they had nothing in common. He would never be able to offer her what she truly wanted...all of him. Mello was married to the streets, and they would always come first.

"Yeah. Don't it feel good to you too?" Tiffany cooed.

His onyx gaze traveled over to her and landed on the hand on his chest. "Watching my businesses grow feels good to me. Getting that call that the bag is ready feels good to me."

Tiffany's hand instantly stopped caressing his chest. Her lips formed a pout. "Why is it always about money, Mello? When are you going to get serious? I'm over thirty, I don't have any kids, and I want to get married one day. You know I'm not going to play this game forever," she told him matter-of-factly.

"I never stopped you from going out and getting your happily ever after. You're a beautiful girl. You deserve all that." Mello shrugged, taking another puff from his blunt.

"Asshole." Tiffany blew out a breath of air, rolling her eyes. She pulled the covers from around her waist, exposing the dips and curves of her chocolate frame. Mello would never deny that she was blessed with a body carved straight from the heavens above. She just wasn't his heaven to indulge in beyond occasional late-night bouts in the sheets.

"I'm going home. I can't deal with you today," she continued to rant. It bruised her pride that Mello just sat there. She wanted him to tell her to stay or that he was joking. She wanted him just to show some type of damned emotion.

He didn't, and he wouldn't. Things worked out perfectly. He no longer had to ask her to leave.

CHAPTER THREE

SOPHIE'S CHEEKS FLUSHED with embarrassment as she watched the salesclerk swipe her card for the fourth time with a sympathetic expression plastered on her lemon-tinted face. Declined. No matter how often the lady slid the credit card through the machine, the results remained the same. Her husband had turned off her card, which he often did when he wanted to flex his power. She was a stay-at-home mom with no source of income. He was the provider, and she had nothing without him.

The argument the night before caused Sophie's nostrils to flare as irritation surged through her being. Ricardo Sr. was so toxic. He got caught cheating, and now *she* had to suffer for it. The day she met Ricardo Morgan was the worst day of her life, and quite frankly, if she could go back, she would have left his ass at the liquor store where she met him.

Sorry mothafucka, Sophie muttered to herself, pushing the bush of curls atop her head from out of her face. "You know what? Never mind. I must have grabbed the wrong card," she shot, reaching out for the clerk to return it.

"Are you sure? I can—"

"I said never mind!" Sophie cut the lady off, snatching her card and marching out of Sak's with her heels clinking against the marble floor. "Come on, Ricky Jr. Stop walking so damned slow," she muttered, dragging their five-year-old by his tiny yellow hand.

14

"But I can't walk that fast, Momma. Slow down," he whined, to no avail.

Sophie couldn't wait to get to her car and curse Ricardo out. He was the one that didn't want her to work. He was the one that promised that all her needs would be taken care of. Nowhere in their agreement did it state that he could take away that promise whenever he got mad at her.

Ricardo Morgan was a corner boy hustler-turned-rapper. Ever since his name started to create a buzz around Detroit, his arrogance multiplied, and his ego was the worst. Sophie knew their marriage was going to shit, and she cursed herself for signing a prenup. The thought of starting over in the run-down Eastside housing project caused a rumble in the pit of her chest. She hated him. She fucking hated Ricardo.

As soon as her seat belt clicked, her freshly manicured nails were pounding on her cell phone, dialing her husband. It only took two rings for the baritone of his voice to greet her.

"What's up, Fe-Fe? I'm in a meeting," he answered, annoyed.

"Why would you turn off my card, Ricky? You knew I would pick up some clothes for Jr., and you allowed me to play myself in front of all them white folks."

"You right. You played yourself. You the one wanted to be on bullshit last night, Ms. I-Spy Private Eye. You don't need my ends since you think you can check some shit."

"*Your* ends?" Sophie squeaked. "I was buying clothes for your fucking son," she yelled, smacking the steering wheel. "You know what? You're right. I got it. Goodbye, Ricardo."

Sophie hung up the phone before he could respond. Arguing with him only stroked his ego. It was like he got his rocks off by belittling her.

"Momma, I'm hungry," Ricardo Jr. whined, reminding her that her heartbeat was sitting behind her. A pang of guilt hit her, realizing how she had carried things for the past fifteen minutes. She never lost her cool in front of her son. Jr. was her prized possession, and she loved him with everything in her.

Releasing a flustered breath of air, Sophie forced a smile. "OK, whatever you want to eat, we'll get it."

"It's okay, Momma. You don't have no money. I'll ask my daddy for pizza when I get home."

That cut. "Momma does have money, and if you want pizza, pizza is what we're getting." She tried her best to keep the smile on her face as she texted her best friend Angel to Cash App her forty dollars until later. When her phone vibrated with a notification from Cash App, Sophie let out a sigh of relief, making a left onto Coolidge Highway and heading to Pizza Hut, Jr.'s favorite.

She also sent an emergency girls' night text to their group chat.

Sophie, Diamond, and Angel were like three peas in a pod. Diamond and Angel were the closest things to a sister she had. Blood couldn't make them closer.

"I swear, I never liked that nigga from the day you brought his fat ass to the crib." Angel frowned as she sipped from her glass of red wine. When Sophie texted that she needed her girls, Diamond and Angel dropped everything and went to Sophie's for wine and girl talk.

Sophie rolled her eyes. "He wasn't that bad at first." She looked around at the expensive décor of their Bloomfield Hills home.

"Not that bad, Sophie?" Diamond cut in. "So, you're going to act like he didn't make our asses walk from downtown because I didn't want to talk to his ugly-ass friend?"

They all burst into laughter because that was a night for the books. They didn't have twenty dollars to their name between the three of them. They made it back home off a prayer and a freaky old man that Angel flashed her titties to for thirty dollars.

"Oh my goodness. I forgot about that. I bet that old man still be having wet dreams thinking about Angel's crazy ass. I still can't believe you did that," Sophie giggled.

"I had to take one for the team. There wasn't no way I was walking back to Seven Mile all the way from downtown," Angel shot. "And speaking of taking one for the team, y'all heffas need to loosen up and come out with me. Y'all turning into some boring, old bitties."

"Uh-uh. Nope. Not going to happen." Diamond shook her head, knowing her girl. "Whatever nigga you trying to rob is not about to be coming for *my* head."

"Really, bitch? When have I ever involved y'all in something like that?"

Diamond's head twisted to the side in disbelief. "Oh, I see both of you heffas got amnesia tonight. Black Ty? Does *that* name sound familiar?" Diamond clapped as she spoke to get her point across.

"Oop," Sophie covered her mouth to keep from bursting out with laughter. The trio had created crazy memories, but that was the glue that held them together. No matter how bad times got, they had one another's backs. "Oh my goodness. I really needed this tonight. Ricardo has me about to lose my top," Sophie groaned.

She felt trapped. She didn't have a life outside of Ricardo. He snatched her out of the hood at twenty, got her pregnant by twenty-one, and married her before the baby was born. She was so vulnerable when they met. It was a welcomed distraction from heartache, loss, and disappointment.

"That's why we need a girl's night! I can't do Shanell's extra ass. I need my day ones. Plus, y'all know I keep the niggas with money around me, and they don't mind spending."

"So, that's what type of shit you be on when you with your girls, huh?" Ricardo's deep raspy voice startled everyone. He leaned against the wall, staring at the girls with those low-set eyes. No one heard him walk through the door or ease his way into the den.

Sophie immediately set her drink on the table and hopped up. "I didn't hear you come in." She nervously tucked her hair behind her ear. "I thought you was staying out late tonight." She sauntered over to him, feeling like a kid caught with her hand in the cookie jar.

"Where my son at?"

"He's upstairs, asleep." Sophie went in to kiss his cheek, but he moved his face away, causing her to catch the air. She frowned in disbelief, watching as he left her standing there looking stupid in front of her girls.

"I am so sorry, boo. I did not hear him walk into the house. The floors should have creaked or something with his fat ass," Angel whispered.

Diamond swatted at her, stifling a giggle. "Will you shut up?"

Ricardo wasn't really fat. He just wasn't small, either. He was a solid two-hundred-and-sixty pounds, with a bald head and a thick beard. No one could deny his swag or the fact that he knew how to get to a bag.

"Give me a second, y'all," Sophie sighed, disappearing to find her husband. She peeked into every room until she found him pulling off his shirt in the guest bedroom.

"Why are you in here? So, you're mad now?" Her arms folded across her chest. He ignored her, continuing to undress. "You don't hear me talking to you, Ricardo? You really mad at me after what *you* did earlier?"

Ricardo kicked the Sak's bags on the floor by his foot before pulling the covers back and sliding into the bed. She hadn't even noticed them, and knowing Ricky, he purchased everything she had left behind and an extra gift for her. Just like a master manipulator, he wanted to play with her emotions. She wasn't his personal yo-yo. The mind games were going to drive her up a fucking wall.

"Why I got to come home to those bitches in my house, Fe? I don't want them around my son, and if you want to go out with them bopping-ass sluts, you can get outta my crib right with 'em."

"*Your* crib? So now you trying to put me and your son out?"

"Nah, my son good. You can take your ass on with your rat-ass friends and be around all the niggas with money you want."

"Let me get this right. So, you can be out here in all these hoes' face, making me look stupid. Yet, just the *thought* of me doing you like you do me is a problem?"

"This my shit. You don't like it? Leave."

"Your shit this and your shit that. You're just going to make it known that poor-ass Sophie ain't got nothing without her husband, huh?"

Ricardo smirked, pissing her off more. "You said that not me. Now gon' with your bullshit before you wake my son. And get them outta my house." The finality in his voice let her know that the conversation was over, and quite frankly, Sophie was exhausted.

CHAPTER FOUR

"SHIT, MANNY. WHAT'CHU trying to do to me?" Diamond hissed as her long, coffin-shaped nails sank into his shoulders. The nigga slurped on her pussy like it would be his last meal, driving her crazy.

Diamond allowed her hips to grind until it stirred up a dizzying rumble between her thighs. She tried pushing his head away, but he wasn't having that. Manny wanted to be rewarded with the sweet nectar of her juices, and only then would his job be done.

The two had been creeping on the low for an entire year. They weren't together, but at the same time, neither of them were fucking with anyone else. It just sort of worked out like that. They both had busy lifestyles and weren't trying to deal with the hassle of commitment.

Just when Diamond thought she couldn't take anymore, Manny flipped her over, placing his hand on her stomach to give her an arch, and slid into her wet, warm mound from the back. He gave her slow, hard strokes, winding his hips like a pro. Diamond swore his dick came straight from the devil himself. She had never been fucked so good in her life...even worse, every single time he hit, it got better and better.

By the time they passed out in a euphoric high, it was well into the wee hours of the morning. Diamond couldn't get enough of the man. She pretended to be heartless. She wished she could just climb into his skin with him. However, she was well seasoned in the game of men, which left a scar on her heart. She didn't trust too many with it. It was entirely too fragile.

She knew a nigga would look you dead in the face, confessing his love, only to be fucking your mother. Diamond had too much going on in her life to deal with that, like the mortgage company for her salon on her neck for the last few months' rent or her car payment that was past due.

Her eyes remained open as she listened to Manny's light snores. The back of her hand tenderly slid down his face. He was beautiful and had his shit together in a major way. Maybe in a different lifetime, they would be soul mates.

Diamond's phone buzzed, snapping her out of her thoughts. It was just after nine o'clock in the morning, and she knew exactly who was calling. The bill collectors were getting more savage by the day.

"Damn, you got a hotline going on. Tell that nigga you busy and to call you after twelve," Manny groaned, groggily burying his head into Diamond's chest.

She sucked her teeth. "Ain't no niggas calling my phone. I'm not a thot like you."

"Here you go. You ain't never had an issue with another broad with me, so don't even try it, my baby. Don't think I don't be peeping you ducking and dodging calls."

"Let me find out you clocking me," Diamond teased, playing with his soft, curly hair.

"Oh, for sure. Watching yo' thick ass like a hawk, nigga. That's *my* pussy," Manny shot, causing Diamond's heart to flutter. She loved when he talked like that.

She giggled. "Ol' stalking-ass nigga."

"And you love it. So shut up," Manny shot, reluctantly pulling himself from the comfort of her warm body to get dressed.

Diamond studied his tall frame as he slid on his jeans and pulled his white tee over his head. Her bottom lip poked out, and she didn't even realize it. She loved to see him coming and hated it when it was time for him to leave.

"I got to make a few runs today, but I'll be back later. You can stay here if you want until I get back. If not, lock the door." They were at Manny's spare condo. That was their relaxation spot when they didn't want to be bothered. It was ducked off, and he claimed no one knew about it.

"I have runs to make too. I might come back later. I don't know. I don't want you to get too addicted to all this goodness."

"Yeah, whatever. That's you. Kissing niggas' foreheads and rubbing faces while they sleep," Manny called her out, causing her to throw a pillow at him and shriek in embarrassment.

"Shut up, nigga. I can't stand you."

"Yes, you can. You love me," he told her matter-of-factly, pausing for a second as if he was thinking. "And I love you too," he added, catching Diamond completely off guard.

Her heart nearly jumped out of her chest. He had never said that to her. The smile that crept on her face was uncontrollable. She was too stubborn to tell him that she loved him too. However, no words were needed. They both knew what was up.

Manny reached into his jeans pockets, pulling out a fat knot and peeling off ten crisp hundred-dollar bills. "Here, go do whatever you be doing. Them feet getting rough. Almost cut my legs. Had to do a throat check on yo' ass, make sure I wasn't fucking a nigga," he teased.

Diamond's mouth hung open in shock and amusement. It had been a minute since her last pedicure, but her feet were still pretty. She burst into uncontrollable laughter. "You always coming for me when I ain't sent for yo' monkey ass."

"It's all love. Go get yourself something nice." He held the bills out, and Diamond just looked at them.

"I told you to stop giving me money, Manny. I'm good."

"You ain't got to be tough all the time. I fuck with you harder than you think, ma. Go pay your car note before we have to handle the repo man." With that, he placed the money on the dresser, kissed her on the forehead, grabbed his keys, and left the room.

Diamond didn't know how to feel. She was so tired of struggling.

Diamond was never the spiritual type, but she found herself praying her way out of many dark spaces lately. Life wasn't supposed to be so hard. Why her? God had her seriously side-eyeing him. He was pushing her to the limit, and she was nearly ready to fold.

She blew out a haughty breath of air as the automated system read off her bank balance. She had just deposited money, so she couldn't understand how it was already in the negative.

Dammit, she forgot she had withdrawals for her cell phone, the lights and gas, and car insurance coming out. They all hit at once. It was like the bills never stopped.

"I'm about ready to rob a damn bank." She rolled her eyes, walking into her salon. Immediately, she fixed her face, straightened her shoulders, and put on the smile that was supposed to cover her pain.

The Beauty Bar was Diamond's pride and joy. She watched her mother put blood, sweat, and tears into bringing it to life and was right by her side, helping to hold it together until her mother took her last breath. Now, the shop was the only memory she had left of the woman...her mother, her best friend, her sister, her confidante. Damn, she missed that crazy lady.

"Whew, chile, if it ain't Ms. Superstar," Brittany, one of the stylists, sang. "You look cute today, boo. Where you coming from?"

Diamond playfully rolled her eyes. "Dang, with your nosy ass. Can I get in the door good? Hello, Brittany. Hi, Mika. Hello to you too, Sharita." She greeted the other stylists.

"Oh, I was going to speak. But we still want to know where you coming from, all glowing and stuff," Brittany retorted.

Diamond and her staff were like family. Her mother hired them when she opened the salon, and they had been riding with Diamond, helping her get through her mother's death, the lights getting cut off in the salon, to now.

"For your information, I was with my little friend," Diamond gushed.

"Your friend, huh? Your friend who? The fine one or that ugly, old nigga?" Brittany smirked.

Diamond's skin instantly began to crawl. She knew exactly who the old man Brittany was referring to was. "Don't play with me, heffa."

Brittany burst into laughter. "I'm just saying. Either he your daddy, or you fucking him. He came up in here the other day looking for you. I meant to tell you that."

Diamond shuddered inwardly at the thought. "Let's not talk about him. Y'all heffas gon' stop with the jokes." She picked up the mail from the counter, going through it.

"Well, I wasn't going to say nothing, but you family. Be careful with that other nigga too. Me and my homegirl saw him out at the mall the other day with some broad. My homegirl knows the chick. That nigga married as hell." Mika's lip twisted as she leaned back in her seat.

A sharp sensation beat at the bottom of Diamond's belly as her heart sank. She blinked twice before plastering on a smile. "That's not my problem either. He's not my nigga. But anyways, let me get my books together." Diamond made a beeline for the back of the salon. She needed to get to her office and fast. She felt as if she would suffocate. Manny was married? She hoped it was a lie.

CHAPTER FIVE

IT WAS DAMN near two o'clock in the morning, and the club was about to let out. The strip club was at its full capacity, and the vibe was hype. Angel had just built up enough nerve to slip the first half of the pill into the man's drink, and they were waiting for it to take effect. Her feet were on fire, and she was two seconds from slapping one of his little flunkies. His entourage was making it next to impossible to get close to him. Luckily, Shanell had no problem laying it on thick...with her drunk ass.

Angel frowned as she watched their victim stick his hand under Shanell's dress. He was playing with her pussy in the middle of the club with no shame. She blew out an annoyed breath of air, tapping Shanell's shoulder.

"Yo, wrap this up before I say fuck it," Angel whispered.

Shanell giggled. "Chill, boo. Stop being so uptight. You got his pit bull looking at us funny." Shanell rolled her eyes, turning back to the man. She leaned in, whispering in his ear. "You trying to go back to the room with me and my homegirl? We ain't leaving Ohio without no dick."

His eyes lit up like fireworks on the Fourth of July. "Oh yeah. Me and my mans got plenty dick. What's up?"

Shanell shook her head, placing her hand on top of his. She pulled it from under her dress, guiding his finger to his lips to taste her sweetness. "Taste good, right?"

26

He smirked. "Yo, you wild," he slurred, running his hand over his face.

"I'm saying, we ain't feeling yo' homeboys. You the fucking boss. We see you shining. Fuck them. We trying to get some top-notch boss dick, and if you really got it like I think you do...it's whatever." Her voice was low and sultry as she began to suck on his neck.

"Damn, you got me on brick, ma. Come on. Tell yo' homegirl we out." He staggered but straightened before grabbing his duffle bag full of cash. Shanell made sure that he didn't waste a single dollar on any of those strip hoes. They would be secure in her pocket when the night was over.

"Yo, Nitty, where you going?" his homeboy frowned. He was the quiet one. Angel had been studying him the entire night. He made her feel queasy because there was no mistaking the fact that he was the shooter.

"We about to get the night popping. I'll holla at y'all tomorrow," Nitty shot as Angel and Shanell stood by his side.

"Nah, you shit-faced. We ain't about to do that. Get up with these hoes another night."

Nitty frowned, feeling himself. He was the boss and wasn't above showing off his power. "Since when you bark orders, nigga? I'm out." With that, he allowed the ladies to hook their arms around his and walked off like the king of motherfucking Ohio. The baddest bitches in the club were leaving with him.

"Shit, is he dead?" Angel frowned, poking at the man passed out in the bed, naked as the day he was born. She checked his pulse and was relieved to find one.

"That nigga good. I didn't give him that much. Forget him. Where he put that bag he came in here with? He had to have at least fifteen thousand in it," Shanell shot.

"It's over there. I saw him put it in the nightstand," Angel whispered, tiptoeing to the other side of the room. She was trying her damnedest not to make a sound as Shanell searched for his duffle bag.

"Bitch, I don't see it. His slick ass must have put it up when we went to the bathroom," Shanell shot back, wincing in pain as her pinky toe connected with the nightstand "Shit," she grumbled.

"Well, keep looking. It got to be in here. I'm not going home empty-handed." Angel frowned, lifting his jeans and relieving them of the thick knot of bills. She calculated at least five thousand dollars. However, she needed a bigger payout for the risk they were taking. After the split with Shanell, walking away with only twenty-five hundred dollars wasn't it.

"Where his car keys at? We can check the car on our way out. I got his jewelry, and you got the money from his pants. We need to be leaving, Shanell."

Shanell wanted to protest, but Angel was right. She took one last look at the man on the bed and shook her head, thankful that he had passed out before things got ugly.

"Come on. I swear, this nigga jewelry better be real. Yo' licks been real suspect lately." Angel grimaced, pulling the hotel room door open—only to frantically leap backward, seeing the big, burly man hovering over the door.

"I told this nigga y'all hoes wasn't shit." He frowned. Before Angel could react, she felt his meaty hands wrap around her hair, yanking her head back and pulling her into the room. Her scalp was on fire, and her heart was racing.

"Ahhh," she shrieked, trying her damnedest to get free. But her little hits weren't fazing him.

"Chill the fuck out before I body yo' scheming ass," he boomed, tossing her to the ground and settling his dark eyes on Shanell. "Y'all hoes got two seconds to run my nigga's shit."

"I don't have nothing of his. We came to fuck, and he passed out, so we're out." Shanell shrugged, keeping calm. She didn't know if he was packing, and her purse with her Glock inside was on the other side of the room.

"Stop lying," the man roared, sending a backhand to her cheek that echoed throughout the room, giving her whiplash. Shanell fell to the ground. "Now, we gon' be in this bitch until y'all give up the money and whatever else y'all thieving asses took," he added as his friend began to stir on the bed. He was coming to, and Angel knew she needed to get the situation under control. There was no way they would be able to handle two angry niggas.

She reached into the pockets of her jeans, reluctantly pulling out the knot she had lifted. "All we got is the little money he gave us to fuck." She looked at Shanell, giving her the eye. "Where is your cut at? You put it in your purse, right?"

Shanell immediately caught on. She nodded almost too eagerly. All she had to do was get to her purse with the pistol. "Yeah, but he gave that to us. Fuck that. We earned that money fair and square." She played along.

Angel sucked her teeth. "Girl, if you don't give this nigga that little money. I knew these motherfuckas were on some bullshit. That's why I don't mess around." Angel was praying that their game was working. She watched as Shanell stomped toward her purse, pretending to be upset...only to cringe in horror when the big, burly man slammed his fist into Shanell's face. The sound of knuckles and bones colliding was horrific. It was like all hell broke loose in the blink of an eye.

He was beating Shanell mercilessly, and Angel used that as her cue to get to their protection before he killed the poor girl.

Grabbing the Glock, she threw the purse on the floor and cocked the gun.

"Let her the fuck go," Angel boomed, hands steady. She had been in too many tight situations to panic. She continued once she was sure the man understood how close to death he was. "Now, what we're about to do is leave, and you better pray my girl don't want to kill your punk ass for what you just did. Are you good, Nelly?"

"Hell nah. Oh my goodness. I know he fucked up my face," Shanell cried, taking her foot and kicking him in the balls as hard as she could. She hoped she'd kicked a nut sack off. He immediately doubled over in pain. "Bitch-ass nigga," she shot, hawking and spitting on him. "*Now* we can go," she stated, snatching her purse from the floor, along with Angel's from the table.

The two nearly ran to the parking lot and sped off, adrenaline on ten. This part of the game wasn't pretty, but they both knew what they were getting into. That's why no discussion was needed on the three-hour drive back to Detroit. They'd get rid of the jewelry, split the money down the middle, and pray that the next lick held no complications.

Angel looked at the stacks of twenties and fifties lying on her bed and couldn't help the burst of excitement that flowed through her. "*Fuck it up. Fuck it up. Ayeeee,*" she cooed, swaying her body to the beat as a mixture of tequila and Nicki Minaj had her turned up.

The events of the night before were the least of her worries. What she thought was a measly couple of thousand-dollar lick turned out to be a twenty thousand-dollar lick. The watch, chain, and pinky ring they had lifted were authentic and expensive. Her poor victim was going to be in his feelings about that loss. Too bad he would never see Mariah from Atlanta again...at least, that's who he *thought* she was.

Diamond stared at her best friend with amusement. "What the hell you so happy for? You must have got some dick last night," she teased.

Angel frowned. "Girl, bye. Dick don't make me this happy." She pulled out the banded cash, doing a little twerk. "*Bandz a make her dance, ayyyeeee!*"

"Damn, girl. Where did you get that from this time?"

Angel shrugged. "Some nigga in Ohio."

"Did he give you that cut on the side of your head too?" Diamond questioned.

"Don't start, Diamond. I'm here, I'm paid, and that's all that matters. Now, have you decided if you dangling with me this weekend? My homegirl only deal with big bosses."

"But what's the catch? I really don't want to be caught up in no bullshit."

"How many times are you going to say that? I would never bring no smoke to your door. You're my sister, Diamond, and that's what you never have to question," Angel explained.

"I know. I just worry sometimes. After all the scheming you've done, you're not concerned about somebody recognizing you one day and doing something to you? Niggas don't play about their money. It's a cold world out here."

"And that's why I'm an even colder bitch. I struggled and got abused enough growing up, Dicie. We both did. I'm proud of you for what you're trying to do. But when are you going to stop fronting?"

"Fronting?"

"Yes, fronting. I saw the letter from the mortgage company. And let's not forget how you listed me as a reference when you signed for that Benz. They call me every time you late on a payment.

Hell, even Sophie. Why she gotta deal with a nigga who feels the need to dangle the carrot in her face and jerk it away every time he gets mad? We deserve more, and my name ain't Angel Monroe if I don't get it for us. Y'all heffas will fall in line one day."

"If you say so."

Angel smiled, picking up a stack of fifties. She tossed it at Diamond and continued to shake her ass. "Go buy something cute. Tomorrow is about to be a movie. Watch."

CHAPTER SIX

MELLO PACED THE floor of the old warehouse with his arms folded over his chest, then lifting one, stroking his beard. He took his time before speaking, knowing he had to choose his words wisely. His team had fucked up, and now they would have to suffer a major loss due to a narcotics sting orchestrated by the chief of police. Robinson had warned him that the heat was coming. Yet, he did not mention the sting, and now, Mello was out of a million dollars in cocaine and cash.

A grimace formed on his face as he stared at the commander who was among the thirteen men he called to the meeting. What was the purpose of him being on payroll if he couldn't safeguard shit like that?

Mello allowed the silence to linger for a few seconds more for effect. No one knew where his head was, and he preferred it that way. He looked into every single eye that was in the room. For the most part, he considered his team solid. He just needed them to understand that mistakes like the one the night before weren't acceptable.

"So, let me get this straight—four men on lookout. Six men in the warehouse and a whole police commander on the team, and no one saw them mothafuckas coming? Better yet, how in the fuck did they know to hit the warehouse *exactly* when the shipment came in? Make that make sense to me." Mello stopped pacing.

Dressed to the nines in a Brunello Cucinelli custom-tailored suit, complete with a pair of Dolce & Gabbana shoes, he looked as if he belonged on Wall Street somewhere and definitely not in the dirty warehouse, overseeing one of the most prominent underworld operations in the city of Detroit.

Bando, his lieutenant in charge of the warehouse operations, spoke up first. "Everyone was on their job, G. Them niggas snuck us. I don't thin—"

Pow!

The sound of Mello's hammer was deafening. The bullet that flashed from its barrel silenced the man instantly...and permanently. His body fell to the floor with a loud plop. The smell of fear was thick in the air. Any one of them could be next.

"I don't pay none of you motherfuckers to think!" Mello shouted, pointing his pistol at Commander Robinson. "You better handle this shit before *your* body be the next one slumped." He stared at the old man, making sure that his point was understood. "Pull all my paper from the streets. Make sure everyone pay up, then shut it down until we figure out what's going on. Meeting over. Get the fuck outta my face." The coldness in his tone chilled the room. He had just taken the life of a man on his team from the beginning. Bando had eaten at the table with his family. One bullet made it clear that no one was safe.

Mello headed toward the exit. Both Commander Robinson and Rock followed. Robinson tapped him on the shoulder once they reached Mello's black Maserati. He was a ball of nerves.

"Jesus Christ, Mello. Did you really have to blow his fucking brains out? You just caught a body in front of thirteen men at a time when it's uncertain who will stay down or who will fold. Then, Santiago is talking about putting the pressure on, and you're making it worse."

"Yeah, my nigga," Rock agreed. "Bando, though? He was part of our come-up, bro. I ain't never questioning you, but I am looking kind of sideways." Rock shook his head as the summer breeze kissed their skin.

Mello waved them off. "That nigga was supposed to been murked. I just prolonged it 'til the right time. His thieving ass just made himself an example to everyone. Let them niggas know to tighten up."

"You one crazy mafucka," Rock chuckled. "I'm out, G. I'll keep my ears to the streets to see what's up."

Mello nodded, slapping fives with Rock. Then he focused on Robinson. "I done gave you too much paper, and now it's time for you to put that shit to work. Make that nigga Santiago disappear like yesterday."

"I keep telling you, it's not that easy. First things first. Did you invite the girls for this weekend? We need girls that are down...if you know what I mean."

"Down for what? You still ain't told me shit."

Robinson smiled, rubbing his hands together. "Turns out we got the upper hand. I think the CBF boys over there on Mack are working with someone at the office that greenlighted that raid."

Mello's brow raised in confusion. "What? Them niggas don't move weight. They move guns."

"Exactly. But I heard Santiago is trying to cross over. A little birdy told me that this weekend will have all the key players there and a nice shipment of product for sale. Guns and dope."

"I'm still lost."

"We hit Santiago back where it hurts and let him know that we're on to his bullshit while making a big payoff in the process. I have a buyer for the guns; you take the drugs. You get your money back from the raid; I get my cut from the guns. That's where the girls come in. Pussy has power, and they'll never suspect their drinks to be spiked, nor will they know what hit them. We'll be long gone before they realize what happened," Robinson explained his plan as if it were genius.

"So basically, you want us to start a war? We do that, then what? Get the fuck out of here," Mello chuckled as his tall frame dropped into the driver's seat.

Robinson held on to the door to keep him from closing it. "Hear me out. It's going to work. Didn't you just take a million-dollar loss? You just be there with your crew and some beautiful ladies."

Mello didn't know what Robinson was trying to get him into, and quite frankly, he didn't care as long as their problem was resolved. He thought of Angel. She was slick and smooth with it. He'd watched her get down on countless men since she started working at the club. He knew that she was perfect for whatever Robinson was trying to pull. No real attachments, she didn't know shit about him, and she wasn't green. He made a mental note to make a trip to the club, talk to her, invite her to dinner, and make a proposal.

Mello found himself at his bar as if the earlier events never happened. A mother had lost her son, a child had lost its father, and Mello was carrying on as if he wasn't the cause of the grief to follow. The club was jam-packed as he studied Angel. She was up to her usual tricks...using her smile to milk the pockets of his guests.

Her curves were on full display, and her innocent, caramel face was beautiful. There was no mistaking what had men smitten. However, Mello would never take her seriously. Trust was big with him. How could he ever trust a woman that was a professional manipulator?

Mello let out a small laugh as Rock tapped his shoulder. "I see you peeping her. That's not the move, bro. Her and her homegirl be on some bullshit. You see what happened the other night."

Mello pulled on the hairs of his beard. "Yeah, they do. But she smooth with it. That other broad be the one on bullshit."

"So, if you pull her in, you don't think she gon' let her friend get down too?"

"It ain't up to her. I ain't fucking with that pill-popping broad."

Mello slid out of the booth he and his crew were chilling in. He found his way to the bar. Angel had just put in an order for drinks and was joking with the bartender.

"I'm gon' have to start charging yo' ass," he whispered, leaning against the bar beside her, facing the crowd.

Angel's attention shot over to Mello, shocked that he had approached her. She smiled, planting her hands on her hips. "Charging me for what?"

"Game recognize game." Mello pulled out his cell phone. "As a matter of fact, put your number in here." Angel didn't ask any questions. Mello was the lick of all licks, and she excitedly did as she was told, punching in her phone number and saving it.

Mello pushed off the bar. "All right, li'l momma. I'll be hollering at you. Answer that phone." He didn't even give her a chance to respond before walking away. No response was needed. Mello knew she'd be waiting like a sick puppy for that phone to ring.

CHAPTER SEVEN

"**I**'M GON' KILL this nigga!" Sophie screamed as a set of fresh tears slid down her cheeks and kissed the corners of her mouth. She couldn't believe that he had the audacity to be parading another bitch around the city as if he weren't married with a whole family. "You that fuckin' bold, huh? You couldn't even get a pretty bitch. You want to fuck around with rats," she continued, scrolling through the girl's Instagram feed.

Apparently, Ricardo had a side bitch, and she didn't know her place. She felt it was necessary to post him online. How the hell was Sophie getting played by a nigga she didn't even want at first?

It nearly killed Sophie to admit that the chocolate, short-haired woman was actually pretty. She had spunk...and confidence. Sophie studied the girl down to the cute dimple on her left cheek. It was safe to say that Ricardo had a type.

Sophie's chest tightened the more she investigated. A part of her wondered what it was about the chick that intrigued Ricardo. Her insecurities were at an all-time high.

Jealousy began to tickle her belly and make its way into a ball of nerves as she continued to study the girl's page. She and Ricardo had been on trips out of town, he had just purchased her the same Benz that he copped Sophie, and even worse, he'd bought the girl a salon.

"No, this motherfucker ain't out here buying whole businesses for hoes, and I have to beg for a dollar!" That was like a sucker punch to the gut. More tears fell from her eyes as she continued to torture herself.

"What's wrong, Mommy?" Ricky Jr.'s voice snapped her out of her trance, causing Sophie to look up at her son through tear-stained eyes. "Are you okay?" he added, trotting into the room and climbing beside her in the bed.

Sophie put down her phone, tried to wipe the pain away, and forced a smile. However, Ricardo had inflicted a hurt that was almost impossible to brush off. It cut deep. When was enough going to be enough? Sophie was so tired of the constant chaos.

"You know Auntie Donna?" Jr. asked, staring at Sophie's phone screen.

"Auntie Donna?" Sophie shrieked. "That's *not* your damned auntie." She said it with so much venom that Jr. cringed a bit. Sophie knew she had to get herself in check. "I'm sorry, baby. I didn't mean to yell. How do you know Donna?"

"Daddy. We be going over to her house sometimes. She give me ice cream." Jr.'s voice was just above a whisper. It was almost as if he didn't want to say it.

"Well, Grandma has ice cream too. How about you get dressed to spend the night with her?" Sophie wasn't in any shape to play mommy. She also knew that it would be World War III if Ricardo walked through the door. She planned to fuck up some shit.

Jr. excitedly shot out of the room, leaving Sophie to sulk in misery. Not only was her husband cheating, but he was investing in the ho and bringing their son around her. It was bad enough that he had her out there looking stupid, but to drag their son into it? That was downright disrespectful. Sophie felt as if she would throw up as her fingers slammed against her cell screen, dialing

Ricardo for the fifth time. Her heart fluttered when he finally answered.

"Why you blowing my phone up, Sophie? If I ain't answer, obviously, I'm busy." He had the nerve to be agitated. Sophie couldn't believe the audacity.

"So, you got our son around your hoes now? You're buying salons for these bitches, yet I have to ask you for money to buy our son clothes at the store? *This* how you playing it?"

Ricardo sucked his teeth. "Man, Fe. Get off my line with that bullshit." He hung up. The ugly motherfucker actually had the nerve to hang up on her. She wondered when the roles had reversed and how their relationship spiraled so far out of control. There was a time when Ricardo would hang off her every word. He worshipped the ground she walked on.

Frustrated, Sophie swung her arm, knocking everything off the dresser. "I was loyal to your bitch ass, and *this* how you do me? You was lucky to have a broad like me. Niggas get a little radio play, and now, they want to act brand new? I got your ass, nigga." She went off in a rant, marching to the closet and grabbing her suitcase. Tears fell, and spit flew as she packed her bags while cursing Ricardo out at the same time. She didn't know where she was going or what she would do without Ricky. All Sophie knew was that she had to get the fuck away before she ended up in jail.

"I feel so fucking dead inside." Sophie's eyes trailed off as she rocked back and forth. The bags under her lids revealed evidence of the tears she shed over her failed relationship. The money wasn't even worth it anymore. She was done, and it ripped at her soul and scared her shitless.

Sophie sat at her mother's house until she couldn't stare at the walls any longer. When Angel called for her to meet at the bar, she eagerly welcomed the distraction. She played with the rim of her Pink Lady drink, contemplating her next move. She was dead broke with a son and had no means of getting money. Sophie knew she wouldn't last long without Ricardo, and there was no way she would give him the satisfaction of crawling back and begging. Fuck that.

"So, what are you going to do, friend?" Angel asked.

"I don't know. I can't stay with my mom. She will drive me up a fucking wall with all that preaching. I don't need to hear the I-told-you-so's."

"You know Diamond and I got that spare bedroom. You can always come stay with us." Angel shrugged, smiling at one of her regulars who held a hand up for her to come to him. "Hold that thought. Let me see what this nigga want."

Sophie watched Angel seductively saunter over to the table across from the bar. Her smile was so fake, but the man instantly began to pull bills from his pocket, handing them over to Angel. The wheels in Sophie's head were spinning. She could do it. Working at the bar didn't seem too bad until she figured out her next move.

Ricardo would lose his top. It didn't matter if she was shaking her ass or not. He didn't like her being around no other nigga. Sophie rolled her eyes. "Fuck his weak ass," she muttered, tossing back her drink.

Seconds later, Angel returned to the bar with a big alley-cat grin. "Ol' boy said what you sipping on? Drinks on him tonight. He got you."

Sophie's head whipped around, and the man held his glass up with a wink. He was cute, and it caused Sophie to blush. She had forgotten how good it felt to get a little attention outside of Ricardo.

"I don't know that nigga." Sophie smiled.

"So?" Angel smirked deviously. "He said what you sippin' on. Order some steak bites while you at it. You can't drink liquor without food on your stomach." She held a finger up. "I got one better. Go talk to the nigga. BJ got money. We can hit his pockets tonight. He shit-faced out of his mind."

"I'm not robbing nobody," Sophie whispered, looking around like she would get in trouble.

"Girl, shut up." Angel rolled her eyes, pouring two drinks. "And follow me. Let me show you how to work a crowd."

Sophie did as she was told, following Angel's lead. After her third drink, she had thrown caution to the wind. She had nothing else to lose and everything to gain.

CHAPTER EIGHT

"**W**HY THE FUCK you avoiding me, D?" Manny boomed into the phone as soon as she picked up. It had been three whole days since she talked to him, and as much as she missed his company, she wasn't in a rush to hear his lies.

Married? Diamond wasn't the type to mess with another woman's man. She was too selfish to share.

"Because I'm just trying to figure out how your wife would feel if she knew you was fucking me every other night and trying to be my whole man." Her voice was sarcastic yet calm. She didn't scream and cut up like she wanted to.

"My wife? What you talking about? Who been in your ear?"

Diamond rolled her eyes. "That don't even matter. Are you married, Emmanuel? And if you are, don't you think that's something you should have told me before you started sticking your dick in me?"

"Mannnn," Manny blew out a breath of air. "Look, people need to stay out of other folks' business. Me and that girl been separated for two years. I don't fuck with her, and she don't fuck with me," he tried explaining.

"Separated? Nigga, you got a whole wife! That shit is so bold. Goodbye, Emmanuel. I'm not dealing with this shit right now." Diamond ended the call just as she pulled into the salon's parking lot.

She sucked in a deep breath of air, hopping out of her car to get her day started. As if that wasn't bad enough, the white piece of paper attached to the salon's door squeezed her lungs and twisted. "Lord, whatever trick you trying to play on me, I surrender. Because look, I don't know how much more I can take."

Diamond snatched the white piece of paper off the door, rolling her eyes. She knew she was behind on rent, but they didn't have to let the whole world know that she had a court date for nonpayment. "I'm going to get y'all the money," she grumbled, walking into her shop and flicking on the lights. Luckily, none of the other stylists had made it in yet. The last thing she wanted them to know was that she couldn't afford to pay her bills.

Tossing the paper onto her desk in the back office, Sophie plopped down into the swivel chair, pulling out the money Angel had given her. She began to count it. There was a total of two thousand dollars. She owed the mortgage company five thousand and still needed to buy an outfit for the night. She had already used the money Manny gave her to catch up on her car note.

Tapping her nails against the desk, she debated her next move. Letting the salon go wasn't an option. Diamond's mother was one of the coldest stylists in the city of Detroit. She was a hustler too. Cynthia could turn a dollar into fifteen hundred. That was the problem. She spoiled Diamond so that she wouldn't know what struggle felt like. But in reality, when those men gunned Cynthia down, she left behind a sheltered child who didn't know the first about independence.

Growing frustrated, Diamond pushed from the chair, making her way to the front of the salon. She stopped dead in her tracks when the door chimed, and Carlos walked in.

Carlos...her mother's ex-pimp. Yes, Cynthia was fortunate enough to break away from the ho lifestyle and create a life for herself after setting Carlos up to go to jail. But that one mistake had cost her life and brought Diamond chaos too.

"Ms. Diamond," Carlos greeted her with that slimy grin. He still rocked a slicked-back ponytail that was beginning to thin and an out-of-date suit. You could tell that he was a handsome man in his prime. However, the years weren't kind to him. Drugs, jail, and life had aged him horribly.

"What do you want, Carlos? I paid you for the month already," she sighed.

"Yeah? Well, it wasn't enough. You know, ya momma owed me a lot of money before she died. I see you reaping the benefits of my money." He looked around the salon. "I don't want to keep hearing excuses. I need that money back with interest. That dead bitch still got to pay."

Diamond's chest began to thump with pure hatred. Her mother's death was still a sore spot. Although she had no proof, Diamond felt in the depths of her soul that Carlos had something to do with it. However, she knew the man was off his rocker. She watched some of the most horrid things he had done to his whores over the years. He believed in instilling fear through violence; somehow, that fear trickled down to Diamond.

"Don't talk like that about my mother," Diamond stated just above a whisper.

"Fuck that bitch. I need some paper."

Diamond shook her head. "I don't have any money. I'm barely keeping the mortgage on the shop and my rent paid."

"That's not my problem." Carlos shrugged as he started toward the back office.

Diamond immediately began to panic. She had left her money on the desk, and if Carlos saw it, he was taking it. She couldn't let that happen. It was every penny she had to her name.

Diamond backed up, attempting to block his path. "Uh-uh, where are you going? You can't just walk around my shit like that."

With one swift motion, Carlos gave Diamond a hard shove, sending her flying into the wall before crashing to the ground. She wailed as her ankle gave out on the way down.

"Carlos! Carlos, no!" she screamed after him, cursing herself for not putting up her money.

When Carlos emerged from the back room with her bills in his hands, Diamond's heart dropped. "Carlos, please don't take my money. I need that."

"I need it too," he muttered.

Diamond felt so helpless. She wouldn't allow the tears to fall from her eyes, but she was dying on the inside. "How much longer are you going to do this to me? Give me an amount. Tell me how much I need to pay for you to stay the fuck away from me."

Carlos showcased that grimy grin again. "Fifty thousand. Come up with fifty thousand, and I'll leave you alone and let that bitch's soul rest in peace," he told her cynically.

"Fifty thousand?! I don't have that type of money! What about all the money I already gave you? I'm not the one that owed you."

"You asked for a number, and I told you. Figure it out, or I'll see you every fucking month until I don't feel like it anymore." He took in Diamond's frame hungrily, causing her to cringe. "You lucky my dick don't work."

The echo of his laughter followed him out the door. Diamond couldn't help the tears streaming down her face or the violent shake in her hands. She had to figure out how to get the money and quickly.

CHAPTER NINE

ANGEL'S BROWS FURROWED as her heels clinked against the restaurant's marble floors. She adjusted her dress to cover more of her cleavage as she approached the table that seated one man too many. She wondered if she had mistaken Mello's dinner invite for more than what it was.

What's he doing here? Angel tried to hide her disdain as she greeted Mello and Robinson. Mello barely even acknowledged her. No hug, no smile, and after a quick nod, his attention was back on his cell phone.

"Wow, you didn't have to get all dressed up for me. You shouldn't have," Robinson shot, causing Angel to roll her eyes.

"I didn't," she retorted, focusing on Mello. He was always so calm, so kept, so...unexplainable. She didn't like that about him, not knowing where he was coming from or where to take him. "So, let's be clear. I was under the impression that this was a date. Clearly, it's not, and before you niggas come at me wrong, I don't sell pussy. I don't take my clothes off and shake my ass for any reason."

Mello respected that. "Since we clearing the air, no offense, li'l momma, but this will never be that. You a tough one, but you ain't my style. I got business on the floor, and I know you about your paper. So, let's discuss business."

Angel's lips twisted. She didn't know if she should be offended or feel honored that he saw fit to offer her a proposition. However,

47

she didn't have time to process her emotions. Mello spoke the magic words. At the end of the day, money made her come. That was all a nigga would ever be to her...a dollar sign.

"What kind of business?" she asked after placing her order.

"The type that can put seventy-five grand in your pockets if it's done right," Robinson smirked, knowing the dollar signs were ringing in her head like the slot machines in a casino.

Angel's lids turned into slits. That was a lot of money, and she knew they weren't giving it up for nothing. However, seventy-five thousand dollars was the big score she was scheming for. So, hell yeah, she was down for whatever.

"Yeah," Mello added. "But we need to be able to trust you, and you need to trust whatever homegirls you bring with you. And I ain't talking about that fiend-out broad you be hanging with. Shit go wrong, bodies might hit the ground, and before I take an L, I'll get rid of all the witnesses, feel me?" Mello's gaze was calm, but his warning was clear and deadly. "If you feel like you and yo' people can't fill the shoes, it's cool. We can forget this conversation ever happene—"

Angel's chest beat with greed. "You must ain't know, but I'm through with it. I got other friends. You still not saying what you need from me."

"We gon' need y'all to look good, talk good, and slip a little extra in the drinks of who we give y'all the go for."

Seventy-five thousand to slip a couple of pills in drinks? That was a lot of money for something so simple. Angel knew there had to be a catch. She met eyes with Mello, who remained stone-faced.

"So, what's the word? You think you and your homegirls down? It's not like you'll come by that much money on a regular day. That's a big payoff for you to barely get your hands dirty."

Angel bit her bottom lip, contemplating. Her head cocked to the side. "You want me to drug some niggas and ain't no telling who else. Not only that, but you also want me to involve my girls? I'm not putting their lives at risk like that." She shook her head, going through mental warfare. Greed had the palms of her hands itching. She was desperate. Hell, Sophie and Diamond were desperate too. They needed this come-up. "Besides, if you're offering to pay seventy-five, y'all must be about to come up on millions. Let me see. After giving my people their cut, that's only me walking away with a twenty-five thousand." She cut off a piece of the prime rib she had been nibbling on and stuffed it into her mouth, chewing daintily. "Nope. No deal. If shit goes bad, I'm not risking my freedom or my sisters' lives."

Robinson smirked. "You work at a strip club. You serve drinks for pennies. Twenty-five thousand is a lot of money for a girl like you," he reasoned, focusing on Mello. "She don't seem like she's with the program. Do we need to find someone more grateful?"

Mello stared straight ahead. His posture was perfect, and his jawline distinct. "She thinking. Maybe it's a good thing li'l mama ain't no dummy. That party starts in a couple of hours. Hit her off with a few more ends, and let's get this paper. I got shit to do."

"Fine," Robinson grumbled. "Two hundred thousand. I can't go any higher. Plus, it will come from your cut, Mello."

Angel smiled. "You got yourself a deal. Nice doing business with you, fellas. I'll see you boys later."

Mello smirked. "Leave ol' girl at the crib. I ain't fucking with her."

Angel pushed her way from the table. She didn't know exactly how to take what Mello and Robinson were offering. On the one hand, the money was calling her. She knew that it would help her and her girls in different ways. They all had their problems.

Sophie was practically homeless. She'd been sleeping in Angel and Diamond's spare room for the past few days. Then there was Diamond...Something was going on with her. But she was so private and had so much pride that there wasn't no telling what was up. Angel knew that no matter how much Diamond tried to play it off, her girl was broke. This lick tonight was the come-up that they all needed.

"Where you at, heffa? It's money in here tonight, and I need my bitch!" Shanell squeaked with heavy noise in her background.

"Something came up. I'll tell you about it tomorrow. What the fuck you doing back to work so soon? You supposed to be resting and healing."

Shanell smacked her lips. "I'm as healed as I'm going to get. You know my situation. I had to get back to this bag."

"Yeah, I feel you." Angel's voice trailed off as she watched Diamond enter the bedroom. "Look, I'll hit you back, cow. Break 'em down tonight. Sorry I couldn't be there to get to it with you," she added before hanging up and frowning at Diamond.

"Sooooo, that's the bullshit you came up with?" Angel's nose scrunched as she took in the Fashion Nova special that her girl had on. There was no denying that Diamond was gorgeous. Her face was the prettiest almond. Her curves weren't build-a-body thick, but they stood out in all the right places. For an average day, she looked cute. However, Angel wasn't looking for cute. She needed her girls to be on sexy, bad-bitch status. Only bad bitches would pull off tonight's assignment.

Diamond turned toward the mirror, taking herself in. No, she wasn't dressed to the nines like Angel and Sophie, but she thought she looked good. They were just going to the club. Diamond really wasn't interested in trying to impress anyone. She had too much of her own shit to worry about.

She shrugged. "I look good. Forget what you talking about, Ms. Extra as Fuck."

"Yeah, you are cute...for an Applebee's date with a regular nigga," Angel agreed. "But we're not going there. We're about to be in the company of men in an entirely different league. We serving drinks and illusions. Any and everybody is going to be there, from politicians to the king of the streets. So we need to be on point."

Sophie frowned. "Bitch, I thought you said we was just going to a party."

"We are. But just a slight change in plans. My homeboy want us to be the bottle girls for this big event, and I promise, it's going to be popping. We all got to be on point if y'all expect to make fifty thousand," Angel stated matter-of-factly, rummaging through her closet for the Fendi dress and shoes she purchased for Diamond to change into after her last lick in Miami.

"Fifty thousand?!" both Sophie and Diamond shrieked in unison.

"Yep," Angel confirmed, popping the *p*. "Fifty thousand."

Sophie finished smearing on a coat of red lipstick, focusing on Angel. "So, you're telling me these niggas giving up almost twenty grand apiece just to chill with them for the night? What's the catch?"

"No. That's fifty thousand *apiece* for you *and* Diamond and a hundred for me with my finder's fee. So, are you heffas down or what?"

"Hell yeah, I'm down," Sophie beamed. "I can put some on a house for me and my baby and have a little pocket change until I find a job. Plus, I don't have to go do something strange to Ricardo's sorry ass. A bitch was two seconds from doing it too."

"That's what I'm talking about, Fe Fe, because that's what we *not* gon' do. What about you? Are you down, Dicie?"

Diamond shrugged. "I don't know. Ain't nobody giving that type of money for free. What do we have to do?"

"Does it matter? You're two seconds from getting your mother's shit snatched, and Lord forbid the repo man find you. Are you trying to get this money or not?"

"Wow, tell me how you *really* feel."

Angel blew out a breath of air. "I didn't mean it like that. All I'm saying is that we all can use the money, and I would never put either of you in a bad situation to get it. I love y'all heffas. So, are you down or what?" Angel gave her the puppy dog face.

Diamond cracked a smile. "Fine, then, heffa. Don't you ever come for me like that even though my broke ass does need the money. And just so you know, I'm not fucking nobody, and I don't want to hurt anyone."

"Girl, hush and put on this dress. I got y'all," Angel smiled.

Nothing in the world made her come harder than when she had money in her pockets with a whole lot of it to blow. She was feeling like Queen Latifah because she would set it the fuck off, however, and whenever. It helped that she finally had her girls on board with her...people she really trusted.

CHAPTER TEN

MELLO WASN'T EXACTLY considered the "life of the party." He was more the type that sat back and observed. However, there was no doubt that his presence could be felt wherever he stepped foot. Opting for a relaxed yet sophisticated look for the night, he decided on a pair of Armani slacks, a button-up with the top two buttons undone and the sleeves rolled up, and he completed the look with a fresh cut, his nine, smooth chocolate skin, and a Rolex that was low-key but screamed at the same time.

He had no idea what to expect from the night. There were never any major issues with Robinson. But Mello was smart enough to know that the sun wouldn't always shine. The game was constantly changing, and so were the players. Gone were the original gangsters that got money and stayed low-key. The new wave of get-money niggas was young, loud, dumb, and unpredictable...even worse, it seemed as if snitching was the new cool. Not only was he dodging the police, but he also had to dodge those types of niggas too.

So he had prepared for the rainy days. His eyes cut over to the safe where he kept his most prized possessions. A passport, a driver's license, and a bank card that had access to over five million dollars...in another man's name. If shit ever hit the fan, D'Anthony Jamison would be in the wind, and Kenneth "Mello" Davis would be a thing of the past.

"Nigga, you dressed like one of them niggas off *Men in Black*. Fuck you think you is? James St. Patrick?" Rock chuckled as he leaned into the room, taking a hard toke from his blunt filled with moonrock weed. He kept it simple with his attire. If shit hit the fan, he was ready for whatever.

"Here you go." Mello shook his head. "And you look like you about to go shoot dice and smoke a pound of weed on the corner. What I tell you, Rock?"

Rock waved off Mello as he continued to puff his weed. "I'm not about to put on my Sunday best for nobody. Besides, what we got to get all *GQ* for to hit a lick? You trust Robinson? Nigga been moving funny lately. I ain't feeling boy."

"You've been my right hand since the sandbox. You should know that I don't trust nobody. I deal accordingly."

"Damn, so now you don't trust *me*, nigga?"

"You ain't just anybody. You're my brother," Mello countered.

"You damn right. It's always us and never them," Rock confirmed.

It was true. Life had bonded them to loyalty. Their friendship went far past getting money. Mello had been the only person in Rock's corner since he could remember. His struggle was Mello's struggle, and vice versa.

Mello's lips curved into a frown. "Nigga, you sound like you want to be my bitch. Let me find out."

"Let you find out what? You got me fucked up."

Mello burst into laughter. "It's always us. Never them." He mocked Rock as they began to slapbox. It was all fun and games, though. Mello knew exactly what Rock meant, and the feeling was mutual.

"Fuck you, nigga."

"Nah, for real." Mello straightened up. "Robinson a sneaky nigga, but he can't fuck us without fucking himself. I put it on my soul. I'll splatter his brains."

Rock pointed at Mello. "My point exactly. We know too much about that crooked nigga. He might be ready to take us out or double-cross us or some shit. If it go bad tonight, we beefin' with CBF *and* the law."

"You scared?" Mello asked with a raised brow, amused.

"Never that. It ain't about being scared. You know I bust them thangs. It's about being smart. And furthermore, why you got that ho from the club in this shit? Why you ain't call Jess and her homegirls? You don't know nothing 'bout 'em. I'll body a bitch."

"That's exactly why I didn't call Jess. She know every fucking thing. She a liability. Angel don't know nothing about us. Plus, Jess ain't got the look. She cool to fuck on, but Jess don't turn heads."

"Yeah, you got a point there. Li'l mama fine as fuck, and her slick ass be getting down on these thirsty niggas. RJ and Durk be coming off a grip in that club." Rock paused, cocking his head to the side as if he was thinking. "You know what? Fuck it. Just so you know, I'm popping her. You can have her homegirls. I bet they bad too."

Mello waved off Rock. "Pussy is the last thing on my mind, especially from a broad like that. Birds of a feather, my nigga. My shit exclusive."

"Here you go." Rock shook his head. "Well, hurry up, exclusive-ass nigga. The crew should be pulling up in a few. RJ and Durk coming in with us, and the rest gon' be posted outside. You know if anything go down, they trained to go."

"No doubt. I wouldn't have it no other way."

CHAPTER ELEVEN

A NGEL AND HER crew stepped into the doors of the plush three-story mansion as if they owned the place. The trio had set everything on the table and left no crumbs. You couldn't tell them they weren't those girls. Pulling her cell phone from her Prada clutch, she scanned her messages for the text from Mello. He instructed her to meet him by the pool when she arrived.

The atmosphere was relaxed. Jazz flowed from the speakers, small chatter hummed through the room, and the smell of cigars lingered just a bit over a cinnamon-apple scent. Angel knew that she would not have even sniffed the same air as the attendees under different circumstances. Not that she was beneath anyone. There were just levels to the game.

She surveyed the crowd, and an instant smile danced across her face. Shanell would have been on the money like a bloodhound. Her girl knew *exactly* what to do to work a crowd.

Settling her gaze on the bar, Angel guided the girls over for a drink. Hips swayed and smooth, silky skin in various flavors mesmerized the room. Of course, they weren't the only women in attendance. However, they were the sexiest...and still the classiest. Thirst oozed from the competition in their next-to-nothing attire, all drooling for a chance to be chosen.

"This is nice." Sophie took a minute to assess her surroundings.

"It is," Diamond agreed, adjusting the straps to her dress. "Don't you have to let your people know we here? I'm ready to get this over with and get back home." Fifty thousand dollars kept running through her mind. One night was going to get Carlos off her back and give her a little breathing room. That alone was reason enough not to be nervous. She'd drop the little pill in every cup in the room if that's what needed to happen.

"We will. Let me get adjusted first," Angel shot, waving for the bartender to come over to her. She ordered apple martinis for the girls and a shot of Patrón straight up for herself. She needed something a little stronger. "You see how these niggas coming? Room smell like money. Niggas looking like walking licks. Got my pussy wet." She began to fan herself. It didn't take much to find Mello and his crew standing by the pool, talking. He stared intensely in their direction, and Angel winked before turning back to face her girls.

"So, where is this nigga that you been talking about?" Diamond squinted as she took in a well-groomed mahogany man with broad shoulders and thick, curly hair. "Is that Duane Kemp? Don't he play for the Pistons?"

"Yes, that's Duane. Mello is standing over there by the pool, though. Look at his big fine ass. I think he gay or something because the nigga sure don't like pussy."

"Damn. Girl, he *is* fine," Diamond agreed.

"Is he gay or—" Sophie paused midsentence. "Kenny? Please tell me you are not talking about Kenneth's ugly ass." Her heart began to race with feelings she thought were buried long ago. The last time she set eyes on him, he crushed her heart into a million pieces. Kenneth Davis was her forbidden fruit...the tie to her soul that wouldn't let go. Even after marriage and a kid, the nigga still had a grip on her emotions...a piece of her heart. At that very moment, the realization made her stomach queasy.

"Kenny who?" Angel frowned. "No, I'm talking about Mello, the dark skin one wearing the button-up."

Sophie ran her hand over her face, letting out an exasperated sigh. "Ughhhh, I'm *not* doing this. That's not no damn Mello. His name is Kenneth Davis, and I'm not playing with him tonight." She pushed off the bar. She didn't want to breathe the same air as him.

"I know you not about to pass on this money because you mad at some random nigga." Angel stood in front of Sophie, blocking her path. "You committed, Sophie. We can't do this without you."

Sophie shook her head. "He's not no random. It was that bad between us."

"If that nigga didn't kill you or shoot a baby in your momma, nothing is bad enough. Last time I checked, you and Natalie was still alive and kicking with no extra kids." Angel frowned, swallowing the twinge of hurt that admitting her truth caused.

"Yeah, Soph, we're here now," Diamond concurred.

"So, throw that damn drink back, loosen up, and let's get this money so you can get that house for your son. Remember, ain't no going back to Ricky. We bad bitches, and we do what we gotta do. Fuck these niggas."

Sophie lifted her glass and sipped from her martini. Her eyes settled on Mello, and she nearly jumped out of her skin when she found his intense gaze on her. Did he remember her? It had been almost ten years since they'd seen each other. Did he even care how much he hurt her?

He turned away first, and she instantly felt hurt, as if he just dismissed her and their past. That almost cut as much as the day he abandoned her in the hospital. Sophie was not about to let Kenneth Davis continue to ruin her life or her emotions.

"Y'all ready to see what these niggas on?" Angel asked.

Sophie wasn't, but she kept her game face on. She was nervous. Scheming wasn't exactly her area of expertise. Plus, Kenneth showing up had to be a sign. What was the universe trying to tell her?

The ladies finally sauntered over to where Mello and his crew were standing. Sophie's heart began to race with each second he breathed the same air as her. She kept staring at him, wanting him to acknowledge her, apologize, curse her out—anything. He never did. He went on into a speech about staying on their game and assigning the women sections to keep an eye on.

Sophie's head began to spin. Between Mello, Kenneth, or whatever he called himself these days, his instructions, and her own thoughts, she felt like she couldn't breathe. She couldn't do it. She just couldn't.

"You hear me, baby girl?" Their eyes connected. The color of her face faded. He really didn't remember her after everything they'd been through. At one point in time, they were stuck at the hip. You never saw one without the other.

Sophie had had enough. Shaking her head, she began to back away. "I can't, y'all. I need to go."

"Look, y'all, go get on y'all sections." He pointed at Diamond. "And you, make sure you stay close to your guy. He like tricking off. If you hear anything, see anything, or feel anything out of the way, let me know." He handed Angel and Diamond baggies with pills in them. They took the packages and walked off.

Diamond nodded, and Mello focused back on Sophie. "Come talk to me for a second, ma." He didn't wait for a response. Mello grabbed her hand and pulled her away toward the front of the yard.

Sophie swore she could feel her entire body tingle at his touch. She was pissed. He didn't get to do this to her a second time.

Mello guided them to a quiet corner on the side of the house. For what seemed like an eternity, neither spoke. They just stared at each other. Time stopped, and the world seemed to spin. His eyes were so intense. Sophie didn't remember him being so...so grown and gotdamned sexy.

"You look familiar. Where I know you from?" Mello broke the silence.

Sophie frowned. "If you don't already know, then from nowhere." Her face tightened. She was so over it. Fuck the money, and fuck him. She'd figure out another way to get the funds she needed to secure her and Jr.'s future.

Sophie started to walk away. "Ayo, Sophie, wait." Mello stopped her by cupping her arm. "I'm bullshitting with you. How you been, love?" His gaze roamed her entire body.

"Are you sure you want to ask that question?" Her arms were folded tightly across her chest.

"Nah, that's a conversation for another time. Right now, we got money on the floor, and your homegirls need you...I need you."

"I really needed you too."

Mello licked his lips, pulling on the hairs of his beard. "I know, love. I apologize. I promise we will talk about it on a different day, in a different environment. But right now, your homegirls need you to come through for them, a'ight?"

"Whatever. I just want to get this over with so I don't ever have to see you again."

"Never say never, love." Mello winked, passing her a baggie.

Angel was in her zone as she made it over to the bar. The man she was assigned to, Faison, was that nigga, and his thirsty ass was on her heavy. Working her charm had never been a challenge. That's why when he asked her to get his drink while he talked to his friend, she did it without hesitation. That was her chance to slip him the pill and cut the fuck out so that she could set up a few licks.

"I need a glass of Champagne and a glass of red wine," she called out to the bartender before scanning the crowd. Her pussy was getting moist with all the money flowing through the place. Of course, she had been around ballers, but these were an entirely different caliber of niggas for her.

"Here you go, sweetie. Anything else?" the bartender asked, handing over the two glasses with their drinks.

After scanning the room, she opted for the hallway that led to the backyard. It took less than a minute to make it over there, crush the pill, and stir. After she was satisfied that the pill was dissolved, Angel adjusted her dress and headed back to the party.

"Still a scheming-ass broad. Where you think you going, bitch?"

Angel's entire body rang with fear at the deadly sound of his voice. It was so familiar, yet she had gotten over on so many men that she couldn't place who it belonged to. She never got a chance to turn around. She felt her long weave gripped and yanked with so much force that her feet lifted before she crashed down into the cement. Pain instantly exploded from her scalp down to her ass cheeks as the glasses shattered on the ground.

"Wha...What's going on?" she finally stuttered—only for her heart to drop to the pit of her stomach, finally catching eyes with the chocolate monster from Ohio...or maybe it was Atlanta, New York, Vegas even. Shit. She couldn't place where she had gotten down on him at, but she knew she hit him for a grip. She knew all her victims. She just didn't understand how he found her. She never ate anywhere near Detroit.

"Damn, yo conniving ass done got down on that many niggas? Dumb bitch. Took a million dollars worth of jewelry from me and got pennies for it. Because a gutter-ass scheming bitch like you don't shit about real money." He reached down and smacked her face so hard that her nose began to trickle with blood. "That's for being so fucking dumb," he gritted, pointing to one of his goons. "Yo, grab her ass up and take her to the back," he ordered.

Domo never expected to run into Angel at the event. He received the invitation and was down for copping a little extra artillery for himself and his team and maybe gaining a new buyer for his drugs. But when he saw her walk into the room with her girls, he instantly knew who she was. He had etched every detail of her pretty, conniving features into his memory bank.

"I didn't take nothing from you. I don't even know you," she pleaded as strong hands snatched her up. "I-I swear, it wasn't me."

"Shut up before you piss me off," Domo spat, mushing her head. "One thing about Domo, he always gets the last laugh. You obviously didn't know who you was fucking with, huh?" he scowled as his goons threw her onto the grass. Then he leaned to smack her again, but Angel balled herself into the fetal position, attempting to protect her face as she screamed out.

"Please, please, don't hit me again." There was no one to save her. The night was quiet. Everyone was inside, enjoying the party, oblivious to what was about to happen. The agonizing truth had her stomach hollow.

Her begging for mercy seemed to piss him off more. He nodded, giving the go for his goons to get her. They began to kick, punch, and stomp her wherever they saw fit. Angel's entire body was on fire, her eyes felt as if they were wired shut, and her nose felt broken.

"That's enough for now." He held up his hand. "It looks like we about to play a little game." He chuckled, holding up her wallet, just as a gun cocked, then another, and before he knew it, four pistols were pointing at him and his team. Domo threw his hands in the air, and his crew followed suit, leaving a badly beaten and bruised Angel writhing on the ground, nearly losing consciousness.

"This don't got nothing to do with you, bro," Domo said as he looked into Mello's eyes and pistol. Domo wasn't disrespectful; however, he was stern with his words. He was from the streets just as Mello was, and although he didn't have the upper hand, he wasn't a soft nigga either. Atlanta had been good to him, and he ran the streets...his streets...with an iron fist. There was no way it would settle in his soul that two scheming bitches got down on him. He had laid people to rest for far less.

"Yeah, it do. She with me." Mello didn't know why he was taking on Angel's problems. A part of him even questioned the notion. He was a man that tried his best to stay clear of bullshit and sucka shit. However, Sophie crossed his mind. Sophie had been through a lot, and helping her homegirl was the least he could do.

"I'll respect that for now. But me and her have unfinished business. Unless you plan on having your people protect her every waking second of the day, I *will* see her again, and that's on my life. You gots to know I don't play about that."

"We'll see when we cross that path, but right now, this ain't that, my nigga."

"You got it." Domo and his crew backed down, but Mello understood that they were two street niggas, and there was a particular code to the streets. He knew that ol' boy could be a potential problem; however, now was not the time to stress it. They were in the middle of something far too important for Angel's scheming-ass ways to fuck it up.

"Thank you," Angel's whisper was almost inaudible as Rock leaned down to help her up.

Mello frowned. "Don't thank me. I didn't do that shit for you."

Angel looked off, but Diamond was marching over to them before she could respond. She had a nervous look plastered on her face. "Where's Sophie?" She completely ignored Mello. "Wait, what the fuck happened to you? I know you didn't put your hands on my fucking sister!" she yelled, hyped, ready to knock Mello's fucking head off.

"No, he didn't. Chill out, Diamond. I'm good. What's wrong?"

"We getting up out of here." She turned to Mello. "I see that y'all niggas on some for real bullshit. Angel sitting here beat the fuck up, and Sophie nowhere to be found. You trying to get us killed."

"What are you talking about?" Angel and Mello echoed at the same time.

"Your mans. You know, the one you told me to stick by. Yeah, that's not ya mans. He plotting on you."

"Plotting on me?" Mello grimaced.

"OK, I was walking over just to peep the scene. I guess he didn't see me coming, and him and some other nigga was talking. Your name Kenneth, right?" She didn't wait for him to confirm. "Well, Kenneth, after you and ya mans do whatever shady shit y'all about to do, you not making it to your car, and neither are the bitches you supposedly had brought along with you. I don't know about you, but me and my homegirls trying to live."

"You heard that nigga say that out of his mouth?" A brow raised.

"I sure did. He told the mafucka he was talking to that they needed to catch us at the door, grab some bags from y'all, and lay everybody out. That's some bullshit. You got us wrapped up in this scandalous shit."

Mello's jaw flexed. "Did either of you get to slip the pills in the drinks?"

"Fuck those drinks!" Diamond yelled.

"These broads here." Mello sighed. "Go get your homegirl. Hurry up and make sure she good. JR, stay with them until they get to the car. I'll handle it from here."

Both ladies watched as Mello smoothly walked off. When he disappeared into the crowd, Diamond turned to Angel. "When you get all healed up, I'm going to fuck you up. You almost got us killed with this bullshit. Them niggas was talking about straight laying our asses down."

"I know, Diamond. Please, just go get Sophie, so I can get myself together and get the fuck out of here," Angel groaned.

Robinson was a ball of nerves as he greedily awaited everything to play out. Tonight would be the end-all, and he could feel his manhood tingling at the thought. He pulled the flute of Champagne to his lips and allowed the bubbly liquid to slide down his throat before focusing on the young goon before him.

"I'm ready to get this show on the road and be out. What's up with ya mans? Did his broads handle that yet?" Santiago's voice was raspy, rugged even.

Robinson and Santiago had stepped outside away from the party for a brief conversation before the show started. Things had to run smoothly. The move was the be-all and end-all. It was his last hope.

"That's what I'm trying to find out." Mello's voice appeared from thin air, causing Robinson to choke on his drink. He coughed and grunted before getting himself together, focusing on Mello and his crew, accompanied by Tiffany's father, Graham, and a few of CBF's founders.

"So, you making moves on your own, Santiago? You making side deals and shit? We picked you as the face, but you got to know it's still a process, and you violating." Graham stood in front of Mello with his arms folded across his chest. He had his nine on his hip and was ready to let it go. He wasn't so much disappointed that Santiago was plotting on Mello. It was more so the principle. He felt disrespected. Nothing moved without the permission of the founders. CBF had an order, and Santiago was violating.

"Nah, OG. We was just kicking it on some other stuff." Santiago shrugged as Robinson took a step back. He looked like a deer with its head caught in the headlights.

"Stuff like what? Since when we just kicking it with the pigs?" Graham's brow raised. "And since we kicking it," Graham pulled out his nine. No one saw or heard the shot coming from the silenced gun...until Santiago's body slumped with a loud thud; blood splattered and dripped from the man's head. "Let's get rid of the snakes first, then get down to business. Shut everything down and reschedule. We not moving shit tonight. If anybody got an issue, handle 'em."

"Jesus Christ!" Robinson squeaked, throwing his hands in the air. "What's going on, Kenneth? We-We're good, right?"

Mello shrugged. "I don't know. Are we? I'm hearing you gave the order to lay me down as soon as we hit these fine people for their product." Ten guns rose, all aimed at Robinson's head as soon as the words left Mello's mouth. "Damn, after all the money we got together, you on some snake shit like that?" Rock's gun cocked. Mello held up his hand for him to chill. "See, I knew you was on some bullshit the minute you came up with this crazy-ass idea. Fuck I look like robbing my own people? What, you didn't know we fucked with CBF, huh? And let me guess. Santiago ain't have shit on me either? Let me find out it was you that hit my spots, nigga."

"This is how you want to play it?" Robinson was caught. "You *do* know, if you kill me now, there's over a dozen men just like me on standby and ready to call backup if needed to throw every last motherfucker in this building under the jail. You wasn't the only one with a plan B and C." Robinson looked down at the bloody, lifeless soul only inches away. "That was just my plan C. I was never going to cross you, Kenneth."

"But you was going to cross *me*?" Graham barked.

"It looks like you got this handled from here, OG." Mello reached out his hand, slapping fives with Graham, then focusing on Robinson. "Oh, from this day forward, if they decide to let you walk away, act like you don't know me when you see me. I don't give a fuck about a prison cell. I'll let these bitches ring until the best man is left standing." He gritted before tapping Rock and signaling for his crew to leave.

No one saw Domo waiting, lurking in the shadows. Revenge fueled his anger. He was so close to snapping Angel's neck, and having Mello put a gun to his face just didn't sit well. Never did he think he would stumble across the scene that just unfolded...a dead body, a dirty cop, and the nigga who pulled a gun on him.

His steps were slow and calculated. His crew was on alert and following right behind him as he approached the badly beaten man. Leaning down, he checked his pulse before kicking him. Robinson grunted, rolling over to his side. Something had to be broken. His rib cage was on fire. The pain almost made him wish for death.

"No more. I'm a cop. I'll have every last one of you in a cell by tomorrow." Robinson threatened through gasps. His eyes were so swollen that he couldn't see who was towering over him.

"Good thing I'm here to help. They fucked you up pretty badly, Mr. Officer," Domo chuckled, tapping his right hand. "Yo, help this man up and take him to the car. It look like we have a little business we can use each other for."

Domo watched as his men did as he ordered. His stay in Detroit had just gotten a little longer. He could feel his entire body tingle with the thought of sweet revenge.

CHAPTER TWELVE

DIAMOND CUT HER eyes over to Angel as Sophie helped to nurse her wounds. Her girl looked terrible, and if she weren't already so fucked up, Angel would have had to throw a fair one with her because Diamond was beyond pissed as she paced the floor. "I'm not getting where you thought this was cool, Angel. Your shit almost got all three of us killed. I mean, look at you," she chastised.

"You really sitting up here mad at me because I put money in your fucking pocket? Look at my face! Look at *me*! Y'all left that party untouched, but everything on my fucking body hurts. You think I got the energy to argue with you about what could have happened when it didn't?"

"This bitch here is really pushing it. Talk to your friend, Sophie, because her bullshit is not about to get me fucked up. My momma died the same way you trying to live, too worried about a fucking dollar. You are not...and I repeat, NOT, about to turn me into her. I'm about to go get a hotel room for a couple of days because right now, I want to touch yo' crazy ass," Diamond snarled.

"I got this under control. You just go worry about the twenty-five thousand you got paid to do absolutely nothing." Angel rolled her eyes. Even that hurt to do. Although they didn't leave with the fifty thousand that was initially offered, Mello still gave them half for their troubles. "You're welcome!" she called out to Diamond's back. Truthfully, she wasn't thinking about Diamond. With a man like Domo finding her, she had way bigger fish to fry.

The next day...

Diamond's eyes traveled over to the neatly stacked bills on the dresser. She didn't know how to feel. However, she didn't want to feel. She didn't want to think. She didn't want to do anything. It felt like her life was on a roller coaster, and she didn't know how to jump off.

After she checked into the Marriott Hotel the night before, all she remembered was the bottle of tequila she had drunk and Manny. She remembered calling him too. She drunkenly poured out her feelings to him, and as she thought about the situation, she hated she did that. He was her drug of choice, and as much as she hated to admit it, she missed him. She needed him to take her away and escape her reality...with his lying, married ass.

Her mother was on her mind heavily. She missed her so much. The last two years were the hardest curveballs life had ever thrown at Diamond. At times like the present, she would have been stretched out on her mother's bed, listening to whatever great advice she had to offer. The lady always had an answer for every problem, no matter how big or small. However, she was gone, and Diamond was left to solve the world's mysteries alone.

"What am I going to do without you, girl?" She blew out a breath of air. The twenty-five thousand from the night before crossed her mind. Was it worth it? Was it going to come back to bite them in the ass? Angel failed to realize that Diamond loved the girl like a blood sister. Diamond was more scared than she was mad. What if something happened to either of her girls? She already had enough on her plate. That would have broken her.

"Crazy bitch always into something." Diamond shook her head. A twinge of guilt tickled her spine. As mad as she was, she knew she would do it again, and *that* scared her. She didn't want to be money hungry. She tried her damnedest to stay humble and all that good girl shit. But where was that getting her? Swimming in bills and a washed-up pimp on her head.

Three light taps at the door caused her to roll her eyes. It was him. That was Manny's signature knock. She missed touching him...Her pussy missed him being inside of her. That was dangerous.

"What do your married ass want?" Diamond mumbled, tightening her robe and releasing a breath of air before swinging open the door. "Why are you even here?" She cracked it a bit, leaving the chain attached.

For a second, they caught eyes. Neither spoke. Emotions surged between them. Diamond broke the silence. "You still married?"

Manny blew out a husky breath of air. "You still on that, man? I told you I just wanted to see you. Let me talk to you."

"I need to protect my heart. You sitting hear love bombing, promising the sun, moon, and stars. But you got papers on you that says you belong to another woman. Why did you just pop up? You don't care that I need space and time to decide if I even *want* to deal with you." She rolled her eyes, swallowing the lump forming in her throat.

"So, you not gon' let me in?" Manny ignored her statement, licking his thick lips.

Diamond's kitty began to purr. She smirked. "Nope, because you gon' do it to me."

Manny cracked a smile too. "I want to...but that's not what I'm on. I really fuck with you, Diamond. Come on, ma. Stop playing. You know I got you. Haven't I been solid from jump?"

"Not a hundred percent. Why didn't you tell me you had a wife, Emmanuel? Why not let *me* decide if I want to deal with that?"

Manny sighed. "Me and that girl been having problems for a long time. On paper, she my wife, but in real life, we ain't been rocking for years."

"That doesn't make it better. Why not divorce? Do y'all live together? I mean, I don't know nothing, and as much as I try to tell myself that this was just a fuck for me, I can't. You got my heart involved, and I don't like to be played with."

"Damn, you love a nigga?"

"Sometimes I think I do, and sometimes I don't know. However, I *do* know that I'm not dealing with a married man." Diamond sassed with her hands on her hips as she stared into his sexy, charcoal eyes.

"I hear you, and you don't. Have you ever had any issues?" Diamond shook her head. "Exactly, now, stop playing. A nigga been sick not being able to lay up with you," he told her.

"I feel like I'm betraying myself, fucking with you. But I just can't let go, and I hate that. I don't want to end whatever we're doing, but I will leave yo' married ass and act like I never knew you." She pointed an accusing finger. "Get your shit together, Emmanuel."

As soon as Diamond opened the door, Manny was on her, his hands exploring her body underneath the robe and his lips hungrily caressing hers. She took a step back, and he moved with her.

"What are you doing?" Diamond whispered, her tough role completely melting.

"Making us both feel good. I missed you, D." His hand stroked her nipple as he placed deep kisses on her lips.

"We can't do this. I'm maddddd," she whined, but Manny wasn't trying to hear it.

"Man, watch out." Manny ignored Diamond's fake protests, lifting her in the air and carrying her back to the bedroom. He placed her on the bed, admiring her frame as it played peek-a-boo in the short robe. He took his time sliding out of his jeans. Diamond was anxious. Her sex was dripping, and he wasn't moving fast enough for her. So she pulled him on top of her.

Manny chuckled. "Ol' fronting ass. Tell me you want this dick," he moaned, slipping into her wetness and immediately pulling out, teasing her. "Say it, Diamond. Tell daddy that you want it," he urged.

Diamond never responded. She pulled him into her and closed her eyes in ecstasy as he slid in and began to rock inside her, filling her walls to capacity. His mouth was all over her...her neck, her lips, her breasts.

"Chill out. Let me enjoy my pussy," Manny whispered, grabbing her hips to steady her movement.

Diamond was in her zone. She had so much built-up tension to release. She ignored him, continuing to rock to his beat.

Manny slammed into her deep and hard. "This what you want, huh?" He pulled out and slammed into her again. "Huh? You missed daddy dick? That's why you tripping?"

Diamond yelped in ecstasy. "Yesssssss."

Just like that, they were back rocking like they never missed a beat. Nothing mattered other than the fact that Manny made Diamond feel good. She didn't have the energy to care about anything else.

Diamond and Manny were cruising through the city in his Spider with the wind blowing and Future's latest hit blaring through the speakers. He had his hand resting on her thigh and his body cocked to the right with one hand on the steering wheel.

They were out joyriding since the shop was closed for the day, and he had tied up all his loose ends in the streets. Their schedules were so tight lately that they hadn't been able to get up with each other. However, tonight, Manny was a well needed distraction from everything that was going on in her life.

Diamond snapped her fingers to the music as her hair blew in the wind. She was on chill, enjoying her little peace to the fullest. Her gaze landed on Manny's fine ass, and a smile crept on her face. She couldn't wait to get back to his house and fuck the shit out of him. Just the sight of him gave her pussy a heartbeat.

Manny turned down the music as they stopped at a red light. "Why you always staring at a nigga? Let me find out you in love," he smirked as his hand caressed her thigh.

"What? Humph, I think *you* the one in love and shit," she retorted, not fully ready to admit it. Manny was her baby.

"You already know what's up with me. You the one scared to make it official."

"Make what official?" she played dumb.

Manny's hand traveled up her thigh, cupping her warm mound through her shorts and squeezing. "This. You know I wrote my name all over this ma'fucka. Stamped it all up in this shit. But you playing with a nigga."

Diamond blushed as he pulled off. "So, I'm just some pussy to you?"

Manny's face turned into a sour frown. "Get the fuck out of here with that bullshit. Pussy come from anywhere, and pussy can go just like it came. I'm a fresh-ass nigga. Don't play me like that. I'm trying to be yo' nigga, and you keep putting up this wall."

"Who I'm with all the time? What wall am I putting up?" Diamond quizzed.

Manny shot her a look before focusing on the road. "Come on, ma. You can't even tell me you love me when I know for a fact you do. I don't know who hurt you in the past, but I'm not that nigga. If I can't add to your life, then I'm not gon' fuck with you."

Diamond licked her bottom lip, swallowing hard. "Is your divorce final yet?" That was a subject that he was trying to avoid at all costs. He never mentioned his wife, ex-wife, estranged wife, or whatever the broad was. But she knew the lady existed, and Diamond wasn't letting up until he handled that situation.

"I don't fuck with that girl, and you know it."

"That's beside the point. Legally, that woman owns you. So, until you have a finalized document stating that you're a free agent, let's just enjoy each other's company while we can."

Diamond reached out and turned up the radio. She didn't want to continue the conversation. She was protecting her heart for a reason. Her life was too hectic to add any extra stress. When she didn't have expectations, it saved her disappointment.

"You hungry, ma?" Manny interrupted her train of thought.

Diamond shrugged. "I can eat something. I don't know what I got a taste for, though."

Manny's eyes landed between her thighs. He bit on his bottom lip. "I know what *I* got a taste for."

Diamond blushed. "With your freaky ass. I thought we was talking about food, nigga."

"Oh shit. My bad." He let out a small laugh. "You want to go to Eddie V's? I know you like their steaks."

"We can."

"Bet." Manny paused before speaking again. "And when I get these papers back, I don't want to hear no more excuses, Diamond. I ain't the one to be up in limbo, guessing and wondering. If that's my shit, let me know. I ain't just talking about no pussy, either. I want yo' heart, yo' mind, yo' body...all that shit."

His intense glare made her nervous. She swallowed hard. "Get the papers back, and we can go from there."

After spending the night with Manny, Diamond was drained. The nigga literally tried to fuck her soul clean out of her body. He made love to her until her legs were wobbly, and her pussy was sore. Then he ate her until tears of pure ecstasy slid down the creases of her eyes. Whatever point he was trying to prove, he had made it loud and clear. Another nigga couldn't even sniff her coochie. He had written his name all in it and stamped it MANNY'S SHIT. Her bud tingled at just the thought of their lovemaking.

"Shit. This nigga play too much," Diamond whispered to herself as she entered the salon, turning to lock the door. She nearly jumped out of her skin when she saw the figure standing behind her. "Dammit, Carlos. Why do you always do that shit?" she frowned, grabbing her chest.

Carlos's grimy smile caused her to cringe. "You never pay attention to your surroundings. That's why you're an easy target." He pushed past her, plopping down into one of the stylist chairs. "I see you left your bodyguard at home today. Don't let that happen again. I'd hate for him to turn up in the Detroit River."

Diamond rolled her eyes. "He just popped up, like you just did. What are you doing here? I'm not due again yet."

"You got that money we discussed?"

"What? I just paid you. I never said that I would have that amount right now. I just asked how much to leave me alone."

"Right. And I told you fifty thousand. That's not a lot of money for a woman like you. You just don't know how to use your pussy. Maybe I need to put you to work like I used to do your mother back in the day," he smirked sinisterly.

"Fuck you, Carlos. You could never. I'd die before I sell my pussy. I can't wait to get you the rest so that you can get the fuck away from me. All I have is five thousand."

Carlos rubbed his hands together as greed settled in. He never actually expected her to come up with the fifty thousand. Diamond was a gorgeous girl with a sick frame. She didn't know her power, and that's why she would always be broke, and he'd always be able to manipulate her. She was nothing like her mother. Cynthia was a gutter bitch that knew how to get to a bag. Her only problem was biting the hand that fed her without preparing for the repercussions.

Carlos stood from the chair. "We'll revisit that when you get me my money. Go get that five while I'm here. Hurry up. I have things to do."

Diamond hated his entire existence. She never knew it was possible not to like someone as much as she didn't like him. How could her mother even deal with a slimy bum like him?

"Damn, that ass so phat," he called after her as she stomped past him.

Diamond nearly lost it when she felt his hand cup her butt. She skipped two steps, jumping forward, before whipping around.

"Don't you *ever* in your life touch me again." She pointed an accusing finger, adrenaline pumping.

Carlos laughed in her face. "And what'chu going to do if I did? Shit. Go get my money, little girl, before I decide not to be nice and have my little goons come up here and do some real damage."

Diamond felt the tears threatening to escape, but she was determined not to allow them to fall. "I hate you. I hate you so much."

"And I don't give a fuck. Get my money, bitch."

CHAPTER THIRTEEN

MELLO'S RANGE ROVER cruised through Detroit as he took a blunt to the face. The evening's sun was starting to disappear, causing a smoked gray tint to cast over Detroit's skyline. The city was quiet to the outside eye, and as he turned down the quaint block with big brick homes in Sherwood Forest, he leaned his seat back and cocked his body to the side.

"Bitch-ass nigga," he snarled, watching as Robinson made his way into the brownstone with a woman and two teenage boys.

Mello had to see for himself. He hadn't counted on Graham allowing the man to leave the party alive. Things were about to get gritty. One of them had to go, and it for sure wasn't going to be Mello.

"So, what we gon' do, my nigga? You see he alive and kicking," Rock snorted, taking a pull from his blunt.

Mello shrugged. "We wait. Nigga gon' come knocking."

"This just ain't sitting right, my G. He got down on us, and we just sitting ducks? This ain't even us."

"I'm hip."

"So, you just gon' act like everything good?" Rock's brow raised.

"No."

"Well, what the fuck? We shut the blocks down. Ain't no money coming in for the soldiers. We don't know what he 'bout to be on. Then what about CBF? Tiff daddy handle them?"

"We straight with CBF; that's fam. I'll let you know how we gon' move with Robinson when I figure it out."

Mello watched as Robinson's door closed, and his family disappeared into the house. Then he coasted into traffic. He'd contact Robinson in due time. Until then, he was just scoping the temperature.

Exactly two hours later, Mello found himself walking into Club Ice with his crew to unwind and talk a little shit. His mood was instantly shot when he locked eyes on Sophie.

"The fuck she doing here?" he mumbled under his breath as his jaw flexed, watching Sophie work the crowd in a pair of boy shorts that had the bottom of her voluptuous ass hanging out. Her cleavage was on high display, and how she smiled serving drinks and flirting had him beyond irked. Quite frankly, she had him fucked up.

"The new girl fine as a motherfucka, right? Angel brought her in last night, and I put her to work," Barry, Mello's co-owner, smirked, tapping Mello on the back.

Mello shrugged. "She can't work here." His voice was calm yet firm.

"Man, they're loving her. If we can get her on the pole, I bet she make us a killing," Barry insisted.

"If I ever come up in this bitch and she anywhere near a pole, I'm fucking you up, B. Now get her up out of here. I'm trying to chill."

"So, that's what it is? You threatening me now?" Barry threw his hands in the air, talking to Mello's back.

Mello never responded. He made his way to the office with a chip on his shoulder. Things were too hectic in his world for her to come barging back in. She still had a piece of his soul, and that was dangerous.

CHAPTER FOURTEEN

"**I**F YOU DON'T let my arm go," Sophie grimaced, snatching away from the big, thick-necked bouncer. When he first approached her and told her that she had to leave, she thought it was a joke. However, when he began to grab her and push her toward the door, she was ready to set it the fuck off.

"I'm only following orders, ma. You gon' have to take it up with Mello. But until then, I will need you to get to moving."

Sophie stood firm, planting her hands on her hip. "So, the nigga too much of a pussy to tell me himself? Where is he? Tell him if he wants me out of this club, he's going to have to put me out himself!" Sophie was livid. She couldn't believe he would stoop so low as to have the security guard put her out.

Sophie would never forget that last day she had spoken to him ten years ago. She was in a hospital mourning the loss of their unborn, begging for him to come and comfort her, and he never came. He told her that their baby was better off dead, and she had misinterpreted their long nights of lovemaking and deep conversations for something it wasn't. Mello said he didn't believe in love, so she needed to find somebody who did.

Mello had really damaged her. A part of Sophie wondered if that was why she held on to Ricardo for as long as she did. He wasn't shit, but at least he stuck around and ensured she and their son were taken care of. She would never fully love again because of Mello.

Pain surged through her body as if the wound were still fresh. The cut of betrayal would never go away. Fuck that. Mello didn't get to hurt her twice. She was going to him if he wasn't man enough to face her.

Her face sported a frown as she marched toward the double doors, ignoring the guard making no real effort to stop her. "Kenneth!" she screamed, drowned out by the base of the speakers. She pushed the door open to his office so hard that it made a loud thud against the wall.

"You motherfucker! I let the other day slide with you pretending you didn't know who the fuck I am and almost getting me and my girls killed. But what you will *not* do is play with me. I never did anything to your raggedy ass. I—"

"Are you done?" Mello asked, uninterested. He leaned back in his chair with an amused expression.

This ugly motherfucker think I'm a joke. Before the thought fully left her mind, Sophie had taken off her shoe and chucked it at Mello's head. He ducked. It missed his ear by an inch. She was so overcome by raw anger and emotion that tears streamed down her eyes.

"You know what?! Fine, I'll leave. You are a heartless devil. No good will ever come your way. Karma is a bitch. You don't do people the way you do them." She was crying so hard that she couldn't move.

The last thing she wanted to do was break down in front of him. When he pushed from his seat and made his way over to her, she wanted to run. She needed to get as far away from him as possible. But her feet were like cement, too heavy to move.

"Don't come over here, Kenneth," she warned before his tall frame suffocated her being. She never expected to be in his arms again, him comforting her like he should have done years ago.

She was outraged. "Get the fuck off of me, nigga," she screamed, flailing her arms. Her hits weren't affecting Mello nearly as much as his presence was doing to her. Each second of his strong arms wrapped around her caused her anger to melt until she was no longer fighting, just releasing a deeply rooted sob.

"Chill, love," he whispered in her ear. He couldn't take her breaking down because of him. Why the fuck did Angel have to bring Sophie out of all the females she could have got?

"Don't tell me to chill. I hate you, Kenneth. I swear I do."

He began to rub her back as she relaxed in his embrace. "No, you don't. But, we ain't going there tonight. Look," he cupped her chin, pulling her face toward his own, staring into her doe-shaped eyes, "my bad about what happened. I was young and dumb. Losing our baby—"

Sophie shook her head. "Don't you dare mention my unborn. You made me go through that alone. You never even had the decency to ask if I was okay, to say hi, kiss my ass, or anything. How the fuck do you think that made me feel?" She tried pulling away, but Mello held her tight.

"That wasn't just your loss, Sophie."

Sophie closed her eyes tightly. She wished she could open them and disappear. She still loved him. She didn't want to, but she did. How did that work?

"I can't do this with you. If you want me out of your club, fine. I'm gone." She tried pulling away a second time, but Mello wasn't having that. He wasn't in control of his own body. Once they touched, it was like the missing piece of his puzzle had finally been claimed, and there was no way to remove it.

"Why you out here on bullshit with a broad like Angel?" Mello asked, changing the subject. "What happened to going to Spellman or whatever the fuck it's called?"

"You don't care." Her voice was just above a whisper.

"I wouldn't have asked if I didn't. What's going on with you?"

"I have a son, Kenneth. I need money." She used the back of her hand to wipe her eyes. "I should be asking you the same thing. That's what you do? Still using women? You almost got us killed."

"Nah, you almost got yourself killed. Didn't you say you had a son? Where his daddy? Ain't no way I'm gon' have my baby momma out here struggling to take care of my seed."

Sophie wagged a finger at him. "Uh-uh. You don't get to have this conversation with me. You left your seed. I had to mourn his death alone. Don't you *ever* speak on what you would do."

"I'll take that. How have you been, Sophie?"

"I'm not doing it." She took a step back. "I didn't come in here for this. We aren't in the movies. We're not about to have this kumbaya moment where we stare into each other's eyes, fuck, and live happily ever after. You want me gone, goodbye. Just make sure you keep my sister out of your bullshit in the future."

With that, Sophie forced herself to walk away and, hopefully, out of his life for good. This time, it was her choice. She just couldn't understand how it was equally as painful as the first.

Sophie paced the floor of Angel's three-bedroom town house, a ball of nerves. She didn't know whether to be angry, hurt, or excited. Mello had her going through every emotion in the world, and she hated it.

"This nigga doing it again, and I'm letting him. Fuck that nigga, Fe Fe," she coached herself, pointing at the wall. No one was there to calm her down. Diamond was out with Manny, and Angel was somewhere at the club. Sophie was so worked up that she didn't even think to tell Angel what was going on.

Her cell phone ringing tore her from her thoughts, and Sophie welcomed the distraction...until she saw Ricardo's name dance across the screen.

"What? It's almost two o'clock in the morning. I don't have your son with me. Why are you calling?" she went off, although her anger wasn't necessarily geared toward him.

"I know you don't got him. I got the li'l nigga. Man, Sophie, why yo' momma calling me to pick up my son because yo' ass nowhere to be found? Get around them hoes and forget you a mother, huh?"

"Do you get off on trying to tear me down or some shit? *You're* his father. Thank you for doing what you're supposed to do."

"I swear, you ain't shit. But I got something for you. Keep fucking with me, and I'll go to court and take my son from you. Yo' broke ass ain't got no crib, no bread, and you and yo' freak-ass friends probably be over there sucking dick in his face."

Ricardo's words were so hateful lately. They cut. "That's how you feel about your wife and the mother of your child?"

"You ain't my wife. I don't know who the fuck you are."

"And the feeling is mutual, Ricky D, the wackest rapper in the city of Detroit. No, you keep fucking with me, and half of everything don't sound bad...husband."

Ricardo burst into laughter. "You wouldn't get half of shit. You forgot, you signed them papers when you was begging me to marry you and take yo' poor ass outta the ghetto. You leaving with the same thing you came with—nothing." He popped her bubble before hanging up on her.

Sophie was past mad. She nearly broke a nail as she dialed her mother's phone number. Natalie answered on the second ring.

"Now your little hot ass wants to call me. What's up, Sophie?"

"Why would you give Ricardo my son?! If you didn't want to keep him no more, you should have called me."

"Girl, bye. You dropped him off a week ago, and you just *now* wondering where he's at? So, hell yeah, I called his daddy. You would know if you called your child," Natalie spat.

"You knew that I was trying to get myself settled and together. I told you I was working on a way to get us a place to stay."

"That's not my problem, Sophie. I don't know what's gotten into you. But playing with the babies is a no-no. Get your shit together," Natalie fussed. She hoped Ricardo and Sophie would get back together. Ricardo was a provider if he wasn't anything else. He kept her bills paid too. Natalie wasn't about to lose her meal ticket because Sophie wanted to be hot in the ass. So what he cheated? All men cheated. A woman just had to pick her poison. You could cry in a Benz, or you could cry in a Neon.

Sophie sucked her teeth. "Bye, Ma. Now I have to fight with this man to get my baby back."

"You need to be fighting to return home where you belong."

Sophie heard her mother, but she chose to hang up. She couldn't give her advice on a man. Natalie never had one long enough to get anything other than a wet ass or a meal here and there.

"Why you tripping, Sophie? That nigga is going to bring that baby back. He's too busy tricking with these hoes to be keeping up with a kid." Angel waved Sophie off. Her homegirl had been walking around as if she lost her best friend.

"You don't know Ricardo's spiteful ass. He'll have some bitch with my son just to spite me. Selfish nigga always want control. Don't want to leave me alone and don't want to treat me right either."

"Sounds just like a nigga. Well, what we not about to do is sit around and look all crazy. You got a few extra dollars in your pocket. Have you looked for a house yet? Went shopping? What?"

Sophie's brows knitted together. "You trying to put me out, heffa?"

"Never that. You know whatever I got, you got. That was the goal, though, right? To start making your own paper and get you and my nephew a crib? Well, I got a way for you to keep the money coming in."

Sophie finally smiled. "With the way I'm feeling. I'm down for whatever. I need to get my money up."

"That's all I've been trying to help you and Diamond with since forever. You see how sweet the other night was? Y'all heffas got paid twenty-five thousand to do absolutely nothing. I ain't trying to be the only one walking around in Gucci. I want to share the wealth with my bitches."

"You so damn extra," Sophie giggled. Then her face straightened. "What do I have to do? I'm in as long as we don't have to involve punk-ass Kenneth." She rolled her eyes. "I'm not doing that one."

"Maybe the universe trying to tell you something."

Sophie frowned. "Something like what? I would never in my life touch that nigga again, even with somebody else's pussy."

"Who said anything about touching him? Maybe that's your chance to do him like he did you. I saw the way he was looking at you. I'm still wondering how I never made the connection."

Sophie shrugged. "Our friendship was so rocky back then." She paused to reflect on it. "You was mad with the world, and I didn't understand it back then. You know what all you went through. We were going through our own little issues. You had your life, and I had mine." Sophie could feel a tear threatening to escape. "But no matter how hard we was beefing, when I called you into that hospital, you never left my side from that day forward, and I will always love you for that."

Angel let off a wry grin. "Yeah, life was just life-ing back then. My boyfriend fucked my mother, and I have a whole little brother by my ex. My childhood...Sometimes, it still fucks with me. But it is what it is. That's why I don't give a fuck about a nigga. I treat a dog like a dog and get my coins."

"Yeah, that was pretty messed up, Angel. But all men are not the same. Don't you want to get married one day? Have kids and the little house on the hill?" Sophie questioned.

"You can believe in that fairy-tale bullshit if you want, but this ain't *The Brady Bunch* or *The Cosby Show*. This real life, and we get these niggas before they get us."

"If you say so, boo. Thanks for the pep talk. Let me get my ass up and do something productive. I'm not about to play with Ricardo's ass. He's just mad because he called me up the other night trying to get some coochie, and I curved him. Hating ass wants me to fail and come crawling back so badly."

"And that will never happen. You better let his ass know you got *real* friends this way, boo!" Angel sang in a singsong voice.

"Period!"

CHAPTER FIFTEEN

A BLUNT HUNG FROM Angel's lips as she traced the scar that decorated her right arm. It had been a constant reminder of the night that changed everything fourteen years ago. The pain and humiliation would never go away, just like the scar.

Her chest began to tighten as she allowed her mind to drift...

"You sure she down for it?" The deep baritone was eager. Angel heard him. She rolled her eyes. There wasn't no telling who the voice belonged to or what the man was talking about. Her mother's room was like a revolving door. So many men had come and gone that she lost count.

"You said five hundred, right? Well, she ain't got no choice but to be down the fuck. She living in my house."

Angel's body went rigid as her mind went into overdrive. The only "she" that lived in the house was her. She just knew her mother wasn't doing what she thought she was doing. At the ripe age of fifteen, she had never been involved with any of her mother's shenanigans, and she wasn't about to start now. The hairs on her neck began to stand as she slid off the bed and placed her ear to the door to hear better.

"What'chu mean, she ain't got no choice? I ain't into raping bitches."

Angel heard her mother's laugh. "But you sitting here trying to pay five hundred dollars to fuck a fifteen-year-old. Nigga, that's rape, any way you put it."

"Man, here you go. Look, I'm not beat for this shit. I'm out."

Angel's heart raced, and her breathing became labored as she held her breath, listening for her mother's response. A million thoughts flashed through her mind. She was a proud virgin. She wasn't shit like her freak of a mother, and that was her way of feeling better about herself. Shannon, her mother, could put her down all she wanted. She could call her every bitch in the book: dumb bitch, ugly bitch, lazy bitch... but she could never call her a rotten pussy bitch, and that was what kept Angel's head held high. That was the one thing that no one could take.

Sadness began to course through her entire being. Angel wondered what she had done so bad for her mother to hate her so much. It seemed as if every chance Shannon got to put her down, she didn't hesitate to do it. But now, she was trying to destroy her.

"Well, are you trying to get that young pussy or not? Shit untouched and all."

"Damn, so li'l momma a virgin?" the man questioned.

"Hell yeah. You would be the first and only nigga to touch her. Shit, if you keep the money coming right, I'll keep it that way too. Bitch got to start earning her keep around this ma'fucka. Maybe a li'l dick will humble her uppity ass."

Angel's feet were like cement. She felt dejected. A tear ran down her face, realizing she had no one in this cold world, not even a mother that was supposed to protect her. She wanted to run just to get the fuck out of that house. But where would she go? How would she survive?

The door creaked open, and the man that was entirely too fine to be paying for pussy walked into her bedroom. He approached her. He grabbed and prodded on her. She fought as much as a little girl could against a grown-ass man until the fight was beaten out of her entire body. She accepted her fate. She lay there and allowed the man to violate her in ways that should never have happened to an innocent fifteen-year-old...

That night caused irreversible damage that would taunt Angel for years after the fact. The rape invoked insecurities, hatred, anger, and other forms of bad seed into her existence. It didn't help that misfortune and mishap became the story of her life. She'd experienced so much pain that she would never be the same. She closed off her heart to the outside world until Diamond and Sophie came along and showed her that there were still a few good human beings in this world. However, she didn't let anyone else in, and she didn't give a fuck about what she had to do to get hers because nobody ever gave a fuck about her.

Two hours later, the pain of Angel's past was pushed far into the back of her mind. She burned the stores down at Somerset Mall, and bags decorating her backseat showcased it. She mastered turning her thoughts off and on by staying busy. However, now, she had business to discuss with Shanell. Domo had her frazzled. The fact that he could touch her sent a chill up her spine. The same chill she got when they robbed him.

"Bitch, we got a serious problem. That lick back in Atlanta that your cousin put us on...I'm sitting here nursing wounds because the nigga popped up on me the other night."

"What?!" Shanell shrieked. "Girl, stop playing. You ain't hardly ran into that nigga, Domo. Besides, where was you at to even run into him?"

"Me and my girls were on a mission, and he just popped up out of nowhere."

"Damn. See, that's what you get for trying to be slick and go on plays without me. Who put you on to that lick anyway?" Angel had to pull the phone away from her ear. Shanell was missing her entire point.

"Does it fucking matter?" Angel gritted. "I need to know what's up with ol' boy. He's not playing, Shanell. He's going to end up killing us."

"Us?" Shanell began to cackle with laughter. "He don't know shit about me. I want to feel bad for you, sis, but I see you on some slick shit, trying to undercut the master. News flash: the reason you never had this problem before was because *I* made that shit happen. That's why *I* set up the licks. You don't know shit but what I teach you."

"That's how you feel? Bitch, I ain't yo' little flunky. I hope he find your dumb ass first and hit you right in them dicksuckers." Angel hung up the phone on ten. If the two were face-to-face, she would have definitely punched her in it.

Before Angel could get the thought out, her phone was ringing again, and she started to answer it and go the fuck off, but Shanell was talking before she could say hello.

"Look, heffa, this not what we do. We don't beef with each other; we beef with these niggas. I ain't gon' front, though. I am a little salty."

"Whatever. I ain't feeling you right now. You need to call Pooh and see if you can get that jewelry back so we can get the nigga off our head."

"That boy ain't coming for nobody. That was a coincidence. We took a few funky-ass cheap pieces of jewelry. Oh, the fuck well!"

"Obviously you didn't have your facts right. It was worth a couple hundred thousand dollars, and we got less than a few thousand!"

"That is cap as fuck. That shit wasn't worth that much. Pooh wouldn't play us like that," Shanell shrieked into the phone.

"Well, you tell him that Domo is in Detroit, and he wants his shit. Call your people and handle that, Shanell," Angel demanded.

"You know good and well that once he gave us the money, that shit was a wrap. Ain't no getting nothing back."

This bitch here. Angel rolled her eyes over the conversation. "Look, I got to go. Just call and see." Angel hung up without waiting for a response.

After two trips to the car, she was done bringing everything into the house, and she couldn't wait to kick her feet up and relax. She had been on edge ever since she ran into Domo, constantly looking over her shoulder, ducking and dodging the club. Angel was ready to handle his ass so she could return to her regularly scheduled program. Of course, she had a few dollars saved, but it wasn't nearly enough for what she was trying to do.

A knock at the front door jarred her from her thoughts. Diamond wasn't home, and she wasn't expecting any company. Her heart instantly began to flutter until she realized Domo didn't know where she lived.

Grabbing her pistol from her dresser, she sauntered over to the front door, peering out. The tall figure caused her brows to furrow. "How this nigga know where I stay at?" she mumbled to herself, wondering why Robinson was at her front door.

Cocking the pistol, she crept to her room to grab her cell phone to call Mello. He needed to get his homeboy. Why the fuck was he there?

"What up?" Mello answered on the first ring.

"First off, you avoiding me and putting my sister out of the club is childish. But never mind that. Why is that cop nigga standing outside my door? Why would you tell him where I stay at?" She went off just as the doorbell rang for a second time.

"Outside yo' house? The fuck?" Mello paused, and Angel heard shuffling. "Sophie and lil man ain't there, are they?"

"You don't care."

"Here you go. Don't answer that door. Shoot me yo' address. I'm on my way."

"No. I'm about to see what the fuck he wants, and if he ain't talking right, you gon' have a dead homie to clean up. I'm not about to play with y'all niggas."

"*Hardheaded broads*," Mello thought as he hung up without a fight.

Angel swung open her front door with the pistol pointed directly at Robinson's head. His eyes bugged in surprise before an amused smile settled on his face. "Is that any way to greet a guest, Ms. Angel?" he teased.

"Sure the fuck is. You showing up at my house, and I didn't invite you. What do you want?"

"To talk."

Angel's lips curved into a frown. "Nigga, I don't know you. We ain't got shit to talk about."

Robinson shook his head. "But I think we do, bitch."

"*Bitch*?" Angel's head cocked, confused with the sudden switch up. A chill shivered up her spine. She never had to use her gun, but she was ready to kill a cop tonight...until the dark figure appeared from the shadows of the night, face finally illuminating from the flicker of light on the porch. It was Domo. Her fears had finally come to fruition. All that scheming and plotting had finally caught up with her.

She tried slamming the door shut, but Robinson's foot held it open. Angel's heart raced, danger thickening the air.

"Stupid bitch," Robinson spat, snatching Angel up and taking her gun. "I should kill you for pointing a gun at me, but I'm a gentleman." His arm tightened around her neck, causing her to cough and claw at his hands. "Plus, we have business to take care of."

"You got that right. Where my shit at, bitch?" Domo frowned. He started toward Angel, but Robinson held up his hand for him to chill.

"As much as I agree that she needs a thorough ass whooping, we'll hold off on that." Robinson released Angel, pushing her into the front room and fully stepping into her house, along with Domo, locking the door. "Now, you've been a busy bee. Stealing, running your mouth. You know, you and your friends cost me a major deal. Millions of dollars are on the line, and some very dangerous people are no longer happy." He pointed at Domo. "And it seems my friend Domonic here has a similar problem, so we decided to join forces to solve them."

Angel's heart raced. "I already tried to get the jewelry back. It's gone. I mean, I can try to get the money, but I don't know where I'm going to find a million dollars."

"Oh, you for damn sure gon' get me my money *and* some. You work for *me* now, scheming bitch. As a matter of fact, you, your homegirls, and Captain Save a Ho," Domo gritted.

Angel shook her head. She couldn't mix her girls into her bullshit. "It don't have nothing to do with him or them. Tell me what I got to do. I got somebody that can help me pull it off." This was all Shanell's fault, and Angel would make damn sure she paid her dues too.

"This ain't no debate. It is what it is," Robinson smirked. "Mello and I have unresolved issues. He put himself in this position. Don't worry. We'll give you all a little incentive to motivate you. I'll be getting in touch real soon." He reached into his back pocket, pulling out a stack of rolled-up papers. "Just a little reassurance. I suggest you try to talk some sense into your friends because things can end up really ugly."

"It's already like that with me. You better be thanking God this cop nigga helped me to see the bigger picture," Domo snarled, jumping at Angel. He broke out into a sinister laugh, seeing her cower. "You played me on the pussy that night. I started to take it from you, but I don't even want that rotten shit no more. You got a month to get me my cheese. He nice...I don't give a fuck. Remember that."

Angel watched as they turned to leave. Her heart was sitting in the pit of her stomach as she waited, holding her breath, for them to leave. Just when she thought she was in the clear, a single shot whizzed past her head, causing her to drop to the ground into the fetal position for cover.

After her heart rate normalized, Angel finally picked up the papers that Robinson threw on her table. *Murder, prostitution, robbery?*

"What the fuck just happened?" Angel spoke to herself, grabbing her chest. She couldn't help the rumble of unease that tickled her toes and traveled all the way up to the throbbing in her right temple. There life was...not giving a fuck about li'l old Angel again.

Thirty minutes later, Angel was pacing the floor, going off as Mello and Rock listened. She went from panic to cursing and back to panic. The only thing that was clear was they were in some deep shit.

"Nigga, so what we about to do? You got a team too. Let's go shoot up some shit and get this over with. He throwing bogus-ass Fed time, another nigga threatening to kill us. Fuck that," Angel frowned.

Mello wanted to tell her to shut the fuck up, but he let her vent. He did his own research. Robinson could be handled without a problem, but Domo was a different kind of beast. His family's name alone held weight in the underworld. Of course, they could go to war, exchange a few gunshots, and lose some lives in the process, but Mello wasn't so sure his team was big enough to go up against the police *and* Domo's connections.

Mello stood up. "You done?"

"Am I done? Hell no, I'm not done. What are we going to do about this shit?"

"You the one that know everything. *You* tell me." Mello was so calm yet menacing. Angel didn't speak. She couldn't. She didn't have an answer. "Exactly, now shut up. Have you said anything to your girls yet?"

Angel didn't plan on involving them, so there wasn't anything to say. How hard was it to shoot two niggas and go on about your life?

"No, I haven't. Why would I do that when they don't have nothing to do with this? We can handle it on our own."

"So, you think it's cool for them to walk around not knowing nothing? Somebody run up on 'em, and they completely in the blind? That's more selfish than a ma'fucka."

Angel placed her hands on her hips, rolling her eyes. "Nigga, you the *last* person to talk about somebody being selfish. Sophie told me how you left her in the hospital after she miscarried your baby. *I* was the one that held her when she cried. *I* was the one that forced her to eat and get dressed every day. You can't tell me *nothing* about selfishness, nigga."

Rock pushed from the wall. He knew his mans, and Mello was two seconds from going off. "Look, all this back-and-forth ain't solving nothing. It ain't gon' make nobody any less guilty, either. Solutions. What we gon' do? Robinson pulled up on me when I was out with my bird. He knew not to do that on no other type of time. We got to get a handle on this shit ASAP," Rock spat.

"Let me figure out what they want from us." Mello sighed, reaching into his back pocket. He pulled his pistol off his waist, handing it to Angel. "Here. I'll get your heater back from him too."

Angel finally stopped pacing. "Yeah, please do. I'm out."

Angel's SUV pulled into Ice nightclub with a loud screech. The parking lot was packed. She was on a mission as she parked in front of the door and pushed through the entrance, ignoring security.

"Yo, Angel. You gon' have to move the whip. I ain't trying to hear Mello's mouth. You know that's his spot," Cody, the dread-headed bouncer barked.

"I'm only going to be a minute," she called over her shoulder, continuing to walk into the club. She scanned the crowd for Shanell and didn't plan to leave until she found her. Making her way to the locker room, she found her girl past tipsy, leaning on Passion, one of the other dancers.

Angel frowned. "This shit don't make no fucking sense." She stood in front of Shanell, folding her arms over her chest. "Bitch, we got real problems, and you can't stay sober for two minutes?"

Shanell pushed off Passion, staggering a bit in a G-string, six-inch heels, and pasties to cover her nipples. Her body was on point, and her hair was flawless. "Heyyyy, boo. You Miss Superstar now. Can't come back to the club. Me and my boo, P, been cracking heads."

"But have you cracked that nigga's jewelry back? What did yo' people say?"

Shanell sucked her teeth. "You still on that? Fucccck Domo. He ain't gon' do shit."

Angel lunged at Shanell, pinning her against a locker. They struggled a bit, but Angel was too much for a drunken Shanell. "This shit ain't a game, bitch. The nigga came to my house! You lucky I didn't give him yo' location. Get that man his shit back and call yo' people before me and you have a serious problem," Angel gritted through clenched teeth.

Shanell's gaze darted around the dressing room. Passion and one other dancer were the only witnesses, but she was still embarrassed all the same. Who did Angel think she was? She was the OG, and Angel was her protégé. Her chest burned with fury and revenge. Angel was going to pay for the stunt she just pulled.

"You got it tough girl," Shanell smirked, snatching away. "Let's just hope he don't slit your throat before I can get his shit back." She looked Angel up and down. "Let's go get this money, P. Everybody can't afford to sit on their ass like this broad."

Angel's fist collided with a locker as she screamed, frustrated. She could have snapped Shanell's neck and not thought twice about it. The beef with Domo wasn't a game. Nothing ever put much fear in her heart...but he had her worried.

CHAPTER SIXTEEN

"**Y**OU WANT CURLS or to keep it straight?" Brittany asked as she began to flat iron Diamond's hair. They were sitting in the shop after hours, having girl talk.

Diamond shrugged. "Girl, it don't matter. I just want it done."

"I don't know what for. That nigga just gon' mess it right back up. Married dick be so freakin' toxic." Chrissy, Brittany's best friend, shook her head.

Diamond cut her eyes over to Chrissy, attempting to determine if the girl was being underhanded. Manny being married was a sore spot that Diamond desperately tried to ignore. He made her body feel things that no man ever had. He distracted her from the reality of how messed up her life really was.

"Really, heffa?" Brittany swatted at her arm.

Chrissy shrugged. "Really, what? I'm not judging her. Do you, boo. I know it's tight out here, and Manny's tricking ass got that bread. I would be milking him too."

Diamond held up a hand, stopping Brittany before she could check her friend again. "I see you getting a little too comfortable in my business, and all those backhanded comments ain't called for. Say what you got to say."

Chrissy rolled her eyes, pretending to study her nails. "I said what I had to say. My cousin work at the Benz dealership, and she told me you falling a little short or whatever, and I'm not mad at you. Oh, and she said her people saw you out at this party with Angel. You know your homegirl be into some shit. If I was you, I would keep messing with Manny. It's safer."

"Damn, you sure is watching my coochie hard." Diamond pointed at Brittany. "What's up with your homegirl?"

Brittany rolled her eyes, letting out a sigh. "You know you family. We been rocking since Cynthia was alive. I just been hearing stuff in the streets, and I wanted you to hear what was being said. Seriously, Dee. Your homegirl is in some shit. Fuck Manny. You need to check on your peoples."

"What kind of shit?" Diamond frowned.

"Just check on her. You know Chrissy from the same hood as that Shanell girl from the club, and Shanell laying all her shit on the table...talking real greasy."

Diamond didn't know what to think. She knew that Angel got down and dirty. A pang of fear shot through her body. What if what happened at that party was finally coming to bite her in the ass?

After finishing her hair and locking up the shop, Diamond tried calling Angel three times, only to get no answer. So she texted her, telling her to call her ASAP. Instead of going home, she followed Brittany and Chrissy to Club Ice for drinks. Really, Diamond was hoping to run into Angel...or Shanell. She wasn't above popping a bitch in her mouth for playing with her sister.

"Mello know he keep this place jumping." Brittany spoke over the music. "Oh my goodness!" She squealed, grabbing Diamond's arm so tight it felt like she was pinching her. "Look at his fine ass. Him and his crew be looking good. I'd do either one of them."

Diamond let out a chuckle. She still wasn't feeling Chrissy's energy from earlier, but she let the girl slide. "Girl, they cool. They ain't all that."

Just as the words left her mouth, she felt his intensity before she looked over at him. Those low-set chocolate eyes were set on her. She remembered him from the party, but they never really spoke. Rodney...Robert...Rock. She tried coming up with his name. Diamond knew it started with an R. She just couldn't remember which one.

"Ol' boy looking over here hard." Brittany tugged at the crop top she was rocking. "I knew I should have got cute. Damn."

"I ain't worried about him. Where the bartender at?" Diamond turned to face the bar. She had too much going on in her life to be worried about a nigga...especially when she already had one that she just couldn't figure out if she was supposed to love him or cut his married ass off.

After placing her drink order, Diamond turned to face the crowd again but almost stumbled to the ground. There Rock was, in her face, invading her personal space. Distance did the man no justice. He was a piece of art. Sexy, chocolate, rugged...and off-limits.

"Whoa, you OK, li'l momma?" He reached out, catching her. "Diamond, right?"

She nodded.

"I was just coming to speak to yo' fine ass. Whatever you and yo' homegirls need, it's on me tonight." He winked at her. "Yo, Michelle. I got them. Put they shit on my tab," he called to the bartender before coolly walking off, abruptly releasing her from his chokehold.

Brittany and Chrissy began to squeal. "You know Rock? You secretive heffa. His fine ass said it's on him, baby! Let's drink up!" Brittany shot. "Manny cool, but li'l daddy really like that with his thugged-out ass."

"He all right. I'm not thinking about him, though." Diamond waved off Brittany as her eyes self-consciously landed on Rock again. He winked, and she blushed.

CHAPTER SEVENTEEN

COMMANDER GEROME ROBINSON sat at his desk, looking over the files before him. He had enough paperwork on Kenneth Davis to lock him and his so-called crew under a jail cell. They didn't know who they were fucking with. Actually, he had made up files for everyone he encountered, including the Russians, Domo, and those three bitches that Mello hired. His nostrils flared as he looked at the burner cell sitting on his desk, ringing.

He had avoided Nikolay Ivanov's calls long enough. Robinson knew that he was a dangerous man. The Russians were ruthless, and their reach was far. When Mello botched the heist at the party, he caused a world of confusion. They were supposed to make it out of that house with those guns and have them smoking on the next thing to Florida. That lick alone would have secured his financial future, dissolved his debts, and catapulted him into early retirement.

"Stupid motherfuckers," he growled, slamming his fists into the desk and snatching up the cell phone.

"Yes?" he sighed into the phone.

"Where is my fucking package or my money?" the man growled in his thick Russian accent.

What Robinson failed to disclose was that Ivanov had given him two million dollars up front for the guns. He'd gambled a bit and tried to flip the rest. However, that went terribly wrong. So, with the little that he had left...or, from the money that he hit Mello for with the staged raid, he decided to come up with a plan to rob CBF, blame Mello, and get rid of him for good at the same time. The young buck was of no use anymore.

Robinson sighed, feeling his temples pulse with a headache. "I told you, I'm working on it. I need a little more time than expected."

"Two million is a lot of money to be pussy footing around with. Please, do not make this what it doesn't have to be. I slated you to be a man of your word. Are you not that?"

"Have I let you down yet?" Robinson countered as his gaze landed on the file for Ivanov. He would make sure the motherfucker went out with a big bang.

"That is irrelevant. The clock is ticking, Commander Gerome Robinson, son to Dorothy and Samuel Robinson, husband to Sarah, father to Gerome Jr. and Joshua. My condolences on your divorce, even though something tells me that affair with Ms. Anita Rice was the cause of it." Ivanov hung up before Robinson could respond. That was a threat.

"Fuck!" Robinson growled, pushing the files off his desk and leaning back in the swivel chair. He needed to find a faster way to come up with the money...or bring Ivanov's crew down sooner.

"Yo, are you all right, Commander?" Cromer, one of his superiors, leaned his head into the office.

"Yeah, yeah. Everything's fine," Robinson assured him, scrambling to pick up the files full of bogus trumped-up charges.

"Good. Well, Chief wants to see you in his office. He told me to drop by and tell you on my way out."

"All right. Thanks, Cromer." Robinson nodded. He felt as if his world were starting to cave in. Everything was coming at him at once.

"Oh, they're going to get me my money," he snarled, texting Mello a time and date before pulling himself together to face the chief.

"So, this shit gon' be legit, my G?" Domo asked as he sat across from Robinson inside Old Café on the Eastside of Detroit. He had been in the city for longer than expected and wanted to ensure all loose ends were tied up before returning to Georgia. "I mean, I'm with just putting a bullet through everybody head and calling it a day."

Robinson took a sip from his steaming coffee. "They're worth nothing to us dead. I need my fucking money first. Then I'll go to the Russians and connect you with a pipeline that will put all doubt and suspicion to rest. You can regain your trust and respect with your family, and I will disappear to Mexico or some shit."

The chain Angel had stolen wasn't just some random piece of jewelry. It was a family heirloom that had been passed down from generation to generation. It was like a rite-to-passage statement piece given out when you took over the *"family business."*

The piece was so rare and legendary that when Shanell sold it to the buyer, he knew exactly what it was and had hit up Domo's father to return it. That one move caused a world of trouble for Domo. The family had come down on him hard. Losing their trust was like signing a death wish. He had to make something shake... and fast.

Domo remained silent as a million thoughts flowed through his head. He thought about what having a real Russian connect meant and how happy his father would be. He lived his entire life to please that man, and he'd do just about anything for his approval.

"Say no more. I'm leaving a few of my people here in case shit get out of line. Hit me up if you need me. I got to get back to the A." Domo stood, his big frame towering over Robinson. He glowered down at the man. "And listen, my nigga. I'm not him. You cross me, and I'm splattering all yo' shit with no questions asked. Ain't no walking away. You got that?"

Robinson nodded, watching the man as he coolly exited. A flicker of bitter disgust caused his mouth to go dry. He was tired of being threatened. *He* set the rules. *He* was the fucking law.

CHAPTER EIGHTEEN

"**W**HAT THE FUCK?" Mello muttered to himself as he watched the SWAT team run up into the warehouse that he previously used to store his work. They would find nothing, but the warning was still loud and clear. It had only been three days since they reopened shop. When he cut ties with Robinson, he switched up his entire operation. Nothing ran the same, not even the soldiers.

"But you ain't want me to ice that nigga." Rock frowned. "Fuck he thought? We was gon' keep shit like it was?" Rock leaned back into his seat, lighting the blunt he tucked in his ear.

"Yo, put that shit out, bro. It's hot out here." Mello waved the smoke out of his face, pulling out his cell phone to call his lieutenant. "Shut all that shit down, make sure you pick up my money and work from everybody, and bring that shit to the alternate location." He hung up the phone, pissed.

Robinson wasn't only fucking with his money. He was also challenging his manhood. Mello didn't like that. It didn't sit well with his soul.

"And what about that Domo nigga? You keep wiping yo' ass with this shit, and it's making us look weak, bro. Bitch ain't never been in my blood. All a nigga got is his word and his balls. My shit be hanging, my nigga. I don't tuck them bitches for nobody, my guy."

106

Mello pulled on the hairs of his beard. "A man that acts off emotion is foolish. This shit bigger than ego. Chess, not checkers, my nigga. You'll see," Mello said, easing into traffic and riding past the warehouse.

Mello was counting up the money from the streets and putting it in his safe as Rock sat across from him, checking the books. A drought was about to happen, and he was fully prepared to lace up his boots and weather the storm.

"You know that was Robinson that hit the warehouse? We can't just ignore him, bro," Rock complained, growing frustrated with the numbers he kept coming up with.

"I got people on it. Is the count adding up?" Mello asked, neatly banding a stack of hundreds.

"Fuck no. Ain't nothing adding up right now. We gon' lose everything if we don't get back to the blocks and put our soldiers to work. Niggas got whole families to feed."

Mello lit the blunt sitting in the ashtray on his desk before taking a hard pull and releasing a thick cloud of smoke. "I told y'all to save for the rainy days, and right now, it's a thunderstorm."

"Bro, you saying that like we don't sell dope. Like we don't move weight. We got a clientele that depend on us. One thing about a fiend. You can't tell that ma'fucka to stop smoking. He don't give two fucks where he get his high from as long as he get it. We start losing our custos because we not providing the work, then what? They gon' find another plug!"

Mello took another pull. "I understand that."

"I don't think you do, my nigga."

"Oh, but I do. But how we gon' supply the work from behind bars or in a graveyard? Moving out of desperation gets you knocked."

"If you say so." Rock threw a neatly banded stack of money into a duffle bag. "What's up with you and ol' girl?" he added, referring to Sophie.

Mello's brows furrowed. "Ol' girl who?"

"Girlie from the other night. The one you threw out of the club."

"Ain't nothing up." Mello shrugged nonchalantly, even though the thought of Sophie still caused a trickle of energy to surge through his being.

"You sounding in yo' feelings, bro," Rock chuckled.

"Never that," Mello lied.

"Yo, it's messed up Angel's grimy ass ain't telling her people what's up. Baby girl seem like she a decent chick. Her and her homegirl." Rock ran his hand through his wavy hair. "I ain't even gon' front. I'm trying to see about 'ol girl. A nigga ain't never looked at a broad and said I need that...but I *need* that."

Mello's gaze shot over to Rock, surprised. "You the one sounding in yo' feelings."

Rock smirked. "Nah, I ain't in denial like you. I know what I want, and I'm the type of nigga to go get that shit."

For the next hour, Rock and Mello passed the blunt around, got their books together, talked a boatload of shit, and ordered takeout from Mighty Wings before deciding to call it a night. They had worked too hard, invested too much, and were in too deep. Allowing everything to crumble wasn't an option. Mello knew that he had to get shit back in order...and quick.

Detroit was always in the news for its gritty ghettos and the violence that plagued the city. At one point, the murder capital was one of the most feared places in the United States. It was rare that you could capture the beauty of it, and as Mello cruised the streets, cocked to the side, smoking a blunt, that's precisely what he did.

He was born and raised in the ghetto. He came up and made a lot of money in those same Detroit streets. Sometimes, it was where he felt the most comfortable. It would always be his home.

Times like the present, he needed a wife to come home to so she could rub his back and tell him that he would get through whatever storm was brewing against him. The world was cold, and as Mello took another pull from his blunt, he knew he had to be colder.

Mello's jaw flexed as his truck slowed down a few spaces from the black Charger he had been trailing. He reached over to the passenger seat to grab his pistol. Word in the streets was he had a snake in his camp. He had just gotten the call thirty minutes earlier. Robinson hit the warehouse, thinking the shipment was coming through, only to find nothing. Mello purposely switched his operation up and didn't tell anyone but Rock and two other people.

Just as the driver of the Charger opened the door and stepped out of the car, Mello's finger positioned on the trigger, ready to squeeze...until Tiffany climbed out behind the man. Mello had to do a double take.

"This ma'fucka." Mello smirked to himself in disbelief. That was the man's saving grace—Graham's daughter. Tiffany got a pass because of his loyalty to her father, but if Mello found out she was on some bullshit...he'd splatter her brains against the pavement.

Smoothly pulling off, Mello placed his pistol under his seat and made a right onto Grand River Avenue. A million thoughts flowed through his head...until his low fuel light came on. Mello knew he needed to get his head together. He wasn't even the type to let his gas tank go below half.

Pulling into the gas station, he parked at the first pump and hopped out to pay for his gas. It was just past midnight. The gas station was packed, and he was trying to get the hell out of Dodge.

Holding the door for a group of scantily dressed females, he ignored their stares as he exited. That's when he saw her. Ten whole years had passed without contact, and now, he couldn't seem to shake the girl. Even worse, she had the nerve to be looking so damn good.

"Fuck she doing out this late pumping gas?" Mello growled to himself, debating if he should even speak. He wanted to keep going with his life and pretend like she didn't exist. Of course, he couldn't do that, though. That's why he found his way over to her.

"The boogeyman be lurking this time of night. Pretty girls like yourself supposed to be tucked away in bed somewhere," Mello said, sneaking up from behind, startling Sophie.

"Dammit, Kenneth. What are you doing here?" She almost dropped the gas pump, but Mello grabbed it out of her hand, finishing pumping the gas for her.

"Why you ain't get gas earlier? This dangerous, Sophia." He ignored her question.

She rolled her eyes. "You don't care. Ain't you the same person that fired me and put me out of his club the other day?"

"You too good to work in the strip club anyway," he shrugged. "We gon' have to stop running into each other. I'm starting to think you want to give me yo' number so I can take you out or some shit."

Even though she was trying to keep her poker face, Sophie blushed a little. "Really, nigga? I'm not checking for you like that, so you can play me again." She folded her arms over her chest.

"I was a little-ass boy when we met. I'm a grown-ass man now, with too much to lose. I ain't got time to play," he told her matter-of-factly, hanging the pump back up and closing the cap.

Their worlds seemed to stop. The rhythm of the night was the only thing to be heard. Both were trapped in their own thoughts, emotions running wild. After all those years, their chemistry was still thick enough to slice.

Growing frustrated with how he still could pull at the strings of her emotions, Sophie began to shake her head, wagging a finger at his chest. "Are you serious right now? You don't get to do this to me. What do you want?"

"I'm still trying to figure it out."

"Figure it out?" she shrieked incredulously.

"I don't believe in coincidences, Sophia. The universe must be trying to tell me something."

"Boy, if you don't get outta my face. You leaving me in that hospital was the most hurtful thing I've ever had to experience. I will never give you another chance to do me like that again."

"I was young and dumb. That shit was my coward's way out, and I apologize."

"Apology accepted, but my heart, mind, or body aren't available to deal with you. So, thanks for pumping my gas, but I need to go."

"Can I go with you?" Mello pressed his luck with a charming smile. He saw right through her attitude.

"No. For what?"

"Your energy. That shit still can pull a nigga in and have him stuck. Let's talk, Sophie. We got shit to get off our chest."

Sophie sighed, frustrated with how he could still tug at her emotions. "I hate that I still care so much. I hate the way my body feels being this close to you again. I feel so stupid for wanting to hear you out."

"No, you don't. The love was real at the wrong time." Mello took a step closer, filling the space between them. "Get in the car, sweetheart. Let me follow you home and make sure you good. I'm moving on your time right now. You call the shots."

The ringing of Mello's cell phone jarred him from his sleep. He groggily opened his eyes, almost alarmed by the unfamiliar territory. He had fallen asleep with Sophie curled in a ball on one side of the couch, and him uncomfortably stretched on the other. He almost forgot coming to her house with her the night before.

He took a minute to stare at her, taking in every feature of her face. He even noticed the tiny mole just under her left eye. She wasn't outrageously gorgeous, but li'l momma was definitely a ten.

The ringing had stopped, but it started right back up. Mello reached into his pocket, pulling out his cell phone. It was Robinson. He knew they would finally have to talk, and Mello wasn't the one to do too much talking.

"Fuck you want?" he answered with heavy irritation.

"Good job on the switch up. My men said your warehouse was squeaky clean," Robinson started. "Well, that depends on what comes back from the pistol found on the scene. I can turn it in now. But we both know the likelihood of it being clean is slim to none."

"You know this some fuck shit, right? After all the money I put in your pockets, this is what it comes to?" Mello snarled.

"Do you know what those Russian motherfuckers will do to me, you, and those bitches? Not to mention what predicament your whores put my good friend Domo in? I'm their only saving grace. I can do a lot of damage, Kenneth, and I'm trying to give you all the chance to make it right and put a little money in your pockets at the same time. I guess that's my problem, always trying to be the good Samaritan."

"Yea, a'ight."

"I figured you'd see it my way. I texted you the details of what I need you to do. You need to make sure the girls are down because their pictures are a hot commodity on the website."

Mello frowned. "What the fuck are you talking about?"

"The way I see it, you owe me. The girls owe Domo. I figured out a way to work together to make sure everyone is satisfied. Your friends will be the face of our new business venture." Robinson smiled sheepishly. "I texted you the details. Call me after the assignment is complete...and don't fuck it up this time."

Mello ended the call, only to find Sophie's doughy eyes peering at him. He watched as her chest rose and fell, waiting for him to speak. He could tell she had something on her mind.

"Are you in trouble?" Her voice was small, but the question was loud. Was he in trouble?

"I'm grown as hell. I can't get in trouble, love." Mello shot her a wink. The thought of involving her in whatever Robinson had planned didn't sit right with him.

"Something is bothering you. You still can't hide it on your face."

Mello grimaced, throwing his head back, relaxing. "How did you get involved with your homegirl? Y'all so different."

Sophie wagged a perfectly manicured finger at him. "Uh-uh, that's what we're *not* going to do. Angel has her ways, but she actually has a good heart."

"A good heart? Out of all the people in the world she could have asked to come with her that night, you think that's really giving a fuck about you for her to involve you, knowing you got a little shorty to look after?"

"I'm not doing this with you, Kenneth. She didn't put a gun to my head. I needed the money. If you're going to disrespect my sister, then get out. She was the one there for me, *not* you."

"Yeah, but she played on your vulnerability. You all calm and cool, but do you *really* realize what the fuck she got y'all into?"

"Of course, I knew what I was getting myself into. We survived, we're good, and next subject."

Mello's brows furrowed, realizing that she didn't have a clue. "Damn, so you *don't* know? That's fucked up."

"What's fucked up?"

"Did your homegirl tell you about how them niggas ran up on her in the crib?" Mello asked.

"In what crib? Here?!" Sophie shrieked, hopping up.

"Yeah, man. You been having li'l man in this crib all this time, and you ain't know niggas on all our heads?"

"*My* head?" Sophie pointed to her chest. Mello saw the panic in her eyes. "Angel! Get your ass down here now and tell me this nigga lying." When she heard nothing, Sophie marched to the staircase and yelled for Angel. "Heffa, if you don't bring yo' ass down here right now, I know something!" she yelled.

Seconds later, Angel groggily made her way to the living room. The boy shorts and tank she sported showcased her perfect frame, and the bonnet allowed her natural beauty to glow. To be so pretty, Mello couldn't understand how she could be so conniving.

"Girlll, why you yelling this early in the morning? Damn."

Sophie folded her arms across her chest, focusing on Mello. "Tell her what you told me, and you better be lying, Kenneth. I know this heffa don't got me and my son staying in this house, knowing it's not safe."

"Look, li'l momma, this seem like a conversation y'all need to have between you two. I'm about to head out."

"Kenneth Ryan Davis! I know you're good at running, but you'll do no such thing today! You are going to stand here, and we are going to figure whatever it is out together. You don't get to throw a stone and walk away."

Angel rolled her eyes at Mello, blowing out a husky breath of air. "I was going to tell you, sis. I just thought I could handle the situation without involving y'all."

"Involving me in *what*, Angel?" Sophie asked through tight lips.

"This dude me and Shanell hit a few weeks ago, he was at that party. You know, the one that kicked my ass?"

"What about him?"

"They came here the other day. Him and the cop that Mello was working with. I guess the shit we took was worth a lot of money, and now he on my head about getting the money back and the cop helping him. He tried to scare me with all these fake charges on me, you, and Diamond. But I'm not worried. I'll figure it out."

"How much money, Angel?" Sophie demanded.

"A million dollars."

"Bitch! And you thought you was supposed to keep *that* away from me? Where the fuck are we supposed to get a million dollars from? I barely have a hundred to my name! What about Diamond? You don't know if these niggas are serious, and it involves us. We should have been the first to know!" Sophie was wearing a hole in the carpet. Her heart was racing.

"I'm sorry, Fe Fe. I said I'll handle it."

Mello shook his head. "It's not that simple, li'l momma. You fucking with some real killers now. It's not a cut-and-dried fix. If it was, I would have put a toe tag on them niggas and moved on. It's fucked up you didn't tell your homegirl, especially with her having li'l man. I gotta meet with Robinson at twelve to see what's up, and I was under the impression y'all was ready to strap on y'all nuts and get it in if need be."

Sophie shook her head. "I don't have no fucking nuts! I'm a woman. I'm a fucking mother! You said you wouldn't involve us in no shit that would put us in harm's way, Angel! What the fuck?!"

"You think I did this on purpose? Why would I bring harm to my only family?"

"Because you're a money-hungry bitch, and I'm just now starting to realize it. You don't care about nothing and no one but yourself."

Hurt registered on Angel's face. It wasn't too often that it was found. She had blocked her feelings off to the outside world and replaced them with a coldness that protected her from the pain and vulnerability that life had plagued her with. However, hearing her best friend, her sister, speaking to her that way was a low blow, and it cut deep.

"Damn, you're really going to sit up here and say that?" Her voice was pained.

"I don't have time for this shit, Angel. Thank goodness my son is somewhere safe. Lord knows I would have been on your ass if anything happened to that boy by me messing with you."

Mello stood off to the side, watching as everything played out. It wasn't hard to miss that Angel cared for her girl. Maybe he had misjudged her.

"Man, both of y'all chill. Beefing ain't gon' do nothing. Let me see what these ma'fuckas talking about, and we'll come together and come up with something." He turned toward Sophie. "Ain't no way I'm gon' let shit happen to you. You can take that to the bank and cash it."

Sophie blushed at his intensity. "Please, just keep me posted."

"No doubt. Be easy, love."

The ladies watched as his tall, muscular frame disappeared. The tension in the room was thick enough to slice with a knife. However, a calmness washed over Sophie. She knew she shouldn't have trusted a word Mello said, but deep down, she wholeheartedly believed he would protect her. She could feel it in her bones.

CHAPTER NINETEEN

SOPHIE TAPPED HER nails against the kitchen table, staring at her phone and debating whether to call Ricardo. She blew out a breath of air at the thought. That was precisely what he wanted her to do...come crawling back to him.

"You have to do what you have to do, bitch. Suck it up." She closed her eyes, picking up the phone.

"What up? I'm busy." Ricardo answered on the second ring.

"You know I haven't asked for anything since I left, and I really appreciate you keeping Jr. for now, but I need a favor." There wasn't any sense in beating around the bush.

"What kind of favor you need, Sophie?"

"I want to make a proposition. I was trying to see i—"

Ricardo burst into laughter before she could finish her sentence. "You know you really got me fucked up, right? What'chu trying to see, Sophie? I know you not about to fix your mouth to ask me for no money when I never put you out."

"You didn't put me out, but you made my life miserable, Ricardo. Ever since you got your record deal, it was fuck me. You was even posted on the internet hugged up with bitches. Was I supposed to just take that?"

"But who I gave my seed and my last name to? You was worried about the wrong shit because it ain't one time I didn't make sure you and my son was straight."

"You call canceling my credit card and allowing me to look stupid in public straight?"

"Look, it is what it is. If you not coming home, get off my line. I ain't putting no bread in your pocket, Sophie. That's a wrap."

"You are so fucking selfish!" Sophie hung up on him, tossing her phone across the counter. She was frustrated. Ricardo had money. He could easily help her, but he was such an egotistical coward. "I hate I ever fucking met him."

"What'chu sitting up there begging that nigga for?" Mello's voice startled her as he pushed off the wall and fully made it into the kitchen, followed by Diamond, Rock, and Angel. "Didn't I say we was going to figure this out together? Fuck that nigga."

Sophie looked off. "Wasn't nobody begging. I was trying to find a solution to a problem I didn't create."

"Well, you can stop looking. Ain't no way out unless that nigga giving up ten million." Mello shrugged.

"Ten, what?!" Diamond and Sophie shrieked at the same time.

"Yeah, ten million, love. I got a few m's, but it's not nearly enough to pay off these niggas."

"You just said it was only a million yesterday. There is no way we can come up with that kind of money. I don't know about you, but me, that heffa, and this heffa are just regular broads. That shit sound unrealistic as fuck." Sophie threw her hands in the air.

"We take it." Angel stepped in. "We do what we did the other night, but on a more organized level, with backup." Angel's head pointed toward Mello and Rock. "Robinson created a dummy escort company. All we need to do is show up, get these niggas to hand over the cash, and we out. We get paid. We pay them off, and we out. It's going to be like taking candy from a baby, Soph. Watch."

Sophie rolled her eyes. "That's what got us into this situation, ain't it? I'm not doing that shit." She shook her head.

"I said the same thing, but our backs are against the wall. I mean, the way Angel explained it don't seem too bad. I just want to get this shit over with and get back to my regular life. What other choices do we have?" Diamond reasoned.

"To call the fucking police."

Angel sucked her teeth. "Are you *hearing* yourself? He *is* the police. What is calling them going to do? Come on, Fe Fe. We need you. Plus, we'll get a cut from every lick. So really, we'll be covering our debt *and* coming up at the same time. It's a win-win."

"Still so fucking worried about money," Sophie scoffed.

"It's not about money, love. We doing what we got to do," Mello interrupted.

"I don't know. I need a day or two to process everything and think about it."

"You don't have a day. You got about an hour and a half, two at the most. Our plane leaves at seven thirty."

Sophie took a deep breath as she listened to her son's curious voice. Her eyes shifted, watching the other passengers load the plane. She couldn't believe she was going through with everything. Nervous energy surged throughout her entire being.

"Mommy will be back soon, baby. I promise. We can go wherever you want to go too," Sophie cooed into the phone, almost in tears. She had never been separated from her son as much as she had been lately.

"Good, 'cause I don't want to be at Granny's or Auntie Angel and Diamond's house. My daddy said we can come home, but you don't want to."

Sophie rolled her eyes. She couldn't understand how she ignored her child's father's ignorance for so long. It was disgusting. "Don't listen to your daddy, baby."

"Aye, man. Don't tell him not to listen to me. The fuck is your problem?" Ricardo hissed, snatching the phone.

This nigga here. Sophie should have known that he wouldn't let Jr. talk to her without listening in. That would have been too much like right. "Well, stop telling him crazy stuff. Keep him out of our business, Ricardo."

"*You* put him in our business when you left. You heard my son. He don't want to be staying with his fake-ass granny or your ho-ass friends. My son deserve to have a crib of his own and his own room."

"And he will have it."

Ricardo burst into laughter. "How? You was just asking me for money. You don't do shit, don't want to do shit, and ain't got shit," he shot mockingly.

"But you saying that in front of my son, though. I must have been about something. You kept begging my do-nothing ass to come home."

"For my son. I don't want yo' sorry ass. Why you think I stay with a bad bitch in the cut?"

"Why are you still on my phone, Ricardo? I'm not about to go there with you. I'll text you to bring Jr. when I get back."

Sophie looked out the window of the aircraft. The pilot announced for them to prepare for takeoff, but how was she supposed to prepare herself for what they were about to do?

"You really think we can pull this off?" Her innocent eyes connected with Mello. He was such a handsome man.

"Shit, we ain't got no choice but to pull it off, love. Stop stressing yourself out. I told you, I got you."

"Your word doesn't really have value, Kenneth. You don't get to just come back after all these years and think things will just go back to normal and we live happily ever after. This isn't a storybook, and our life isn't exactly a fairy tale right now."

"I never said it was. And to keep it a buck, I never liked them bitches growing up. Life's a motherfucka. Ain't no happy endings."

"If you don't believe in happy endings, then what is the purpose of anything? Why not just let the cards lie how they fall?"

Mello shrugged. "Because life's a bitch, and you got to fuck her before she fuck you."

Four hours later...

It was seven at night, and Sophie was finding it terribly hard to get her nerves in check. They hopped straight off the plane and went to the hotel their mark was staying at. She barely had enough time to complete her hygiene and change.

Ralphael Donaldson was a wealthy politician that dabbled a little in the black market. He chartered into Miami to close on a new venture with his weapons dealer. It just so happens he ordered a little fun before he got to the business in the morning, and out of the three girls on the site, Sophie was the one he chose.

Robinson had created an escort service with the ladies as the face of the company to lure in their licks. Sophie was livid when she found out. The last thing she needed was for her face to be plastered on a ho site.

She sat nervously in the hotel's lobby, waiting for her cue from Angel. The money at the end of their lick was the only thing holding her together. It was taking everything in her not to just run out.

"You waiting on me, beautiful?" The deep masculine voice jarred her from her thoughts.

She looked up at him. The voice belonged to a tall, handsome Italian man. He wore a custom-tailored suit with silky, charcoal, slicked-back hair. Sophie's eyes quickly scanned the room with an unsure pang of nervousness. Her gaze landed across the way to Mello. He nodded, and for some reason, that was all the assurance she needed to pull herself together.

Sophie rose to her feet, accepting his outstretched hand. The Dolce & Gabbana dress that covered her body hugged every dip and curve of her tight frame. There wasn't a hair out of place, and her nails and toes matched the red of her dress. She held a black leather briefcase in her free hand and gripped the handle nervously. Sophie had to remind herself they were in California, and once the caper was over, they'd never be seen again.

"I should call you Ralphael, right?"

The man smiled. "In the flesh. Although I have to say, Olivia, I wasn't expecting you to be so beautiful in person. I'm going to have a lot of fun with you."

Sophie giggled. "We'll see."

"Indeed, we will," Ralphael retorted, guiding them to the elevator and pressing the up button. Before the doors could open, Diamond, Angel, and Mello were lined up, pretending to be kissing, awaiting the elevator to open as well.

"Wow, two of them. You're a wild boy," Ralphael chuckled, giving Mello his nod of approval. "What floor?" he added after stepping on the elevator and pressing seven for their floor.

"Seven," Mello retorted, pretending to be engrossed in the ladies.

They rode the elevators up to the seventh floor in silence, with an occasional giggle from Angel as Mello pretended to play with her hair. Mello was going to end up blowing their cover because if he kept it up, Sophie would straight go upside his head.

She was relieved when the elevator door swung open. Ralphael allowed Mello and the girls to step off first. He ogled their thick frames before shaking his head and turning to go the opposite way. "Lucky man. *Very* lucky man," he commented, studying the room numbers until he reached the one he was looking for...room 716.

Before he could open the door, Angel appeared out of nowhere, sending a skull-shattering blow to the back of his head. She looked both ways to make sure the coast was clear, pushing Ralphael into the hotel room, followed by Diamond and Sophie.

"Shit," Ralphael staggered, falling into the bed. "Wha... What's going on?"

"You know what time it is. Sit down, Ralphie," Angel smiled.

Ralphael's mouth hung open. "What do you want? I don't carry cash on me, you scheming bitches."

Smack! This time, when Angel's beretta crashed into Ralphael's head, it caused blood to gush from his hairline. "That name-calling will get you fucked up. Where's the money?" Angel insisted.

Ralphael grabbed his head, letting off a groan. He had close to a million dollars secured in the hotel's safe. There was no way he could take such a significant loss. He wasn't about to be robbed by three bitches.

"I just told you. I don't carry cash on me," he grumbled, stalling for time.

"Then how was you going to buy them guns, Ralphie? With air? Stop playing with me."

Angel lifted her gun to hit him again, but he threw his hands in the air. "Wait. Wait. Please, my head is already splitting. I have a wife and three kids to go home to."

"Well, if you stop bullshitting and hand over the money, we'll be out of your hair," Angel assured him. When he didn't move, she continued. "Get the fuck up. Go get the money and put it in this case." She cocked the gun.

"All right. All right. Don't shoot me." Ralphael pleaded. Reluctantly, he did as he was told, popping the safe and handing over a million dollars. Just the thought of the loss had him thinking about risking it all...but his three children were his saving grace. Painfully, he watched the ladies close the case and swish their way out of the room. He felt helpless...worthless...He felt like revenge.

Sophie tried to play it cool, but her nerves had her running to the hotel's exit. She didn't know what to expect since she had never stolen a million dollars from a white man before. She didn't exhale until they had safely made it back to their own suite across town, and Mello was handing over the envelope with her cut, indicating that the mission was completed.

"It's hot as fuck out here, and this line too long," Diamond complained, wiping the beads of sweat from her forehead. Summer in California wasn't a joke. The heat was almost unbearable, and it was well after midnight.

Warwick nightclub was a popular bar in Hollywood. Celebs and some of the most elite frequented the bar. At least, that's what Google stated. Angel had researched and narrowed their nightcap down to two different bars, Warwick being her first pick. Supposedly, the afterparty for the Future concert was being hosted there.

"Yes, it is kind of hot out here. I'm not trying to be all sweaty in this club," Sophie agreed. Truth was, she wasn't thinking about a club. They had just robbed a man of a nice grip. Instead of partying, they should have been somewhere ducked off, headed back to Detroit. However, they had to meet the dealer in the morning to pass off the diamonds before they were truly finished with their mission.

"Here y'all go complaining. Relax and have fun! We just made some easy money. Plus, I peeped you and your boo getting all cozy. I told y'all I was going to make it right."

Sophie rolled her eyes. "First of all, he is *not* my boo. I'd never fuck with him again." Sophie tried her best to swallow the lump that settled in her throat at the thought. "Second of all, I just want to go home. What if Ralphael has goons or some shit? How do you know he won't send nobody after us? Domo found you."

"He doesn't even know your real name. Shit, he doesn't know anything about any of us. What we're about to do will be epic; watch," Angel squealed.

Diamond looked around with a chuckle. "Will you shut your crazy ass up?" She lowered her voice. "I'm not going to front. I was mad at first, but this was a little clutch. Got my adrenaline pumping. Now, I can get a few people off my back," Diamond agreed as they finally made it to the front of the line.

After waiting for nearly an hour, Mello, Rock, and three others came waltzing their asses to the front of the line, walking in with the girls. Sophie rolled her eyes. She tried not to notice how fine the man was, but Kenneth Davis was walking perfection. The years had aged him well. He wasn't your average nigga. He was far from the Kenny that used to fuck her on the air mattress inside his little studio apartment.

"So, y'all just gon' walk y'all ugly asses in line when it's time to go in, had us waiting in this heat, feet hurting and everything. Furthermore, I thought you was that nigga. Where yo' pull at?" Angel complained, calling out Mello.

He smirked, his eyes never leaving Sophie's frame. "You talk too much." That's all he offered before falling in line with Sophie's stride. "What's up, pretty girl?"

"Don't call me that," Sophie muttered, missing a step, almost falling over.

Mello grabbed her by the waist, holding her up. "See, trying to be mean. I got you, though, love. I'll never let you fall, baby." He chuckled, causing Sophie to laugh as well.

"Will you leave me alone, boy? Dang."

"I ain't started yet. Watch." He winked as a tall, lemon-skinned man approached Mello, slapping fives with him.

"What's up? My niggas, Ken and Rakim." He greeted Mello, then Rock, calling him by his government name. "You know I got your section laid out for you and the beautiful ladies." He eyed Sophie, Diamond, then Angel. "And I *do* mean beautiful. Welcome to Hollywood, ladies. Follow me."

Rock chuckled. "This nigga still be on some bullshit. Here you go. What up, Gunna?"

"I can't call it. Staying far from Detroit and sucka free. Y'all niggas getting too wild up there," Gunna frowned.

"Tell me about it. I'm on the same tip. About to make a little investment and get the fuck on," Mello confirmed.

"I feel you. If you ever decide to move to Cali, hit my line. You know I'll show you around and introduce you to who you need to know."

"No doubt."

"All right, your section is the last booth to the right. Let me mingle a little. We got them rap niggas in the building, and they be acting like they on their period, thinking they princesses and shit."

The men shared a laugh before slapping fives and watching Gunna walk off. Mello didn't mess with too many people. Niggas weren't loyal. However, Gunna was an exception. They ran in the same circle back in the day, and he proved to be one of the solid ones.

After helping the ladies into the booth, Mello stared at Angel and winked. No words needed to be spoken. She knew what was up.

Angel rolled her eyes. "Whatever, nigga. If you had so much pull, why you make us wait in that long-ass line?"

Mello smirked. "Because I wanted to admire Sophie's ass while I could." He turned to her, placing his chin on her shoulder without permission and sniffing her neck. "You looked good, love."

She blushed, and everybody saw it. Mello was wearing her down, and it irritated Sophie's soul. Her mind told her to run, but her heart wanted him as bad as the air she breathed.

"Why you always talking shit?" she sighed.

"Because I can back it up," he retorted. "Stop bullshitting, and you'll see."

"Whatever. I'm not doing this with you every time I see you."

Mello smiled. "Yeah, every fucking time I see you, I'm on yo' ass. Believe that." He smacked her thigh. "You got to run it back and see I'm for real this time."

Sophie moved his hand from her thigh. "I don't go backward. My mother taught me that."

"Who, Natalie? She ain't taught you shit," Mello chuckled.

Sophie was offended. She could talk about her mom, but no one else could. "Leave my mother out of this, and leave me alone, Kenneth."

"I'll think about it." He turned to his crew. "What y'all sippin' on? It's on me tonight." His gaze landed back on Sophie. "We toasting it up to new beginnings."

Sophie bit down on the folds of her cheeks. How could they ever start a new beginning if the wounds from the old one weren't healed yet?

Sophie didn't know how she ended up in Mello's hotel room with him kissing her in places he had no business touching. One minute, they were drinking and having a good time in the club. The next, they were hot and bothered and back at his place.

For a second, she had to ask herself what she was doing and why she had come...until the sensation of his tongue swiveling around her clit was too much to bear. Chills eased up her spine as he aggressively gripped her ass cheeks and ate her like Thanksgiving dinner.

"Shit, Kenny. We can't do this. Oh my goodness. I don't want to do this with you again," she whined as reality began to sober her. "Wait. Wait, stop. I'm not ready." She pushed his head away, and Mello stopped, falling onto the bed beside her.

"What's on your mind, love?"

Sophie was so overtaken by emotions that she could feel her chest tighten. She couldn't breathe. She had to get away from Kenneth Davis. "I-I-I got to go." She didn't even bother to put her shoes on. She pulled her dress down and leaped toward the door.

"Sophie! Aye, Soph—" Mello's words were cut off by the room door slamming. She heard him, but there was no way she was waiting around to talk to him.

CHAPTER TWENTY

A WEEK LATER, THE girls had safely made it back to Detroit and were up to their regularly scheduled programs. Life had changed drastically for Diamond. In less than a month, over seventy-five thousand dollars had flowed through her hands. That was more money than she had ever seen at one time, which was a cause for her to turn up.

"Boyyyyy, would you. Boss up and get this money..."

The lyrics to the late local Detroit rapper Blade Icewood's hit song blared through the speakers as the club went wild. After over ten years, the city still turned up to the classic song. Everyone was doing the Blade dance and singing along, including Diamond and Manny as they held the VIP section down. It was a celebration. She finally paid off all her debt and had a little breathing room.

Her long, jet-black Brazilian hair swung over her shoulder, and her hips rocked as she scanned the crowd. She wasn't looking for anyone; however, her eyes squinted when they met with a beautiful yellow bone throwing daggers in their section. She frowned right back at the bitch.

After a two-minute stare down, Diamond finally shoved Manny to get his attention. The chick had to be one of his hoes. If they weren't fucking around, they had in the past. She knew that look all too well, and Diamond wasn't the one.

She pointed at the girl, disregarding discreetness. She wanted the bitch to know she was talking about her. "Is that one of ya little hoes about to get her ass beat? Why she staring at me like that, Emmanuel?"

Manny's eyes followed Diamond's fingers, and he had to shake his head. "Mannnnn, that's my fucking wife. Fuck!"

Diamond's brows furrowed. "What you fuckin' for? Y'all not together, right? Y'all getting a divorce, right?" She rolled her eyes. Diamond was never the one to play with her feelings. She had walls up that he decided to knock down. She had given him the outlet to kick it on the low; he wanted more.

Manny waved Diamond off. He felt like a kid caught with his hand in the cookie jar. He kept both worlds separate and counted on them never colliding. "Here you go. Man, don't start that shit, Diamond."

"Start what shit? Yo' wife the one staring over here like she want to get smacked up. The way she looking, it look like you need to go give her some attention or something." Diamond's attitude was heavy. She knew that Manny had a wife. She swore if she had known before she became invested in him, the nigga would have been a wrap. However, as much as she hated to admit it, he had her heart.

Diamond sized up his wife as emotions built in her chest. Why she had to be so pretty, though? Why couldn't she be one of those hoodrat hoes? Diamond's insecurity was eating at her.

Tiera, his wife, began to make her way toward them. Manny was so full of shit. She had left him because his attention was obviously elsewhere. However, he swore that he didn't want no other broad. He swore he was a real nigga. In many ways, he was. However, how could a nigga really love you and constantly cheat? That wasn't love. That was a toxic, narcissistic asshole.

"Oh, she coming to say hello, huh?" Diamond frowned, crossing her arms over her chest as Tiera's thick frame made it to their section.

"What's up, Emmanuel? So, this ya boo you said you didn't have, huh?" Tiera snarled, pointing at Diamond.

"Don't point at me, bitch," Diamond shot, pissed. The music was blasting. Everyone seemed to be oblivious to the altercation that was about to take place.

Tiera let out a small laugh. "You would choose a ghetto-ass broad like that."

Why did she have to say that? Diamond charged at Tiera. They scuffled a bit before Manny snatched Diamond up, pulling her away, kicking and screaming all types of obscenities.

"Ayye yoo. Take your ass home, Tee Tee. I'll holla at you later," Manny growled.

"Tee Tee, huh? You calling the ho pet names and got me fighting over yo' ugly ass? Oh, hell no. What am I doing? You somebody else's whole husband."

"Oh, that's what you telling people, Emmanuel? Did you tell her how you was just at my house begging to eat my coochie a week ago?"

"A week ago?" Diamond snatched away. "What the fuck am I doing? I'm not about to beef with you about your husband, sweetie. He can have you," she shot, stomping off. "Niggas want to bother you just to waste your fucking time. I knew I should have fucked and dipped." She continued with her rant, pushing open the door to the club. She was so thankful that she drove her own car.

"Yo, Dee. Hold up. Diamond!" Manny called after her.

She kept walking, only stopping when she felt his strong hands cup her arm. Diamond spun around so quickly that Manny never got a chance to react to her first slap. However, he caught the second one midair, pinning her against someone's random car.

"Aye, nigga. Chill the fuck out," he growled, and Diamond surprisingly listened. The grimness of his voice calmed her right down. "Don't put your fucking hands on me, Diamond. Respect me like I respect you, a'ight?"

Diamond looked away from his intense glare. Manny cupped her chin and pulled her face back up to his. "Nah, nigga. Don't look away. You steady screamin' that 'just kicking it' bullshit, and I'm trying to make it official. How you get mad at me because you see ol' girl in the club? That's lame."

"No, what's lame is you telling me how much you want to be with me but still fucking with yo' wife, begging to eat her pussy in the next breath."

"How you know we still fuckin' around? That's what you assumin', right?"

Diamond sucked her teeth. "Manny, please! You heard the same shit I just heard. We both know you love havin' yo' face in somebody shit. Furthermore, why she feel the need to come check you if y'all ain't fuckin' around?"

Manny let out a sigh. "You know how y'all females be. I mean, I thought about trying to make it work a few times, but I ain't on that."

"Well, go make it work, Manny. I don't need the headache of an indecisive nigga. If you still in limbo, don't come fucking with me. Go pick that bitch. Bye, Emmanuel."

Manny pushed her car door shut again. "I ain't done talking to you. What's the issue, Diamond? What's really good? You giving off mixed signals, and that shit frustrating as fuck."

"What just happened is why I won't fuck with you. Answer me this. Was you at that lady's house last week, begging like she said? I could have sworn you was with me every other day, talking about how solid you is and how you trying to make it official. Is that why you dragging out that divorce? Keep it a buck. Let me know something."

Manny ran his hands along his face. "I just told you. I tried to see if we could make it work. But you see who I'm out here trying to make it work with. Fuck that girl. I'm on yo' wave right now if you let a nigga in."

"I'm on my own wave too. Give me some space, Manny. Don't be selfish." Diamond finally fell into the soft leather seats of her Benz. She closed the door, firing up the engine, speeding off. Manny stood there stuck. He wasn't fucking with Tiera, but he wasn't ready for the finality of her not being his anymore either. He loved Diamond. He'd choose her first anytime. He'd been trying to show her that. Why couldn't she see that and chill the fuck out?

"Are you going to be okay? It looks like you lost your best friend. We need you focused." Angel leaned over Diamond's shoulder, looking into her phone to see what preoccupied her. She frowned. "Why you stalking that girl's page? Fuck him and his wife."

Diamond placed her phone on the table, facedown. "Ain't nobody stalking her page. I'm just trying to see what's going on. He told me he was getting a divorce, and clearly, he don't hate her as much as he was claiming."

Angel sucked her teeth, pulling a pair of fishnet stockings up her thick thighs. "You the one trying to keep it casual with the nigga. What difference does it make if he still fucking her? You don't want him."

"That's not the point, Angel. My thing is, don't have me thinking you're all in love and it's all about me, but you out here dirty. I'm only messing with him, and if that's not what he's on, leave me alone. Keep it real so I can know how to move."

"Again, why does that matter if y'all not together, and you keep telling this nigga you ain't trying to be? We, as women, get shit confused. If we just dating, then you don't belong to me, and I don't belong to you. So, we can do whatever the fuck we want."

"Yeah, whatever. It's just certain shit you're not supposed to do when you supposedly fuckin' with someone heavy. No matter if we together or not."

"That's why you need to be fuckin' with a winner." Rock eased into their conversation, causing Diamond to jump. No one heard him slip into the room. Sophie and Mello followed behind him. "Li'l thick ass be sprung and all in love and shit."

Diamond took Rock in. He was dressed in jeans and a black top with the newest Jordans. His hair was cut in a low taper, and his waves were spinning. He had a tall, thick frame that was sexy to Diamond. She smirked. He was attractive, but beyond that, she wasn't trying to go there with him.

"Y'all ready?" Angel asked as Diamond's heart raced. It was showtime. They were back out on the prowl. This time, it was some wealthy politician in New York. Mello had flown out a week early to study the man and get everything prepared. According to him, he was just some sucka that liked young, Black pussy. Diamond still couldn't help the jitters, though.

They were standing outside of the mansion's door. One knock and their mission would officially begin. The girls were all scantily dressed as escorts. Their bodies were on full display, oozing sex. He was only expecting Angel, but they would surprise House Rep. Justin Bozenski with the "three-for-one special."

Their job was to seduce him, get him drunk, then make him transfer the money he owed the Russians into an offshore account, plus their fee. Mello and Rock were waiting outside the door as reinforcements if he gave them too much of a struggle.

"Do we have a choice?" Sophie asked, looking back at the rented Malibu that held Mello, Rock, and two of their goons. He winked at her, and she blushed. That was always his signature move right before they hit a lick, and somehow, seeing his face always gave her the reassurance she needed.

Angel lifted her hand to knock, but the door swung open before she could. She approached him, rubbing her perfectly manicured hand down his chest. "I know you ordered one, but my girls were free now, and I figured I would challenge you to three. Can you handle it, daddy?" she cooed seductively.

Bozenski looked around skeptically. The first thing he noticed was the briefcase in Sophie's hand. He was a wise man. He'd done plenty of dirt, won plenty of awards, and hung with a variety of people, including the leaders of prominent crime families to the president of the United States when Trump was in office. He didn't get that far for nothing. There was no way he'd let pussy destroy his years of hard work and scheming.

"No, I only ordered you. The company assured me that my privacy was valued. Now, I have three bitches in my business—"

"Bitches?" Diamond's head cocked, cutting him off.

"You know what? Never mind. How much was I supposed to pay? I'll give you half, but your services are no longer needed," he grumbled, patting his pockets. "Shit." He left his wallet on the table. Turning to grab it, he never saw Angel coming as she pushed him forward into the house, striking him on top of his head with the butt of her gun. Sophie and Diamond followed them into the house, locking the door.

"Wha...What's going on?" Bozenski stuttered, holding his head that now sported a tiny gash with trickles of blood.

Angel held the gun aimed at his face. "These 'bitches' came to collect. Oh, and next time you decide to call me a bitch, make sure you call me *Queen* Bitch."

"I don't have anything but what's in my wallet. You can take that—about five hundred dollars."

"Five hundred? Nigga, please," Angel frowned, signaling for Sophie to bring the briefcase to her. She did. "Have a seat, Justin."

"I'd rather not. What do you want from me? I have a family."

Angel let out a sadistic laugh. "*Now* they matter? Did you have a wife and kids when you thought you was going to get some of this sweet Black pussy? Sit yo' ugly fat ass down," she growled, pushing him into the table.

He started to protest, but Angel took the gun and pushed it into his temple, causing his skin to dent from the pressure. "We can do this the easy way, or we can do this the hard way. Either way, you have three bitches with guns in here, and if you just so happen to get past us, there's a car full of goons that won't be as nice as us."

Bozenski's head fell as he sat defeated in the wooden chair, awaiting his fate. "Good boy. Now, I need you to open this briefcase and log into this laptop," Angel instructed.

Bozenski's heart dropped when he laid eyes on his "secret" laptop that was kept hidden in a safe inside his office. Only a select few knew where to find it and what it held. His entire fortune was just one click away.

"How'd y...Ho...How'd you get that?" He swallowed hard.

"Don't worry your greasy little head." Angel leaned in, pinching his cheek. She had been the one to take the lead in all their licks since she was the more experienced one. Her girls were just reinforcement.

"Now, Justin, I need you to log into this computer and transfer five million into one account and a million into another. Can you do that for me?" She placed a small piece of paper with the account numbers in front of Bozenski.

Bozenski's hands began to shake. That would nearly wipe him out. He had plotted and schemed to get that money. He'd lie in the grass with dogs and never thought about coming out with flees. Yet, here they were in the form of three beautiful Black women.

He couldn't go out like that. His eyes darted around the room, landing on the rack of knives on a table. All the sense left his body with six million dollars on the line. The girls didn't even have a chance to process it before he lunged for the knives, grabbing one and snatching Diamond up with the cold steel to her neck, threatening to penetrate.

"Put the gun down, or I'll slit her throat," his voice cracked.

Sophie panicked. She instantly lowered her gun to the floor. Angel wasn't so easily convinced, though. She held her composure. Bozenski wasn't a killer. His eyes told his story, and his hands were too shaky.

Angel cocked her gun, catching eyes with Diamond, telling her silently that everything would be OK. Then she focused on Bozenski with a menacing scowl. "Do it," Angel urged.

"Bitch, what?" Sophie frowned.

"I want him to do it. He kill her, and he for damn sure won't be leaving out here alive. Then his family not gon' be able to bury him because I'm gon' make it my business to send that wife and them three kids he was hollering about to the grave right with his fat ass. So again—*do* it," she taunted.

Bozenski's thoughts were scattered. However, he thought about his three beautiful daughters and even his wife. They were his world. He quickly wondered how he got into such a fucked-up position when he had everything he needed under one roof. He cursed himself for being so stupid, dropping the knife, defeated.

Once he released Diamond, she smacked the man so hard that the sound echoed throughout the entire house. "That's for having me fucked up." She hit him again. "Don't you *ever* play with me like that." Her heart was racing with fear and adrenaline as her hand shot to her neck, and her breathing slowly steadied.

Angel burst into laughter. "*That's* what I'm talking about. Get gangsta wit"'em, sis. Just wait until after we get what we want." She pointed at the laptop. "I think you need to sit down and do what we asked. We all know you don't want these problems."

"Just so you know," he started, a final attempt to plead his case, "this will bankrupt me...my house, my wife, my three girls. What about my kids? What am I supposed to tell them?"

Angel's smile faded as a menacing scowl replaced it. "Nigga, fuck those kids. Press that button!"

Bozenski looked so pitiful. Losing six million dollars would break the strongest man, and it was damn near killing him to be so helpless. Against his will, he pressed the button that catapulted his future into shambles.

Bozenski had a good run with the Russians. He ran his campaigns with their dirty money, cleaned their money with his legal businesses, and orchestrated white-collar deals. When he figured he had enough saved up, he stopped taking Ivanov's calls and cut himself out of the game, cold turkey. Bozenski wasn't a greedy man. He knew that the game wouldn't last forever. He thought he was five steps ahead. But as he sent his last million dollars to the second account, he realized he was the one being played all along.

"Now, was that so hard?" Sophie smiled, closing the laptop, placing it back into the briefcase, and picking it up. "By the way, I hope your wife leaves you and your dick falls off. You're trifling," she snarled as they made their way to the door, Angel walking backward with the gun pointed at Bozenski. Once outside, they ran to their car and sped off.

"We have been getting it in. We're really good at this. We're good, and it only gets better. Watch," Angel said, texting Mello to let him know the job was complete.

"Girl, bye. I don't plan to get comfortable doing this. I'm saving my money, and once we're in the clear, me and my son are out," Sophie insisted.

"Out?" Angel frowned. "Where else will you get the type of money we've been getting? Why would you want to quit, and we just getting started? We're good at it. At the rate we're going, we'll be millionaires in the next few months."

Sophie rolled her eyes. "Diamond almost died back there, for one. And two, I'm not fucking with them Russian niggas, that Domo nigga, or that cop. We rub him the wrong way and end up dead or in somebody's prison cell. I'm too cute to be fighting off Big Kim every night because she want to suck on my coochie."

Diamond touched her neck. "I thought that man was going to smooth chop off my head, and all I could think about was my mother." Her expression saddened momentarily, then changed to a sly grin. "You was really trying to be Cleo and set off some shit. I'm looking at you sideways now because I almost pissed on myself when you told him to kill me."

"Girllll, that man wasn't hardly going to do nothing to you. I told y'all I got y'all. I fucked up on the first one, but I'll be damned if it happen again," Angel professed.

Diamond shrugged. "What about Karma?"

Angel rolled her eyes, sparking a blunt and taking a pull. "What about her? Your mother is in a grave, my momma got a baby by my ex, and Sophie got some nigga thinking he can play with her top. We been getting fucked over for years. It's time to *be* Karma."

"That simple? You think they just going to let us walk away after the dust settles? We getting deep into this shit."

Angel leaned back, closing her eyes. She didn't know if the high she was experiencing was from the lick she just hit or the weed they were smoking. "I'm not worried about them, either. You know what type of nigga Mello is? He's not going to let anything happen. I wouldn't be surprised if Mello already planned the way he's going to take that man out of here."

Diamond frowned. "I know Mello is cool, but that cop and that other nigga...You don't ever think about how they trying to extort us? Like not even a little?"

Angel shrugged. "Shit happens. I done had a nigga do way worse to me." Her voice trailed off as she blinked away images of being repeatedly raped. Mentally, her mother had fucked her up, and instead of apologizing, she went and had a baby with the only man Angel had ever loved in her life. Her entire being began to tingle. She had to shake that shit off. Emotions were for the weak. "Y'all heffas don't have to get all quiet. I'm over it," Angel added.

"I know you say you're over it, but I know you haven't healed, Angel. You put on this tough cover, but you're hurting and pacifying it with a Band-Aid," Diamond said.

"Every time I watch a nigga come up off that bread, I heal. I'm good. Now, can we get off the Negative Nancy shit? I want to relax and enjoy this high. Let's celebrate them coins that's about to fatten our bank accounts." Angel dismissed the conversation as the car zipped through the busy New York traffic.

"I see you made it back to a nigga," Rock smirked as soon as the ladies walked through the door of the rented condo. Apparently, Mello thought that it would be a good idea for them to share an Airbnb instead of renting separate rooms for everyone. Granted, the condo was spacious and luxurious, with four huge bedrooms;

however, he wasn't slick. Mello was trying to get next to Sophie, and Rock was trying his damnedest to get under Diamond's skin with his fine, thugged-out ass.

"To you?" Diamond let out a small laugh, bending over to take off the heels that were wreaking havoc on her toes. "I keep telling you to stop playing with me, boy. This a whole-ass big-body Benz, and I don't think you can handle that ride," she added, plopping down onto the couch, rubbing her sore feet.

Rock followed her to the couch, sitting too close for comfort. He grabbed her foot, placing it onto his lap. Diamond didn't know what exactly to say when he began to massage it. His strong hands were like magic as they caressed and kneaded at the balls of her feet.

"Ummm, that feels good," she moaned, tossing back her head.

"What you was saying about that big body, 'cause I'm feeling real NASCAR-ish around this bitch," Rock said. Diamond tried to sit up and place her foot on the floor, but Rock held it tighter. "Nah, don't get scared now, baby. Keep fucking with me, and I'm gon' show yo' pretty ass something."

"I got a man, boo."

"I don't give a fuck, boo," Rock shot back, frowning over at Diamond as he examined her closer. "Yo, what the fuck happened to yo' neck?"

Diamond's hands lifted to her neck unconsciously. She shrugged. "Ol' boy tried to chop my head off. I held my own, though."

"Nah, for real, shorty. What happened?"

She finally sat up. "Seriously, ol' boy wasn't trying to give up the money. One minute we thought we had it under control, and the next, he had a knife to my throat. Angel handled it, though."

"That's wild as fuck. Shit like that can't be going down. Why didn't y'all call? We gon' have to do something about that. I'm gon' fuck some shit up if something happen to my future."

"Your *future*? Rock, please. You ain't hardly trying to settle down with nothing but the streets and these tackhead hoes. Don't think I don't peep how your line stay buzzing."

Rock began to knead her foot again. "Nah, I'd settle down for the right female. I just ain't came across nobody worth sitting my ass down and doing the right shit for yet."

Diamond rolled her eyes to the ceiling, getting more comfortable than she cared to admit. "Well, what's the right person?"

"You." Rock laughed at the cute way that Diamond's nose wrinkled. He had been peeping her since he first saw her when she walked into the party. He liked her style. She had layers that he wanted to peel back and nurture. "For real, though. I ain't on no bullshit. I'm digging you, li'l momma. Is it a crime for me to want to get to know you? Got me over here rubbing feet and crying like Keith Sweat."

"Whatever. I swear, you're too much."

"Nah, I'm just enough," he countered.

Rock and Diamond sat up until the wee hours of the morning, talking. He had a vibe, and the conversation just flowed too easily. He felt familiar. He felt good. He felt like trouble because Rock's cocky ass was on a mission to break down her walls...and it was working. They got so cozy that Manny's six calls went unanswered.

CHAPTER TWENTY-ONE

THE DAYS TURNED into weeks, and weeks turned into two whole months since they came up with their big plan to lace up their boots and hit licks. Angel was sitting on top of the world. Everything she thought she wanted was sitting right at her fingertips.

She stood in front of the full-length mirror, admiring how her dress fit every dip and curve of her body. Tonight, she'd gone for sophisticated-sexy. Her long weave was pressed bone straight, and her skin was glowing with just a dab of makeup. Angel truly was a natural beauty outside of all her ratchet tendencies.

She puckered, smearing on a coat of lip gloss and popping her lips. She turned to the side to view her ass, then stood straight, facing the mirror. You couldn't tell her she wasn't the shit, and tonight would prove it.

While shopping at Somerset Mall, she'd run into Taj Mahoney, one of the hottest up-and-coming rappers in the city, at Nordstrom's. She'd just purchased a pair of fly Alexander McQueen pumps and paid for it in cash without hesitating...like the boss bitch she was always destined to be. It must have impressed Taj because he walked over to her, and they exchanged numbers.

That was an entire week ago, and he was finally free for a date tonight. Well, he'd asked her to accompany him to an event out in Bloomfield Hills. He offered to pick her up, but there was no way he was coming to the hood to see her house. When a person thought you were of a certain caliber, they treated you accordingly. All Taj needed to know was that she was a bad bitch.

"Maybe I should look into moving," she muttered before snatching up her purse and heading for the door.

Forty-five minutes later, she was pulling up to an enormous seven-bedroom mansion. She called Taj and told him she was pulling up, and he was waiting outside for her. Tall, handsome, and rich, he looked damn good, and Angel's hotspot began to thump from the possibilities.

"Damn, girl, you sexy as hell," his deep baritone greeted her as she stepped out of her car...a 2022 Benz that she had just driven off the lot three days before, thanks to her last lick. She was moving on up like the Jeffersons, and the transition was addictive.

A seductive smile creased her lips. "Thank you. You're not looking too bad yourself. You weren't waiting long, were you?"

"Nah, you good." Taj took her hand into his, guiding her into the party. Thick clouds of smoke filled the air, and rap music blasted from the speakers. Angel looked around, confused by the crowd of ballers and whores. She just knew damn well he didn't invite her to no freak party.

"Ummmm, I thought we were going to an event. I didn't know it was going to be all this." Angel tried her best to hide her disgust.

Taj smiled. "It *is* an event. Chill, ma. We coolin'. You don't have to do nothing you don't want to do," he assured her as a group of men approached him and began to drown him with conversation.

Angel sort of fell to the background, and she would be a lie if she said she wasn't salty. However, she quickly sucked it up as she began registering how much money was in one room. Scheming was her game, and she was always on the prowl. She looked at Taj, who seemed to be paying her no mind.

"Where the liquor at?" she mumbled, sauntering over to the bar in the corner. She didn't even bother telling Taj she'd be right back. He was so busy entertaining his fan club that he just said fuck her.

"If it ain't Angie Ang. Damn, ma."

Angel's entire being went tense at the sound of the voice too close for comfort. She thought that she'd never hear it again...ever. He was supposed to have caught a life sentence.

"Gamble? What are you doing here?" She played it as cool as possible, considering she was face-to-face with the man she had set up to be robbed, only for him to end with a murder case and a life sentence hanging over his head.

He chuckled. "I should be asking you that. I'm sure whatever nigga you trying to get down on don't know how toxic yo' scheming ass really is."

Butterflies began to churn in her stomach, and not in a good way. Gamble had always been a ruthless man, but he had a soft spot for Angel...until he slept with her mother. Anger, hurt, and jealousy gnawed at her insides.

"I got to go. Nice seeing you again." Angel walked off so quickly that she was almost floating. Fuck a drink, fuck Taj, and fuck that party.

"I'll be seeing you again, Angie Ang."

Angel scrambled to the front door and almost made it to her car. "Dang, ma. You was just going to leave like that without saying goodbye? It's like that?" Taj followed her outside. He saw her speaking with Gamble and was going to ask how she knew his big cousin. But she made a beeline for the door so quickly.

Angel whipped around. "I-I-I wasn't feeling good. I'm going to have to catch up with you some other time," she stuttered, looking back at the door.

Taj followed her gaze. "You tripping off my cousin? Y'all used to kick it or something before he got locked up?"

"Gamble is your cousin?" Angel frowned.

"Yeah. The nigga was locked up on some bullshit for about nine years. He just now getting out. This his coming-home party."

Angel pinched the bridge of her nose, releasing a sigh. "You don't think that's something you should have told me?"

"I mean, you said you wanted to chill. So, we chilling. Come back inside. Whatever you and Gamble had must have been years ago. That shit don't count no more."

Angel shook her head. "It's complicated. Call me. Maybe we can link up some other time," she offered before opening her door and falling into the car. She barely waved goodbye before speeding off.

Angel's past flashed before her eyes as she sat in a tub filled with lavender bubbles. She sipped on a glass of wine, thinking about her soiled relationship with her mother and the roller coaster she went on dealing with Gamble because of it. He was the one that taught her to love and to hate. He was her gift and her curse. Gamble had trained her in the art of survival, whether it was hitting a nigga's pockets, setting him up to be hit, or protecting her heart at all costs.

Gamble was good to her, but he had fucked-up ways about him. Like, in one breath, he promised her the world and made her feel as if she were the only girl in it...and in the next, she caught him fucking her mother. What part of the game was that?

A bitter taste sat on the tip of her tongue. She felt her eyebrows tighten. "Niggas ain't shit but hoes and tricks. Get yo' money up, boo," she coached herself, pretending to be unbothered. Truth was, she was bothered as hell.

Her cell phone rang. She looked over to the counter where it sat, allowing it to go to voicemail. Angel needed peace and quiet. She needed alone time to be one with her thoughts. Her phone dinged with a text. She sighed, deciding it was time for her to get out of the tub anyway. Her skin was beginning to wrinkle.

CHAPTER TWENTY-TWO

MELLO WATCHED AS Tiffany sauntered her thick frame into his living room. He wanted to tell her to leave. However, he was curious to know what she had to say. She was living foul, and it amazed him how she could sit up and beg for him with a straight face.

"You got some other broad? You sure haven't been fucking me," Tiffany squeaked, whipping around to face Mello with her hands planted at her side.

"You ain't my girl. I don't have to answer to you," Mello frowned.

He was surfing into uncharted territory and needed focus. Mello wasn't a jack boy. He was a hustler. He grinded for his. Women were a distraction, and Tiffany...She was a nonfactor to him. All she did was cause chaos and then bring a wet pussy when he needed it.

"All I'm asking is for you to give a fuck and put me in your schedule. Niggas make time for what they want, no matter how busy they are." Tiffany's voice cracked. She had wasted so many years hoping he would finally get his shit together and choose her. He owed her that much.

"Just like you was making time for Bleu? Get out of here with that bullshit, Tiff. He must not be fucking with you no more." Mello chuckled, knowing the answer to that. Bleu was disloyal, and he wouldn't be messing with anyone anymore. His body was at the bottom of the Detroit River, attached to cement bricks.

"Wha...what...What are you talking about?" Tiffany stuttered, eyes bugging.

Mello blew out a breath of air. He began to walk toward his bedroom. They'd be in Miami in forty-eight hours, preparing for yet another caper. This one was the most important one to date. It was worth ten million. He would walk away with a million, his crew of three would have a million to split, and the girls would have a million to split as well.

"Look, I'm about to go to sleep. I got moves to make in the morning. Please don't pop up at my crib again. It's a wrap."

Tiffany's eyes lowered into slits. "A wrap? Boy, please. Anyways, are you really out here robbing people, Mello? My daddy said you was working with that crooked cop." She paused, irritation growing. "That's another thing. I introduced you to my daddy. I'm always looking out for you, and you stay treating me like a random."

Mello stopped walking, turning to face her. "You ain't introduce me to shit. I been knowing Graham since I was a youngin', way before you. And whatever business we handle ain't because of you. I'm a solid-ass nigga, so I'm always good. As a matter of fact, don't do shit else for me. That way, you won't feel so used." He turned to continue to the bathroom, pulling his shirt over his head. "Fuck outta here talking about what you do for me. Not a damn thing but give me a fucking headache."

Tiffany sat on the edge of his bed, hurt. She had asked herself a million times why she stuck around and dealt with his arrogant ass. Each time she thought about walking away and leaving him alone, butterflies would form in the pit of her stomach. She loved him. Mello was a decent man. He fucked her better than any man had ever done, he had his shit together, and just the sight of him gave her pussy a heartbeat. The only problem was he was emotionally unavailable, and the headache of dealing with Kenneth Davis was emotional torture.

She sat and listened as the shower went, deep in her thoughts. Too bad she didn't know much about his illegal activities because she could have sent his ass straight upstate for playing with her. Or she could have had her daddy get at him, but Mello even had him wrapped around his fingers. She rolled her eyes, admitting she'd always only have a piece of him.

Taking off her clothes, she lay back and began to play in her sweetness. Sex was always the Band-Aid to mend the tension between them. She knew exactly how he liked it, and it helped that she got off in the process.

Ten minutes later, the shower turned off, and Mello emerged from the bathroom with a towel wrapped around himself. Beads of water dripped from his chest, and Tiffany flicked her clit harder. Mello took her in but quickly dismissed her. He was tired of her bullshit.

"You still here, man?" he snarled, grabbing the deodorant off the dresser and rolling it under his arms.

Ouch! That cut. Tiffany felt her chest tighten. "*Really*, Mello? Why are you treating me like this? What have I done to you so bad?" Tears began to stream down her cheeks. She sat up, pulling the covers over her chest.

"I got a few moves to shoot." He ignored her question.

Tiffany sat in utter disbelief. "Who is she?" Her voice was just above a whisper. "You must have went and got you a bitch."

Mello smiled. "I don't fuck with bitches. Now, I'm respecting you off the strength of your pops. Gon' about your business, Tiff, before I get real disrespectful."

"You know what? Fuck you, nigga. I can have anybody I want, but I'm sitting around playing myself about you. Remember how you doing me. I'm going to make you stand on that shit." She snatched her dress from the ground and began to get dressed. She was more hurt than angry. Mello was going to get his one way or the other. He needed to learn that you couldn't just go around playing with people's feelings like that.

An hour later, Mello pulled up to Ice and vibed to the music, peeping the scene. He hadn't really chilled at the club in weeks. However, he needed an escape to free his mind.

Sophie would just so happen to be there. After an entire week of dodging his calls, here she was, all up in his space. He once heard if you love something, let it go. If it came back, it was meant to be. That was the universe telling them something.

He lifted his glass of Rémy, taking a sip. She was sitting with Diamond while Angel twerked. Angel had quit the club a month ago. That was expected. The club offered chump change compared to the money they were making. That was the main reason he neglected to tell the ladies that their debt was paid with the last lick, and they were free to go. He needed them, and they would be rewarded for their time. Putting a little money in someone's pocket was never a crime, right?

He wanted to apologize for coming on to her like that in Miami. He wasn't trying to take it there, but she had his little man rock hard and fiending. He had to take a cold shower after she left.

"Fuck that. She gon' talk to me," he muttered, making his way over to the ladies' table.

"Wassup, Big Boss Man?" Angel spotted him first. He waved at her, then nodded at Diamond, saving Sophie for last.

"What up? You avoiding me?" He threw his hands in the air, eyes hard-set on Sophie.

"How can I avoid you when we have to work together?" She rolled her eyes, pretending to be annoyed. Truth was, Sophie had purposely come hoping Mello would be there.

He sat down in the empty seat next to her. "You saw my calls. I even stopped by the crib."

"Actually, I didn't see you calling," she lied. "And what crib did you stop by? I don't stay with Diamond and Angel anymore. I have my own house now."

Mello smiled. "*That's* what's up. I'm proud of you, love. I got to get you a housewarming gift. Where I need to drop it off at?"

Sophie rolled her eyes. "Ha-ha. Nice try, nigga."

"Yo, for real. Let me holla at you. I'm not feeling the way we left off in Miami."

"Me either. Where do you want to talk at?"

"Take a ride with me," he suggested. Sophie was skeptical, but when he held out his hand to help her stand, she obliged.

Sophie couldn't help but stare at Mello as they cruised back to his place in his Range. Here they were, yet again. She wondered what made this time different than Miami. There was no way she should have been so relaxed in his presence.

When she first saw him, she wanted to hate him. But being forced to suck up his energy was tearing her walls down. She still loved him. He obviously still loved her. That scared her. How could she forgive him for abandoning her at the lowest point of her life?

"What'chu looking over here for? I look good, don't I?" Mello teased, rubbing the hairs of his beard. It was two o'clock in the morning. His Range was cruising through the partially empty streets of Detroit as his speakers blasted '90s R&B. Tyrese was serenading the truck.

"Because I'm trying to figure out how we got here again and if I'm really prepared to deal with you mentally. I have a lot of shit with me, Kenneth."

Mello smiled. "Why you always call me that? Everybody else call me Mello, but you want to be different." He changed the subject.

"Because that's your name. I don't know no Mello."

He glanced at her before focusing back on the traffic. "You ain't trying to get to know him, either. I'm not gon' hurt you, Sophie."

"You promised me that years ago." She paused. "Why you have to do me like that? I would have done anything for you. I really loved your stankin' ass." Sophie could feel her emotions stir. She had waited a long time to ask him that question, and she was anxious for an answer.

"When you never had genuine love, you don't know how to receive it or give it back. That shit scary. My own momma never loved me, so how could this little cute-ass girl from the hood love the kid? Fuck that. I wasn't giving you the power to hurt me. So, I got you before you got me."

Sophie frowned. "That was the dumbest, most selfish shit I ever heard. I was never out to get you, dumb ass."

"Don't you think I realize that shit now? I can't change the past, but I can correct the future. Besides, you went out and had a whole baby on me. How you think *I* feel?"

"What?!" Sophie shrieked incredulously. "Do *not* do that. I lost our child because yo—"

"A'ight, a'ight. We not about to go there. My bad for bringing it up. For the record, that shit fucked me up too. I was a coward back then and used it to escape." He swiped his hand across his forehead, shaking his head and letting out a small laugh. "I ain't never did this much begging and explaining in my life."

"So, I'm not worth it?"

"Of course. You wouldn't be in my whip, heading back to my crib if you wasn't."

Sophie chuckled. Mello was so damned cocky. But she secretly loved that about him. It didn't hurt that he was sexy as hell too. "Whatever. Just so you know, you said we was coming to talk, and that's *all* we're doing. I'm not fucking you."

Mello waved her off. He could be a rude boy, but he also knew how to be a gentleman. There was no way he would have even attempted to play her like that after what he put her through. He just wanted to absorb her energy and listen to her little sexy-ass voice screaming at him about how he had her fucked up. After she got it all out, they would go to sleep with him holding her.

Make no mistake. If she threw the coochie at him, he was hitting a home run up in that ma'fucka. She was looking sexy as hell in a pair of black leather shorts and a halter top. Her smooth, creamy legs were on full display, and her skin had a glow about it. He'd eat her until she pleaded for mercy, then fuck her silly. He was a grown-ass man that loved to fuck.

"And if you got a girl, a sneaky link, a piece on the side, a nigga..." She chuckled at the look he gave her before continuing. "I'm just saying. That's a possibility these days."

"You got me fucked up."

"Whatever. Like I was saying, if you got any of those, just leave me alone now or dead that before I find out."

Mello smirked. "I thought you wasn't fucking with me. How you setting guidelines and shit?"

Sophie turned to face the window. She closed her eyes briefly before refocusing them on the passing buildings. "Because this is *my* show. We're playing by *my* rules this time around." She meant it. The second she even sensed Mello was playing games, she was gone.

"OK, Ms. Showrunner. You just make sure you dead all yo' little situations too. I ain't running from a broken heart no more. I'm straight shooting niggas for playing with it."

"Something's wrong with you." Sophie frowned. Mello never responded, and neither did she. Deep in thought, they rode back to his place; both were terrified by the possibilities. However, they were ready to strap on their nuts.

"So, you finally done bullshitting with me, ma?"

Sophie sank into the butter-soft leather of Mello's couch. She tucked her feet underneath her body and leaned her head back. Mello was living like a king. His condo was tastefully decorated with expensive furniture and paintings, giant TVs, and a beautiful saltwater fish tank that Ricky Jr. would love. She looked at Mello, watching how his pink tongue slid across his lips.

"I was never bullshitting. I think I have the right to be cautious when dealing with you. Besides, I'm not rushing into nothing. I just got out of a ten-year relationship that still drains the fuck out of me." She rolled her eyes at just the thought of Ricardo. He was so damned toxic. He didn't want her, yet he didn't want to see her with anyone else.

"So, how you end up with a clown like that nigga?" Mello asked Sophie. "I dog hoes. Hit the bar and slide a credit card down these bitches' booty holes." He mocked the lyrics to one of Ricardo's latest radio songs, causing Sophie to burst into laughter.

"*Really*, nigga?" She tapped him on the shoulder.

"Yeah, really. That nigga don't even seem like yo' type. I just knew you was going to go off to college and get you one of them rich, stuffy niggas. A part of me would have felt better if you did that."

Sophie frowned. "Nope, you're not about to judge me or ask me twenty-one questions about my decisions because, to be honest, I should have had *your* last name and *your* kids. I guess life has its own agenda."

Mello held up his hands in surrender. "You know it ain't no judgment this way. It's all love. We can get to working on the marriage and kids whenever you ready."

"You think you're so freaking smooth, nigga. We can't work on nothing until I figure out what kind of hoes I'm going to have to check and how you deal with my son. If he don't like you, I'm not messing with you."

"I can dig that. I know I can't fuck with you without fucking with your seed, and as far as hoes, I got a jumpoff or two, but that's dead the minute you quit playing. Now what?"

Sophie bit the folds of her cheeks. "So, what have you been doing all this time? I feel like I don't even know you anymore. I remember broke Kenneth on the block grinding for his come-up with me riding shotgun. But it seems like you're on another level now." She pointed around the room. "Did you get all this from stealing? What you like, some Takers meets Mission Impossible-ass nigga now?"

Mello laughed, rising to get the bottled water he'd grabbed from the refrigerator. "Man, you watch too much TV."

"I'm serious. I need to know how deep into the robbing game you are. I'm not trying to be out with you or have my child out, and some fools run up on me because you done took they shit. Karma is a bitch. You know that, right?"

"I worked for everything I had. I ain't never been no thief, love. This shit new to me, just like it's new to you. We got into a little situation, and a nigga doing what he got to do to get out."

"I feel you. Well, I'm not complaining. I didn't know what I would do when I left ol' boy. So I guess thanks are in order for putting me where I need to be."

Mello shook his head, taking a swig from his water. "Nah, ma. That's all you. You and your homegirls been doing ya thang. I just hope you don't make no life career out of it. Ya girl be into some other shit."

"What we *not* going to do is talk about my sister." She pointed an accusing finger, letting off a yawn that seemed to just creep up on her. She was tired as hell, but being in Mello's presence was so soothing. She didn't want the night to end.

"You sleepy?" he asked, tucking a stray strand of hair behind her ear. Energy and chemistry surged wickedly between them by his touch. Neither spoke for what seemed like an eternity. Honestly, Sophie didn't know what to say next. How could she register what was taking place between them so naturally? After ten years, it was like they never even missed a beat.

"I missed you," she whispered. She couldn't look at him. However, she felt his strong arms as he lifted her and pulled her onto his lap, wrapping them around her.

"I missed you too, my baby. Welcome home, ma."

CHAPTER TWENTY-THREE

D IAMOND SILENCED ANOTHER call from Manny as her eyes slanted down to Rock. He was sitting between her thighs while she rubbed his wavy hair. They were watching the new episode of the BMF TV series and talking shit. He had a blunt sparked, and she had a glass of wine. She needed a buzz to deal with his energy.

"Diamond got the hoes, huh?" he chuckled, releasing a cloud of smoke from his nostrils. "And Diamond gon' get fucked up. I don't play that shit," he warned.

She didn't know whether to take it as a joke or not. Being with Rock was a different type of intimacy that Diamond wasn't used to. Yeah, she and Manny had mad chemistry...when they were fucking. But there wasn't much past that. However, Rock? The nigga got her coochie wet, had her talking and thinking about the bigger picture and what she needed to do with her future. He made her feel like he saw *her*, inside and out.

Rock shook up her world. He was her peace and her storm... if that even made sense. Diamond had been hurt so many times; she had taken so many losses that it seemed like a setup. They had been swimming on a fine line ever since they'd gotten back from the last lick, and their closeness scared the shit out of her. Every night, after he finished running the streets and she made it in from the shop, he would be at her door, and they would have the same routine. If he wasn't chilling between her thighs being massaged, she was being massaged while they talked about any and everything. They enjoyed each other so much that they forgot about sex every single time.

"Whatever. That's you, playboy," she finally answered him as her hand continued to slide over the ridges of his wavy hair.

"This shit feels so good, my baby." Rock's eyes opened as he turned to face Diamond. She was in all her natural glory...no makeup, no weave, no lashes, just pure, smooth skin and that sexy, dimpled smile. Her energy was so pure and genuine.

Diamond stared back. "What are we doing, Rock?"

Rock yielded a lazy grin. "Us," he shrugged as if it were that simple. "We doing whatever feels good until it don't feel good no more."

Diamond bit into the folds of her cheek. "And when is that?"

"We ain't got the answer to that. All we can do is try our best to make sure it keep feeling good."

"That's not reassuring. You can decide that tomorrow you done, and then what? You're stirring all these feelings up inside me and getting all close, and then *boom*...It don't feel good, and I'm sitting around looking goofy."

"We been rocking for a couple of months, ma. I ain't got tired of you yet, and that speaks volumes. I got you," Rock assured her.

"We'll see," Diamond smirked. But she couldn't help that blush that settled on her face. Rock just had that effect on her, and she was learning to like it more than she wanted to admit.

Diamond stood over the stove, stirring mashed potatoes and frying chicken. She hummed to a Summer Walker jam as she pranced around the kitchen. For the first time in a long time, she felt good.

She didn't have a bill collector on her back, Carlos was paid off, and she had a man that she could let her femineity flourish with. Rock brought that out of her, and it felt good.

It had been nearly a year since her mother was murdered. She had been living in hell ever since...until now. That was a wound that she wasn't prepared to address. Hell, she never really got a chance to digest it. Two weeks after her funeral, Carlos was knocking at her door, and debt was piling up. She had to use every penny of her savings to bury her mother.

"Let me find out you fine as hell and can cook, acting all domesticated." Rock startled her, reaching over her shoulder and grabbing a piece of the golden fried chicken.

Diamond popped his hand. "Don't be putting your crusty hands in my food. Wait like everybody else."

Rock bit into the hot chicken and immediately began to play hot potato with the meat. "Gotdamn, that shit hot as hell," he grumbled.

"That's what you get," Diamond chuckled. "Ig'nant ass always doing something."

"Yeah, it do smell good." Mello's stomach began to grumble.

Diamond let out a giggle. "Y'all greedy niggas get on my nerves." Ever since they began hitting licks together, the ladies had bonded with Mello and Rock. Being forced to be around one another allowed walls to fall.

Angel came waltzing into the kitchen, laughing. "Girl, we all walked into the house, mouth just a-watering. Who pissed you off, friend? You cooking a whole Sunday dinner. Something got to be up."

"Nah, yo good, sis; just in love." Rock gripped her from behind, kissing her neck in front of everyone.

"Whatever. I just felt like a homecooked meal and figured I would fix one." She eyed Mello and Rock, who sat at the kitchen table.

"Well, damn, I hope you stay feeling like homecooked meals. You trying to get a ring or something?" Rock teased, causing Diamond to blush.

"Will you stop?" Her cheeks were sitting so high from smiling that it hurt. "Have y'all heard back from Robinson?"

"Oh yeah. What's up with your homeboy? I saw him sitting outside of the house a few doors down. It's like he wanted me to know he watching me or something. I will kill that old, ugly man." Angel rolled her eyes. "Something just don't sit right with me about him. He be giving off crackhead vibes. Like how he a whole cop?"

Rock chuckled. "I tried to tell this nigga. Our debt paid off. Why he want to keep fucking with a snake-ass ma'fucka like Robinson?"

Diamond immediately began to frown. "Paid off? So, when was you going to tell us that? I mean, you don't think that was important enough to divulge?"

Mello shrugged. "I was going to tell y'all. I just wanted to go on one last run to test the temperature. I still don't trust the crazy ma'fucka. Besides you've been getting compensated… right? No risk, all pros. Y'all have a problem making money?" he reasoned.

"No, I don't have a problem with it. ButBut it's not what you do. It's how you do it. Tell us the truth and have us decide if we want to continue. Trust goes a long way." Diamond turned to Angel. "So, did you know that we was all paid off?"

Angel shrugged. "Actually, I didn't. But does it really matter, Diamond? Are you where you want to be? As long as we're getting paid, I'm down for whatever."

"That's why I fuck with you." Mello smiled. "Nah, seriously, shit been kind of tight in the streets and I'm not trying to make no moves until I figure Robinson's bitch ass out. The paper got to keep flowing somehow. I ain't trying to see Sophie in this shit too much longer anyway. Just rock with me until I get shit straight... aight?

"Yeah, whatever. Have you heard anything from Domo's ugly ass? What is he on?" Angel wondered out loud.

"Nah, I got people in the A doing research on him and his people, but he been quiet as a church mouse. He straight too, though. Whatever we do is all profit from here on out..

Rock shook his head. "Fuck that. I put it on my momma. The minute I catch either one of them niggas slipping, I'm ending all our cash flow. Ain't nobody about to threaten me, and that's on my soul." Rock kissed his finger and drew an imaginary cross over his chest to solidify his warning.

"Where yo' homegirl at?" Mello asked, pulling out his phone to call Sophie. After three rings, someone finally answered. However, the masculine voice threw him off.

"Yo, where Sophie at?" Mello could feel his jaw flex, but he controlled himself. He had no right to be mad about another man answering her phone.

"She took our son to the bathroom. Who is this?" the man retorted.

"Don't worry about it. Tell her to hit up big daddy." Mello was feeling petty. He and Rock had smoked two blunts before pulling up to Angel's house.

"Big daddy? Nigga, stop playing with me. Do you know who I am?" Ricardo yelled into the phone.

"Is this Jody? The same nigga that got my boo pregnant and can't handle his responsibilities as a man? Nigga, you's a bitch." Mello mocked Snoop Dogg from the movie *Baby Boy*.

Everyone at the table burst into laughter as Mello ended the call. Yeah, he may have been a little childish, but he didn't give a damn.

"I can't believe you just did that!" Angel was howling in laughter. "You know Sophie gon' fuck you up."

Mello shrugged. "She ain't gon' do nothing but act like she got some sense. Watch this," he smiled, connecting Sophie's call. She immediately redialed him, and he placed the phone on speaker.

"Why the hell would you do that, Kenneth? Got this retard going off, and I really don't got the time for it," she fussed.

"Why that nigga answering your phone anyway?"

"Because he crazy and a hater."

"Girl, fuck Ricardo. You kid-free. Come by. You and Diamond boos over here. We about to chill and eat," Angel teased, leaning into the phone.

Diamond sucked her teeth, rolling her eyes. "This heffa always starting shit. You might as well come on through and chill."

"I guess I'll come by for a second. I'm tired, and we have to leave in two days."

Mello smirked. "I knew you wanted to see daddy. I'll see you in a minute, love."

Sophie started to say something slick, but she was cut off by Mello ending the call.

CHAPTER TWENTY-FOUR

Domo sat across from his father at the dinner table, pretending to be engrossed in the steak dinner that the chef had prepared. Things had become tense between them ever since the chain incident arose. However, if Domonic Sr. didn't bring up the obvious, Domo wouldn't either.

"How is your new business dealings going in Detroit, son? You know, it took a lot to convince our partners to agree to that move. However, I believe something good will come out of it, right?" Dominic Sr. was a smooth-talking older man with the perfect shade of salt-and-pepper hair. At the seasoned age of fifty-seven, he still had women flocking to him, men respecting him, and an undeniably large bank account.

"It's been straight. You see the numbers. We done pulled in a couple of million in the last few months," Domo shrugged.

Dominic set his fork down beside his plate, pushing back in his seat. "Oh yeah, what exactly did you say you was doing again?"

Domo sucked his teeth. "You know. Tapping into a little of this and that. Just trying to figure out where to plant my feet. You know weed legal in Michigan. It's a lot of money to be made."

"But that's not what you been doing, son." Domonic stood to his feet, and a chill slithered through Domo's being as he felt his father grip his shoulders. "You just keep creating a deeper and deeper hole for yourself."

"Bu—"

"But nothing! Do you know how proud I was to pass the torch down to my one and only blood son? I fought for you to be in the position you're in, and what happens? You disgrace me." Domo felt the grip on his shoulders becoming tighter.

"Disgrace you? All I do is try to fucking make you happy. I see that ain't gon' never happen. Nothing I do is ever good enough for you."

Slap!

Domo felt his father's meaty hand collide with the back of his head. The sting was hard enough to make him dizzy. "Shut up! Just shut the fuck up! The fucking police? Russians? Starting beef in the streets? What the fuck was you thinking? It was already bad enough you allowed your dick to compromise our empire. But you want to go and add insult to injury, and I'll kill you before I allow you to take down this empire."

"So now you want to kill me?"

"I'll slit your fucking throat," Dominic Sr. gritted.

"Your own son, huh? I'm sitting on a connect to the fucking Russians and a pipeline to the law, and this the thanks I get? Yeah, a couple of bitches caught me lacking, but I'm taking care of that and putting us in position at the same time."

"No, you have created a problem that's beyond my control. I've covered your ass more than I care to count. You're so smart that you're stupid." He paused with a pained frown. "Did you know the cop you befriended reached out to myself and a few of our founders? A fucking crackhead dirty cop that has crossed too many important people. Fuck your connect and your pipelines. Why, Dominic Jr? I'm sorry, son."

Domo felt one last squeeze on his shoulder as his father walked away. Then he heard the footsteps before he even looked up. They didn't belong to Dominic Sr., and Domo knew it.

"Don't make him suffer."

Domo heard the whisper. He could feel the Grim Reaper... the smell the death swimming in the air. Crazily, all Domo's brain could think to do was pray. How could one night of pleasure end with him losing his life? Angel's face flashed through his head, but the complete picture never really showed up. The bullet that lodged into his temple silenced everything forever.

Robinson had been calling Domo for the past ten hours. He hadn't heard from him or any of his men, and an important meeting was coming up with the Russians within the next few hours. Robinson finally had the money to repay them and needed his partners as a backup. He didn't trust those shady motherfuckers and couldn't wait to pay them off. Then he was going to have Mello and the ladies take the money right back, and the grand finale...Domo was going to silence Mello for good, and Robinson would make sure Domo and his family were taken care of. After that, all loose ends would be tied, and Robinson would be off in Mexico or Cuba somewhere, living like a king with ten million dollars.

"Where the fuck are you?" Robinson sighed, pushing away from his desk.

"Hey, Robinson. I need you in my office right quick." The chief leaned into Robinson's space. His voice was stern, leaving Robinson to wonder what could have gone wrong for him to be summoned.

Robinson stumbled a bit before standing straight up and composing himself. "Sure thing, Chief." He offered a half smile, watching as the stubby Caucasian man backed out of his office.

"What the fuck does he want now?" Robinson blew out, snatching his jacket off the chair and reluctantly marching down the hall to the deputy chief's office.

"It's open," the chief yelled before Robinson could knock.

"What's going on, Chief?" Robinson looked around, taking in the two union reps and the Big Chief. He couldn't exactly read the room, and that bothered him.

"Have a seat, Gerome." Chief pointed to the chair in front of him and waited until Robinson was seated. "We've been hearing a lot of not-so-favorable things lately. I didn't want to believe any of it. Still don't. A man with your position and rank has a lot of merit behind your title."

"Unfavorable?" Robinson frowned.

"Unfortunately, you have been suspended until further investigation has been completed. The union rep is here if you want to fight it. However, we need you to turn in your gun and badge until you are cleared."

"Investigation? After twenty years, this is the thanks I get?" Robinson grimaced, his heart racing.

"Turn in your badge and gun. Report to Concentra for a random drug test," the chief sighed apologetically.

"This is bullshit!" Robinson roared. He felt as if his life was slowly crumbling, squeezing him, and he felt suffocated.

CHAPTER TWENTY-FIVE

Angel COULDN'T EXACTLY call how she had been feeling lately. Running into Gamble put her in a bad head space. She thought she had everything figured out. Fuck niggas, get money. Yet, there she was, sitting in a bedroom, attempting to swallow the lump forming in her throat.

Tears. She couldn't believe she had allowed one to fall. As if she wasn't damaged enough, Gamble really came through and finished her. That was years ago, and she felt so weak for allowing a man to control her emotions.

Angel had been thinking so much that her head began to pound. She was two seconds from going to Urgent Care. That was how bad the migraine was beating at her temples.

Bam! Bam! Bam!

Someone banging at the front door caused Angel to cringe. She hoped they would go away. But when the doorbell dinged, she knew she had no such luck. Reluctantly, she grabbed her pistol from the dresser and went to the front door.

Angel frowned, taking in Shanell's silhouette. They hadn't been rocking with each other since she confronted her at the club. She wondered what the heffa wanted.

Swinging the door open, Angel placed her hands on her hips, staring at Shanell. She didn't speak. Quite frankly, Angel had nothing to say to the girl.

"Ewwe, you still on that?" Shanell turned up her lips. "We beefing for what? I miss my girl."

"Humph, I thought you had a new li'l puppy up under you since you calling all the shots and shit," Angel answered sarcastically.

"Dang, I can't even come in now? You start getting money, and now you Hollywood?"

"Whatever." Angel stepped out of the way for Shanell to enter. "My head hurting, and I don't got time for your bullshit. So, what's up? Why you doing pop-ups?" She didn't try to hide the attitude in her voice.

Shanell began to look around the place. She ran her hand along the paintings on the wall. "I peeped your new Benz. It's nice, boo. I'm really proud of you."

"You ain't got to be proud of me. Despite what you think, you may have reintroduced me to the game, but I was getting money way before I met you." Angel's neck rolled as she spoke.

Shanell smirked. "I hear you talking, Big A. Anyways, I came here to tell you that my people in the A said Domo dead. They had his funeral the other day, so we ain't got to worry about that no more. I hate we even did that shit. My intentions were never to beef with you. Despite what you think, you was like my little sister, and we had each other's back. I miss that."

"Oh really? What happened to Passion? I thought y'all was good."

"Girl, bye." Shanell waved Angel off. "You know I was talking shit to get a rise out of you. I don't trust none of them hoes like I trust you. How it's been going working with Mello? Word in the streets, y'all niggas big time now. He don't even be moving weight no more. You need to put your big sis on."

"Big sis?" Angel couldn't believe Shanell had the audacity. She must have eaten a whole humble pie and swallowed it down with courage to come to Angel's house begging. "Yeah, OK. Look, I'm not feeling good. My head banging."

"That's not good, boo. You need to check your stress and blood pressure."

"I got it."

"I know you do. Well, I'm going to get up out of here. Answer your phone and let me know if Mello need another girl. I'm trying to get on yo' level."

"OK, I will." Angel gave Shanell a fake smile. She just wanted the girl gone.

"OK, boo." Shanell began to walk toward the door. "Oh, and just a word of advice...The sun don't shine forever, boo. I know all the money and glam is looking good. But you know the rest." She winked before making her full exit.

Angel didn't know if that was a threat or if she was being genuine. However, her head hurt so badly that she couldn't even process it. Instead, she went to the medicine cabinet, popped two Tylenols, and lay down.

Angel was awakened out of her sleep by her phone dinging with a text. She started to ignore it until she saw it was from Mello, a 911 text for her to meet him at the club in an hour. The pounding in her head had subsided, but she still didn't feel like leaving her bed. Groaning, she dialed Diamond.

"What's up, heffa? I was just about to call you. What Mello texting us 911 for?" Diamond asked as soon as she answered the phone.

Angel sighed. "Who knows? I'm on my way to Ice now. Where's Sophie?"

"You already know where that heffa at. She be up under that nigga like white on rice. I ain't hating, though. They cute."

Angel sucked her teeth. "You the last one to talk. Rock got that ass on lock."

"He do, though," Diamond gushed. "Anyways, I'll see you at the club, heffa."

After hanging up, Angel reluctantly pulled herself together and got dressed. Thirty minutes later, she was walking into the familiar walls of Club Ice. The usuals were there, doing the same thing, just another day, and she didn't miss it at all.

She spotted Mello first. Then her eyes landed on the rest of the crew. She frowned, realizing that they weren't alone. "The fuck he doing here?" she mumbled, making her way to the booth.

"Nice of you to join us, Ms. Angel," Robinson snorted, sipping his drink. "Shall we go to the back as usual?"

"Nah, we all here. What's up?" Mello shot him down. Small talk was over.

"What if I told y'all I had a lick that will set you all straight for the rest of y'all lives if you pull it off? This score is big enough for every single one of us to retire."

"But what's the catch?" Angel wondered out loud.

"Nikolay Ivanov. Russian motherfucker with a lot of protection."

Mello waved Robinson off. "Man, yo' desperate ass on some bullshit. The Russians? How we supposed to pull that off? I bet he stay with an army behind him."

"That's why we must act on it within these next few days. It's his anniversary weekend, and his security will be lax. Snatch him up, get him to wire money into our accounts, and split it halfway. We all win."

"Moving out of desperation gets you fucked up every time. We good," Mello retorted.

"On the low end, you'll make two million apiece. But I'm banking on a ten-million-apiece profit."

Sophie stood to leave. "Nope. Not going to happen. I have a whole son to think about. What is he going to do if something happens to me?"

"Wait a minute, Soph. I'm down for ten million," Angel answered.

"Just for us not to be able to enjoy it because we're dead? I'll pass."

"Hear him out. This is the endgame we all need."

"It really is. I'm trying to help you guys out," Robinson lied. "Look, just let me know if you're down. The clock is ticking," he added, standing to leave.

The crew watched as Robinson went through the crowd, eventually disappearing. They each were in their own little worlds. That was a lot of money.

CHAPTER TWENTY-SIX

SOPHIE'S EYES SCANNED the court documents for the hundredth time. She could feel the anger building in her chest with each word she read. "This motherfucker is so fucking spiteful," she roared, blinking back tears. Apparently, Ricardo Sr. had gone down to the courts petitioning for full custody, claiming that Sophie was unfit and had their son in an unstable environment.

"What's the problem, love?" Mello's voice was laced with concern on the other end of the call.

"Nothing," Sophie sighed, tossing the papers and rolling over to cuddle Jr. in her arms. His little body was wildly sprawled across the bed as he let out light snores. Homeboy was beyond exhausted.

"You ain't never been a good liar. What's the problem?" This time, Mello's voice was firm and demanding.

"My sorry-ass baby daddy trying to take my son away, but I'm not worried."

"What? You're a great mother, Soph. You ain't got nothing to worry about."

Sophie's eyes connected with the walls of her new apartment. Everything was falling into place, and Ricardo would throw a monkey wrench into the program. "The thing is, I do. He has receipts of me going in and out of town, leaving my baby. I don't have a job. You don't know Ricky. He acts just like a catty female." She rolled her eyes, kissing Jr.'s forehead. "Then here I am about to leave him again tomorrow. Sometimes, I feel like I can't win from losing. I take two steps forward, just to take two more steps back."

"So, what you trying to do? Want to get rid of that nigga?"

"Kenneth!" Sophie shrieked with a chuckle. "As good as that sounds, I can't do that to RJ. That's still his father."

"Well, you better tell him to find something safe to play with. It's like that about mine."

"Yours? Who said I was yours, Kenneth Davis?" Sophie's cheeks were hurting from the alley-cat grin plastered on her face. Mello made her feel whole again. He made her feel alive.

"Your heart. I got that ma'fucka, and I ain't letting go this time."

"Whatever. Are you packed and ready for tomorrow? Who is the guy, and what makes this time so important? I don't know why I keep getting this weird feeling."

Mello shrugged. "Honestly, I don't know what that nigga Robinson on. All I know is after we get through tomorrow, we done."

"Why tomorrow? If we're in the clear, why be greedy and keep going?"

Mello paused as if he was thinking about the answer. "Are you walking away from a million yourself?" He didn't wait for Sophie to respond. "Exactly. *That's* the reason I'm doing it. And to be real, after all the moves we done shot, I'm thinking about retiring from the game, chilling out, and doing the family thing."

"With me?" Sophie smirked.

"Nah, with you and li'l man. I might pop one of my own in you and give you my last name too."

"I hear you talking," Sophie mumbled. "Well, let me get off this phone and get our stuff together. I have to call my mom and tell her what's going on with this fool so she can keep him out of my business. Lord forbid he finds out I'm out of town again." She rolled her eyes.

"Yeah, clown shit. But check this out. When we get back, I'm taking you on a real date. We gon' do it all, the taking you shopping for your 'fit, getting your hair and nails done, going out and dancing...all that good shit."

"OK, princess treatment. Let me find out."

"Let you find out what?"

"That big, bad, thugged-out Kenneth Davis knows how to be a gentleman."

Mello let out a small laugh. "Stop playing like I wasn't always a gentleman when it came to your spoiled ass: foot and back rubs, running to the damn corner store for your apple pie and butter pecan ice cream."

"Well, why did you just up and leave me like that? I swear, we were so good, Kenneth. You were my entire world, and I would have given you anything." She sniffled. "RJ should have been yours. We should have been living our happily ever after by now. I want to hate you so bad for being a coward and running away. But my soul won't let me. You have my entire soul, Kenneth Davis. You have all the power, and it scares the fuck out of me."

"Good thing you have the same power. Nobody wins if shit goes south. So I guess we better play it right this time, huh?"

"You better," Sophie's voice was just above a whisper. Her emotions were nearly raging out of control. However, the thought of another chance at forever with him soothed her. She could feel it deep in her soul. Everything was right, and their time was now.

CHAPTER TWENTY-SEVEN

DIAMOND STOOD OUT on the hotel's balcony in a robe and her hair sitting on top of her head, totally taken by the view that illuminated under the half-moon. The waves of the ocean crashed against the sand, and the sound of movement from the nightlife was peaceful. Miami was beautiful, and Mello hadn't held no stops with the rooms he reserved for them for their mission. She knew that the game she was playing was dangerous. But the allure was too powerful.

Her eyes traveled back to the stacks of neatly banded cash sitting on her bed...which was only a fourth of their payout until their job was complete. Money had been plentiful lately. The missions were so simple, and the cash flowed almost too easily. If she hadn't learned anything else, she knew that nothing in life came without a cost. She was dancing with the devil, and Diamond was waiting for him to show his fiery horns.

A knock at the door interrupted her train of thought. Pulling her robe tight, she went to the door, looking through the peephole.

"Fine ass," she mumbled, spotting Rock coolly leaning against the door frame with his hands shoved in his pocket. He had been gone all day with Mello peeping the scene and preparing for their lick.

"What are y—" Her words were cut short by Rock pouncing on her. He attacked her lips, kissing them tenderly yet aggressively. His hands roamed her frame, leaving Diamond stuck.

Her pussy had a pulse, and her heart was racing. She had to stop him before they crossed the line of no return. Giving herself to Rock would change the dynamics of everything. Sex was more than just one night of pleasure. It was the exchange of energies. She would be giving him her energy, and their chemistry would be meshed together in a fucked-up web. That's where things would get tricky; feelings would get involved.

"Wait. Wait. Stop. We can't do this," she finally found the strength to push his tall, thick frame away. "I can't go there with you."

Rock's hands were still cupped snugly around her ass. Chest to chest, they both were breathing heavily. "We both grown as fuck. We can do whatever we want to do." He leaned in and pecked her lips. His kiss deepened, causing her fat clit to thump again.

"Rock, wait...What are you doing?" Diamond whined.

"Making us both feel good. I'm tired of all that gentleman shit. Can I do that? Can I make us feel good?"

She tried holding out. But Rock had a way about himself. He was smooth as fuck with it too because how the hell did she end up bent over with his balls slapping her ass cheeks? In the blink of an eye, they had reached the point of no return, and it felt too good to stop.

Diamond's eyes involuntarily rolled to the back of her head, her lips slightly pouted, and her nails sank deep into Rock's back. She had no choice but to succumb to the euphoric wave of pleasure he created.

The twinkle of the moon hit their bodies as he slid in and out of her wetness...and that motherfucker was wet. It gripped Rock like a glove, yelling, "Welcome home!" every time he hit her wall. Her brown eyes looked down at him as he pushed in and out of her, hitting her G-spot. Nobody had ever pleased her correctly before Manny. Yet, it only took Rock minutes to navigate her body like he was her personal tour guide with his own personal map.

"Dammit, right there," she panted, fucking back. "You are so wrong for thissss. Shit, Rockkk." Diamond called out his name as he began pounding into her.

"Shut up and take this dick," Rock growled, smacking her ass. She was so wet and warm that he knew they had to change positions before he came prematurely.

Scooping up Diamond, he carried her to the bed, laying her down. Her pussy was glistening, her bud playing peek-a-boo. So he slid back in, slow stroking her until they both came in unison, collapsing onto the bed.

"I can't believe we just did that," Diamond panted, covering her face. Guilt slowly crept in as the high of their sexcapade began to trickle down. "Shit, we shouldn't have done that. We didn't use protection either. Oh my goodness."

Rock looked over at her. She had a near-perfect shape, thick in all the right places. Her waist was slim, her ass was phat, and her breasts were just right. Li'l momma was a cold piece. "What you trippin' for? I ain't shoot no club up." He shrugged. "That had to happen sooner or later. You can't keep teasin' a nigga like me 'cause I'm gon' see what's up."

Diamond grabbed the sheets to cover her frame before frantically power walking to the bathroom and turning on the shower. She leaned out the doorway. "That's not the point. We just fucked, Rock. I don't even know your real name, and I'm scared shitless because this all seems too good to be true with you. I have to protect my heart. Furthermore, we gettin' down, rawdogging like diseases ain't real. I don't know where your dick been."

Rock smirked. "Inside you."

Diamond rolled her eyes, letting out a groan. "I'm being serious. What we just did was irresponsible. We can't do that again."

"Did it feel good?"

"Are you even *listening* to me?" Diamond countered, shaking her head.

"I ain't worried about that bullshit you talking." Rock waved her off. "You trying to hit the strip with me? Niggas sleep, and we in a whole-ass Miami."

"I swear I can't stand you." Diamond slammed the bathroom door, stepping into the shower to scrub herself.

"Yeah, yeah. Hurry up. I'm hungry. I need to refill after all that good pussy," he teased, smiling at the fact that he was getting under her skin. He didn't know what it was that had him so attracted to her. Their chemistry was so thick. Quite frankly, he wasn't a little-ass boy. If he wanted something, he was going to grab it. He had always been that way.

"Keep talking that shit, and I'm gon' toss yo' ass in this water to the sharks," Rock bluffed, snatching Diamond up as they stood on the beach. The restaurant they ate at had an excellent selection of seafood and wine. Diamond was stuffed and buzzing. She always enjoyed Rock's crazy, blunt ass.

"You's a lie. You get my hair wet, and I'm gon' fuck you up." Diamond rolled her eyes. "I'm not thinkin' about you."

Rock smirked. "Quit bullshittin' with yo'self. You can't *stop* thinking about me and how I put that good dick on yo' ass. You thinkin' about lettin' me hit right now."

"You so full of yourself that it's crazy. How you worry about pussy, and all I can think about is how we got a big day tomorrow, and we out here playing around."

Diamond looked out onto the beach, watching as the waves crashed against the shore. The breeze was cool and subtle, the atmosphere was serene, and under different circumstances, she may have enjoyed Rock's company a little more.

"Yeah, I ain't trippin'. We good. It's gon' be a in-and-out thing. Watch." He licked his lips. "If you was my girl, this whole risking yo' freedom shit would be a wrap, though."

Diamond finally focused on him. He was a handsome yet rugged man. She could tell that he had deep layers underneath his hood persona. "I thought I was your future. Let me find out I'm tripping. Plus, it wasn't like I had a choice at first. Your friend was on some bullshit."

"My friend?" Rock frowned. "I don't fuck with that nigga. I kept tellin' bro to separate himself from ol' boy. He ain't listen. Now we in some bullshit with the Russians, some fake-ass gangster, and a crazy cop."

"You know, you're smarter than you think, Rock."

"Rakim."

"Huh?" Diamond's nose scrunched in confusion.

"My name is Rakim. You ain't got to call me what these other niggas call me. We fucked, so we passed that now," he smirked.

Diamond giggled, tapping his chest. "Shut up, Rakim."

"Did I do my thing?" he asked, amused.

Diamond's cheeks turned rosy. The nigga had her blushing. "Ewww, why you askin'? After it happen, you're not supposed to talk about it."

"Shhhhhiiitt, I'm gon' talk. That shit was wet as fuck. Macaroni-ass pussy." He rubbed his growing bulge. "Damn, ma. I want to hit it again right now."

Diamond's entire being began to tingle. It wasn't love. It wasn't just infatuation...She didn't know what it was.

CHAPTER TWENTY-EIGHT

"**M**Y STOMACH BUBBLING. Something don't feel right," Sophie mumbled, running her hand across her flat belly. Her stomach was doing somersaults, and she didn't know why. "Like, this time just feels different."

Angel rolled her eyes, smearing on a coat of lip gloss and popping her lips. "Girl, what's so different? We about to make the most money we ever made on any lick, and here you go with the bad vibes."

Diamond nodded her head in agreement. "Yeah, boo. Go pour you a shot and calm down. This is going to put us all where we need to be. I got Carlos's crusty ass off my back, and we don't owe that creepy-ass cop anymore."

"I know. But still, I'm just starting to wonder if it's worth the risk. Did I tell y'all Ricardo sent me court papers? Petitioning for full custody?"

"Fuck Ricky," both Diamond and Angel yelled in unison. He was such a sorry-ass nigga to them.

Sophie chuckled. "Well, damn. Tell me how y'all *really* feel."

"OK," Angel plopped down on the bed next to Sophie. "Since we're giving it straight up, no chasers. I feel like you need to stop playing with Mello. He's really a decent nigga, and I know for a fact that he cares about you. I like him for you."

"Just like you liked Ricky, huh?"

Angel's lips twisted into a frown. "No, heffa. Let's not pretend as if the Ricardo before the little fame and record deal wasn't a good-ass dude. His fat ass used to cherish the ground you walked on. These hoes and that money got to his head and watch. He's going to regret it."

"No, he's not. He don't care, and quite frankly, I'm so over him that I rarely think about the nigga."

"Yeah, because you're too busy thinking about Kennnethhh," Diamond teased.

"Oh, please. While we calling each other out, let's not pretend how that nigga Rock got your nostrils flaring. Oh, I peeped the way you be blushing and giggling when he be talking that talk to you."

"What?! I definitely do not be paying that man no attention. Things are just coming together, and I don't need that wild-ass nigga fucking nothing up."

"You can stop fronting. I know you. Rock got you about to lose your mind...in a good way, though. He's solid and loyal," Angel shot.

"Why you always be up in everybody else's mix? What about *you*, heffa? I ain't never seen you with a nigga. Where is *yo'* man at? I'm starting to think you like coochie or something."

"Yeah, I might do," Angel smirked, then burst into laughter at the screwed-up faces her girls gave her. "Y'all heffas know I'm only playing. There's absolutely nothing a female can do for me. Seriously, I don't do love and relationships. It ain't for me, and I'm fine with it. I get these niggas before they get me and be on to the next before I can blink."

"Don't let that catch up to you, boo. You see what happened with Domo. These Negros ain't playing fair out here. You watch the news, and you be hearing about it in the streets," Sophie warned just as Angel's phone dinged with a text.

"Ewww, I'm not feeling this conversation right before a lick. Change the subject." She held up her phone with a smile. "It's showtime, bitchessss."

Nikolay Ivanov was a tall, thin, and handsome Russian that carried himself with intellect, power, and dignity. He was different from any lick that they had previously gone on. The way Mello explained it, he was smart, his crew was dangerous, and they had to be on their A-game. That was the reason this lick paid so much.

Sophie blew out a breath of nervous energy as she watched him. He wasn't flashy at all. He was low-key. If it wasn't for the picture that Mello provided, under normal circumstances, she would have never given him a second look.

Tonight was a special one. Ivanov was celebrating his fifteenth anniversary in the most exclusive restaurant in Miami. There was no entourage with him and minimal security.

The ladies were dressed to the nines, dripping designer from head to toe. They looked classy and sophisticated. With her hair pulled back into a neat bun and just the right amount of makeup to give her a smooth, golden look, Sophie was simply gorgeous.

"He's with his whole wife. How are we supposed to get to him?" Diamond leaned over and whispered into Sophie's ear.

Sophie shrugged, but Angel spoke up. "We're not. Mello said our job is to stay on his ass. Wherever he goes, we follow. I told y'all heffas, this lick is completely different." She took a sip from her Tequila Sunrise. "Besides, we're in Miami, at one of the best restaurants, and don't have to come up off a dime. Y'all better order some food, relax, and wait for his little white sexy ass to move. His wife better be lucky I don't like pink meat."

"Yeah, you need a real nigga to work yo' pretty ass out," the deep baritone leaned in, whispering in Angel's ear. She was so startled that her knee hit the table, causing it to shake.

"Shit," she muttered, giving her girls a look that screamed, "What the fuck!" She frowned over at him...only to become mesmerized by how fine the big, chocolate dreadhead was. He definitely looked like a pussy monster, and under different circumstances, Angel would have called his bluff.

"Would you and your homegirls like to join me and my partners?" he asked in his thick Caribbean accent as he nodded to a table with three handsome men. They were in a different league. Angel concluded that they were dope boys or something.

"Does it look like we want company?" Angel sassily spat. Her eyes traveled over to Ivanov's table. She had to get rid of ol' boy before he completely messed up the lick.

Mystery Man smiled. "That ma'fucka right there is Big Nick. Whatever you're on, ma...get off it. I'd hate to see anything happen to you beautiful ladies." He winked before walking off with so much swag that he earned a second glance from Angel.

"What the hell was that?!" Sophie hissed through clenched teeth. "I'm not doing this shit." Her leg began to shake uncontrollably.

"Yes, you are. We're already here. Fuck that nigga."

"Did you hear the ma'fucka? That's not what we want. How the hell does he even *know* we're here for that man? Call Mello and tell him it's off," Sophie rustled.

"I'm not calling nobody. Don't do this right now, Sophie. Get your shit together, bitch. Three motherfucking million! That's one apiece. Think about Ricky Jr. and the life you'll be able to provide. Think about those court papers. You won't have to worry about shit for a long time. Just *think*!"

Sophie bit into her bottom lip. "What if it goes wrong?"

"And what if it goes right—just like our other licks?" Angel proposed. "Shit, he's about to leave," she murmured, grabbing her purse and throwing it over her shoulder. "Y'all know the drill. Wait until he leaves to grab your car. I'll be on his ass in mine."

Angel approached the door with a mean sway of her hips. She needed to get to her car before Ivanov got to his. However, she didn't want to seem obvious, so she kept a steady pace toward the rented Maserati.

Sophie and Diamond sat back at the table, whispering amongst themselves. Now wasn't the time to be falling apart. However, they were all over the place.

"Do you really think we about to pull this off? A nigga of that caliber? Angel don't give a damn because all she see is money. My *son*, Diamond! I have to get back to my son," Sophie stressed, just as Ivanov left the building with his hand protectively planted on his wife's back.

The girls watched intensely for who left with him. They counted four men...two Russians, a burly dreadhead, and the man who approached them wasn't too far behind. Sophie couldn't help but wonder if it was coincidence or reality. If Mystery Man was really with Ivanov, they were at a disadvantage. He had already peeped them.

"Come on, boo," Diamond reached over, grabbing Sophie's hands. "Before we leave this restaurant, please get those negative thoughts out of your head. Words, thoughts, all that, are powerful." Diamond winked as she placed two crisp hundred-dollar bills onto the table for their drinks. They didn't even get a chance to order food.

The ladies rushed to their Maserati that matched Angel's. When they were inside, Diamond called Angel to get her location, and Sophie texted Mello about her ill feelings. He promised he would be right there every step of the way once they got the drop on Ivanov, and nothing would happen to her. She sure hoped he was right.

Boom!

The door to the beachfront home went flying open. Mello and his three goons, along with the ladies, came filing into the place with their guns drawn...only to be surprised by the calmness of Ivanov sitting behind an expensive swivel chair with five armed goons right next to him. The man from the restaurant was one of them.

"I was wondering when you would join us," he smirked with a head nod. Seconds later, the seven men and female crew felt the cold steel as it pressed into their temples. They were each relieved of their weapons.

Sophie felt sick to her stomach. She was always taught to listen to her gut. She wanted to kick herself. Ricky Jr. flashed before her eyes, bringing a pang of guilt and hurt throughout her entire being. What if they killed her?

"Now that we have that taken care of, have a seat, Kenneth, Rakim, Sophie, Angel, and Diamond. I'm sorry, I never learned the names of the others, since they aren't really that important." He called off each of their government names, proving that he was on his shit. "I hear Diamonds are a girl's best friend." He chuckled at his own wit.

"Nah, we good." Mello stood with his arms folded over his chest, nostrils flaring. "Obviously, you're not about to murk us because we would be dead by now. So, what the fuck you want from us?"

No one saw it coming...until Mello fell to the ground, holding his head. The goon had come from nowhere, striking him with a pistol in the back of the head. Sophie shrieked, and Rock turned to buck—but was met with cold steel to his forehead.

"Uh-uh. I wouldn't do that if I was you. We will speak respectfully in this house, especially when you all choose to disturb me on such a special day." Ivanov sat up in his seat. "I want you all to know that your business dealings with Gerome have been very impressive. I knew it would only be a matter of time before all them drugs would have him sending you all my way, though. So, I can't really fault you. You are not what you don't know."

"I have a son," Sophie pleaded.

"I know. Handsome little dude, although his father's music sucks. And before anyone else tries to plead their case, Diamond, my condolences to you for your mother. Angel, your mother and brother could use some of your newfound wealth. Family over everything, sweetie. I could go on, but I believe you all catch my drift."

"So, what the fu—" Rock caught himself, turning to the goons behind him. "You hit me, and I'm knocking you the fuck out, straight up," he warned menacingly.

Ivanov chuckled. "You amuse me, son. What do *I* want? I need you to send Robinson a message. It seemed the slickster has my back against the wall. It can cause a lot of confusion if Robinson gets to the wrong person, which isn't good for anyone. If I'm upset, you better believe my crew is upset."

Out of nowhere, one of the men standing behind Ivanov aimed his pistol, pulling the trigger that silenced the man from the restaurant forever. Sophie, Diamond, and Angel all cried out in agony. Blood and brain matter splattered as his body hit the ground with a loud thud. They had never witnessed a murder. They weren't really in the game. They had only scratched the surface.

"Awww, first time witnessing the soul leave a man's body?" Ivanov chuckled. "Well, it appears Onyx couldn't be trusted. Why did he approach you all's table, and please, do not lie."

"He...he...he offered for us to have dinner with him and his friends," Sophie stuttered, hyperventilating. She could feel the contents of her stomach threatening to release.

"Are you sure that was it?"

"That was all," Angel muttered with her heart pounding. Reality finally began to kick in as danger lurked in the shadows. They were really toying with death.

"Then we will ensure that Onyx is sent off properly and his family is taken care of." Ivanov drew a cross over his chest, closed his eyes to say a silent prayer for Onyx's soul, and carried on as if nothing had happened, and there wasn't an innocent dead man only feet away. Sophie had completely zoned out...until they were told that they were free to go. She didn't know if she was coming or going.

CHAPTER TWENTY-NINE

THE EYES OF the man right before the bullet silenced him haunted Angel's thoughts. That was a look she'd never be able to unsee, a sound she would never be able to unhear, even a smell she'd never be able to unsmell. Death. She couldn't help but feel guilty. What if she had just gone over to his table with him? Would things have worked out differently?

Unable to sleep, Angel pulled the covers from over her body and headed to the bathroom. She figured if she took another shower, she could wash away the guilt that her sins caused.

"What the fuck just happened?" she muttered as she broke down into a soul-rumbling sob. It had been years since she cracked away at the hard exterior and allowed herself to be vulnerable. She bottled so much inside, and in that very moment, under the hot stream of water, she finally let it all out.

She scrubbed and cried until her skin felt raw. Angel only stepped out of the tub when the water had become too cold to bear. She wrapped a towel around herself and slow dragged to her bed, not bothering to put on clothes.

An hour later, her cell phone ringing gave her the distraction she needed to escape her thoughts. She answered on the second ring. It was a conference call with Sophie and Diamond on the line.

"How you feeling, boo?" Diamond asked.

"Like I'll never be the same. Someone lost a son, a brother, a father, all because he tried to warn us about that crazy Russian motherfucker."

"You know that wasn't our fault, right?" Diamond offered. "Like I told Sophie, we never intended to kill anyone or almost be killed ourselves. But after losing my own mother to violence, it's safe to say that shit happens, and we can't let this stunt our growth as a person."

Angel's brow furrowed. "I'm not getting where you're going with this. A man lost his life, Diamond. That's it, and that's all?"

Diamond pointed her finger into the camera. "What I'm saying is I lived in guilt for months, wondering what I could have done differently to keep my mother alive. I know how that shit can eat at your soul. We didn't know that man, but that was my whole mother, so imagine how you feeling—just times it by a hundred."

"Yeah, Angel. I'm out. I'm not doing this anymore. That was an eye-opener. We could have gotten ourselves killed. Hell, Mello walking around here like Sir Lump-A-Lot, and he's lucky that's all they did to him." Sophie paused for a second. "I overheard his conversation with Robinson. That man is really pyscho. He's not happy, and that could be bad for us all."

"Fuck Robinson," Angel grimaced. "Look, I'm good. I promise," she lied. "I just need a little time to myself before we hop on the plane tomorrow to recharge. You know I get over and through anything."

"Yes, we do...with your tough ass. I love you, cow," Diamond smiled.

"I love you cows too. Don't have too much fun with those niggas," Angel shot.

"What nigga?" Sophie shrieked.

"Heffa, please don't think I don't know you over there playing nurse with Mello and Diamond over there letting Rock's wild ass rock her world. I'm happy that y'all have them as safe distractions. I like them for y'all."

"I like him too," Sophie finally admitted to herself and her girls. "Make sure you call me if you need to talk, chill, or whatever. Don't sit in that room driving yourself crazy."

"Oh, I'm not." That was another lie that Angel told. After hanging up with her girls, she sat in the room addressing all the bottled-up trauma she'd experienced over the years. Life had really dealt her a shitty hand.

Two days had passed since the ladies returned from Miami. Angel used that time to burn sage, listen to music, and recharge. Now, she was ready to see the outside world, get a few drinks in her system, and talk a little shit. It was a Sunday night, and she was almost back to her old self.

She leaned against her truck, rolling a blunt, as Megan Thee Stallion blared through the speakers. Tonight, the radio station was throwing a free concert at Hart Plaza, and the girls were downtown mingling. The fact that Angel was willing to go out had Sophie and Diamond throwing on their clothes and hitting the streets with the quickness.

Downtown Detroit was packed with all walks of life. Different music blasted from different cars, old schools and new schools. Women and men walked the streets, some dressed to the nines...others not so much.

"Gotdamn, it's thick down here. I hope these fools don't be on no bullshit. You know how your cousins get." Diamond looked around, paranoid. They weren't exactly in the clear. Robinson had become an obsessed psychopath, calling and threatening them. The minute they touched down, he showed up at the airport. He acted like a complete ass. The airport authority actually had to take him away. Then the Russians let them walk with their lives, but it still didn't sit well that they knew everything about them.

"Here you go," Angel smirked, catching eyes with a sexy, caramel dude cruising by in a tricked-out '69 Chevy Impala. "Oooh shit, li'l daddy can get it. Damn, I needed this." She winked at the man, licking her lips. He waved her over, but she was only woofing. Angel didn't plan to talk to anyone for real. She was too fucked up in the head to complicate her life with a relationship, and Miami had her putting her hustle on hold. Therefore, there really wasn't a reason to converse with a man.

"He was kind of sexy," Diamond concluded, turning to face her girls. "I got a serious problem, y'all. While me and Rock was chilling at the crib, Manny decided to just pop up on me. I had to beg, plead, and suck all types of dick for Rock not to kill that man. He's crazy, and I felt so fucked up because I loved every second of it."

Both Angel and Sophie burst into laughter. "Say, you put that little cooter on him, and now the nigga don't know how to act, huh?" Angel teased.

"It's not funny. That boy crazy and even worse...that shit sexy to me. Seriously, though, I feel bad for cutting off Manny without warning and just jumping into whatever it is Rock and I are doing."

Sophie twisted her lips. "Fuck Manny."

Diamond looked off. "Crazy thing is, I've only been like that with Rock for a little while, and the nigga got me feeling butterflies, seeing heaven—the whole nine. That shit scary. I don't want to go up so fast and come crashing down because I rushed things. I barely know him."

"Life's short. Take a chance." Angel shrugged.

"My sentiments exactly. I never thought that I'd ever get back with Kenneth. Yet, here we are...attached at the hip, and it feels so good. I love the man he turned into."

"Whew, chile, all this love shit got me nauseated. Are we having a girl's night, or are y'all gon' talk about y'all niggas alllllll day?" Angel rolled her eyes.

"Uh-uh, Ms. I-Don't-Need-A-Nigga. When was the last time you had a nigga knock your socks off? Is that why you hating? I think that's what you need," Diamond told Angel.

"Almost two years ago, and after that dick, I didn't want no more. Nigga almost had me forgetting to hit the safe," Angel chuckled, fanning herself. She hadn't realized that two years passed since she was intimate. Maybe she *was* due for a good dick down.

"Two years?!" Sophie shrieked. "You're saying your coochie hasn't been licked, fucked, sucked, or nothing in *two whole years*?"

Angel nodded.

"That's why this heffa so damned evil. We got to get you some dick, friend," Sophie teased as her phone rang with a call from Mello.

She answered. "What's up, babe?"

"Yo, where y'all at?" he immediately asked without saying hello.

"Downtown, why?"

"Fuck," Mello growled into the phone. "I told y'all to stay low-key. Why are y'all downtown, Sophie?" His voice was stern. She couldn't read if it were more anger or concern.

"Angel needed to get out. So, we to—"

"Took her to crowded-ass downtown? What the fuck? The freeways closed. I can't fucking get to you. This nigga Robinson on some bullshit. Let that nigga do something to you, I'm murking you *and* his bitch ass."

"Me?" she shrieked.

"Yeah, you. Because you hardheaded. I got some people at the Marriott on Jefferson—the one with the Applebees connected, not the one by the water. Get your homegirls and go there. Wait for me to call you back."

Sophie's heart raced. "What's going on, Kenny?"

"Just go. Now!" He hung up. Sophie looked at her phone before her eyes circled the block cautiously.

"What's going on, Soph?" Angel asked, noticing the change in her demeanor.

"I don't know. All I know is that he said for us to get to the Marriott right now. We have to go." She pushed off Angel's Benz and began to power walk up Brush, making her way to Jefferson.

"What about my car?"

"Girl, forget that car. We have to go now!"

It happened so fast. One second, the girls were just letting their hair down and chilling...the next, they had an overgrown man stalking behind them. Angel spotted him first. Robinson was leaning up against his car. She didn't have enough time to process how long he'd been standing there because he came toward them once they started to walk off.

"Bitch, look!" she squeaked, pointing at the gray-haired menace. She didn't know if he had caught on that he had been spotted. She didn't care. "Where did that ma'fucka come from? Get his ass jumped in front of all these folks." She cursed herself for forgetting to grab her pistol.

Sophie reached back, tugging Angel along. "Mello said for us to get our asses to the Marriott, not be out here fighting some grown-ass man." She finally caught eyes with Robinson, and her heart dropped seeing him. She watched as he reached into his waistline and pulled out his pistol. Words failed her. Thankfully, Angel saw it too and jumped into motion, pulling them through an alley between buildings.

The ladies took off. They were running for their lives. To their advantage, the streets were packed. Pockets of partygoers here and there. Police presence everywhere. However, they couldn't stop for their help because they didn't know who was dirty and who wasn't.

It didn't take long to get to the Marriott. They were almost there and hopefully safe from harm. Well, at least they *thought* they were...until someone yanked Angel by the hair, sending her flying to the ground. Robinson was on her, his hands were around her neck, and the pressure was causing her breathing to go ragged.

"You bitches ruined everything!" he growled. "Where's my money." He squeezed tighter.

Diamond and Sophie both snapped into survivor mode. He was going to kill her if they didn't do something. Robinson attacked Angel, and the ladies attacked him. Diamond was on his back, and Sophie was throwing punches wherever they would land. They just needed him off Angel so that they could make it to the hotel. The scene was almost out of a movie—definitely fit for *Worldstar* or *The Shade Room*.

The struggle lasted two minutes too long before a group of good Samaritans decided to step in and help. One dude came out of nowhere and directed a left hook to Robinson's temple, sending him toppling over.

"Fuck is wrong with you? Those females," he growled menacingly.

Another man pulled up his pants, squaring off with Robinson. His foot lifted to kick but was paused midair when Robinson snatched his pistol from his waist. "Oh shit," he murmured. Everyone began to scatter...even the ladies. That was their chance.

The threesome went diving through the hotel's entrance. Mello didn't tell them who would be waiting for them or where to go once inside. Sophie panicked as she frantically dialed his number. Her eyes were bouncing around the room like a crazed woman.

"What now? He's coming." Diamond panicked.

Angel looked around. She saw the bathroom and pointed. "Let's go in there until we get in touch with Mello. That nigga is real-life crazy." She rubbed her sore neck, which was turning red. "He did that shit in front of everybody. He gave zero fucks." She grimaced, knowing that if Robinson caught them, he'd kill them.

The ladies raced to the bathroom, closing and locking it. Only then were they able to breathe...for just a second. "Why the fuck isn't he answering?" Sophie growled, frustrated. She started to redial Mello, but her phone began to vibrate. He was calling back, and she answered before a full ring could get out.

"That crazy motherfucker just tried to kill us!" she yelled into the phone. "Kenneth, he running around all willy-nilly waving a gun. He choked Angel. We tried to fight him." She was rambling so fast that Mello had to tell her to slow down.

"That's why I told yo' ass to stay low-key until we handled him. Where are you now, and where is he?"

"We're at the Marriott, like you said, hiding in the girl's bathroom on the first floor."

"Stay where y'all at. My niggas Durk and RJ about to come get y'all. I'm pulling up now."

"Please, hurry up, Kenneth."

"I'm here. Stay put," he promised before hanging up.

Minutes later, Mello's black Range Rover pulled into the hotel's valet area with a loud screech. He hopped out, and workers tried to tell him that he couldn't park there. However, he wasn't trying to hear it. He had to get to Sophie and the girls. The last conversation with Robinson didn't go so well. In so many words, Robinson had declared war.

Mello brushed through the hotel lobby just in time to see Durk and RJ escorting the ladies through the area. Sophie spotted him first. She ran to him and jumped into his arms, wrapping her legs around him.

"I'm so sorry for not listening to you," she whispered into the crook of his neck.

"It's all good, ma."

"Excuse me." A squeaky, ill-developed Asian security guard made his way over to them. "I will have to ask you and your party to leave."

Mello frowned. "Leave why?"

"Disturbing our guests. Does anyone have a reservation for tonight?"

Durk waltzed over to where Mello, Sophie, and the guard were standing. "I do, Mr. Top Flight. Room 316," he informed the guard, flashing his room key. He turned to Mello. "We got a couple of freaks waiting. But you know y'all can come up until everything is everything, OG."

Mello started to decline, but after the hell he went through with traffic, he knew that staying put until the festivities ended was best. Too bad they never saw Robinson lurking in the shadows, watching...waiting for the perfect time to pounce. He saw everything, even Mello's look of pure adoration and concern for Sophie.

The rules of the game had just changed.

CHAPTER THIRTY

"WHEN YOU COMING to get your son, Sophie?" Sophie's mother sighed into the phone.

The downtown incident played through her head. As much as she needed her son, Sophie knew now wasn't the time to have him. Mello had Sophie attached to his hip, and they both decided to keep Ricky Jr. as far away from the drama as possible. So as a result, her mother had been looking after the baby for over a week, including when he arrived for their trip to Miami.

Rock and the crew worked overtime to find Robinson and silence him forever. The man seemed to have disappeared from the face of the earth. They staked out his wife's and mother's houses and sat outside the precinct. It was almost like he didn't exist.

Today, Mello finally allowed Sophie a few minutes alone to grab some of her belongings from her condo. He pitched a fit about it, and Sophie made a big fuss right on back. After going at it a few rounds, Sophie won half an hour to grab what she needed. He had a few important runs in the streets to make and wouldn't be able to take her. No one knew about her condo outside of the girls, so he deemed it safe enough.

"Ma, a lot's going on. I just need time to figure everything out. I can bring you some more money to keep him another day or two. Or call his dad. Ain't that what you always do?" Sophie rolled her eyes. Ricardo Sr. had been a real pain in the ass lately, making it hard to coparent ever since he discovered that Mello was a new permanent fixture in her life.

"You know his trifling ass ain't gon' do nothing. Just bring me the money and make sure you come get him in a couple of days, like you said. Shit, all my kids grown. Ain't no way I'm gon' be stuck raising nobody else's, my grandchild included."

Sophie wanted to tell her how she hadn't done much raising, but she opted not to. That would only cause trouble. She needed her mother here and now.

"OK, Ma. I'll be there in a f—" Her words were cut by a hard shove into the door frame. The phone dropped, and she panicked.

She tried running back into the house, but it was no use. Commander Robinson grabbed her by the hair, yanking her to the ground. She yelped in pain, and her heart raced with panic.

"Uh-uh. And where the fuck do you think you're going?" he said mockingly.

Things had gone terribly wrong out in Miami. However, Sophie never guessed that Robinson would come knocking at her door. She had nothing to do with the big blowup. What did he want? Why was he there? She thought about her son. Was he going to kill her? What would Jr. do without her?

"Please, I have a son that needs me. Whatever happened wasn't my fault, I swear. I didn't have anything to do with that," she pleaded, hoping he would have an iota of mercy in his cold heart.

"Yeah, that may be true, but your boyfriend does, and if I'm going to lose everything, so is he—starting with you."

"He's not my boyfriend," Sophie pleaded, scooting backward, away from Robinson's hovering frame. "I have the money from the drop. You can take that."

Robinson laughed. "What you have is pennies compared to what your life is worth. Get up!" He snatched her again by her hair, pulling her from the ground to her feet. Sophie could feel her hair being ripped from her scalp. "The way I see it, your boyfriend owes me ten million dollars, and I'm going to collect. Looks like you'll be taking a little ride with me, bitch." There was no one to help, no one to call, nowhere to run, and Sophie felt helpless.

Panicking had never been Mello's style, but when Angel called, screaming about Sophie's mother saying her daughter was in trouble, he was in full panic mode. He had raced to Sophie's house, only to find her door unlocked and her purse and keys sitting on the table. His first thought was Ricardo. However, he quickly nixed that. Ol' boy wasn't crazy enough to come at Sophie like that. Just as he hopped back into his Range, it hit him. *Robinson!* He was going to kill that fuck nigga.

Mello couldn't dial Robinson's number fast enough. He made a sharp U-turn and headed to his house. His hands were shaking. He'd just found Sophie again. She was the missing piece to his puzzle, and he'd go to war behind her.

"Where the fuck my girl at, fuck nigga?" Mello didn't give Robinson a chance to say hello. As soon as the call connected, he went off.

Robinson let out a small laugh. "That's not the million-dollar question. The question is, what is it that I want? Right?"

"I don't give a damn about what you want. If she say you breathed wrong, I'm taking your head off and sending it to your momma," Mello growled while reaching over and using his burner phone to text Rock, asking him to meet him at Robinson's address.

"You really think you're in the position to issue threats? Have you forgotten who I am? I can kill her now and have a SWAT team pick you up and haul your ass upstate before you blink an eye. Don't allow your arrogance to cost you more than what needs to be spent."

Mello's jaws flexed. He knew that Robinson was right. So he swallowed his pride for the moment. But when he finally got a hold of the old bastard, hell would have no fury...

"What do you want so we can get this over with?" Mello grilled.

The line went silent before Mello heard Robinson's sinister chuckle. "Your life. But first, I want you to suffer. I'm coming for everyone you love, starting with this bitch." Mello heard scuffling before the sound of Sophie crying out in pain broke his heart.

"Sophie! Sophie, I'm coming, baby girl! I swear to God, I'm mur—" Mello's sentence was cut short by Robinson disconnecting the call.

"Think! What else did you hear? You don't remember nothing?" Diamond grilled Sophie's mother. She prayed her best friend was okay and everything was a misunderstanding. However, she could feel it in the pit of her stomach. Something was off—bad.

Diamond knew things would never be the same after everything that transpired with the last lick, but damn, did her sister have to get snatched up? She paced the floor, her heart racing. Mello and the boys were out scouring the streets looking for Sophie, and Angel wasn't answering.

"Shit, I don't know. I told you everything I heard. Her little hot ass done messed with somebody, and now look at her. My nerves too bad for this shit."

Diamond frowned. Sophie's mother was so lucky that she wasn't face-to-face with her. If looks could kill, she'd be burning in hell with the devil.

"What do you mean, look at her now? Your fucking daughter is in trouble! Why you hate her so much? She ain't never did nothing but tried to help you. I would tell her to say fuck your money-hungry ass, but I know how it feels to be without a mother. So I don't want her to miss out on the piece of the one she got." Diamond gritted.

Sophie's mother had always been a jealous-hearted, conniving bitch. Back in her prime, she was a bad bitch. Niggas were lined at her feet, hoping to get a chance with her. However, the years had aged her horribly. She never lost her baby weight, and it was downhill from there.

"I don't need this frustration. Let me know when you find out what's going on with my daughter." Sophie's mother disconnected the call, and Diamond paced in full-panic mode. Her sisters were the only real family that she had. They weren't blood related, but even blood couldn't make them closer.

CHAPTER THIRTY-ONE

MELLO'S HEART RACED as he zipped through the streets of Detroit, searching for Sophie. He had been blowing up Robinson's phone and pulling up to every spot he was known to frequent, including the police station. That was the real shocker. The nigga had gotten himself fired weeks ago. One of his homegirls that had done Mello a few favors told him that.

Mello looked over at Rock, who had an unnamed expression plastered on his face as he hit a puff from his freshly rolled blunt. "That nigga dead. As soon as I find him, I'm murking his bitch ass."

Rock shrugged. "I told you, man. Now, here we are. He done snatched up homegirl, and for what?"

"Because he a bitch," Mello answered, unable to help the overwhelming feeling of guilt.

"Yeah, I been told you that too. But my nigga, you got to slow this ma'fucka down. You whipping like we ain't got all types of heat on us that can throw us under the jail. We gon' find her, and we gon' handle his bitch ass too. I promise you that," Rock said. Mello's emotions were getting the best of him, and, truthfully, Rock had never seen his best friend so thrown off. In that instant, he knew just how much Sophie meant to Mello.

"I'm trying to calm down, bro. This shit blowing me, though. Sophie ain't built for shit like this. Homegirl ain't never busted a grape. She probably scared as fuck, and all I keep doing is picturing her face and how she must feel."

Rock passed Mello the blunt. "Yeah, you got it bad. We gon' get her back, bro. I promise." He tapped the Glock on his waistline as his scowl tightened. Robinson had crossed the line one too many times, and he was ready to handle the nigga like yesterday.

Mello's truck pulled up to a small run-down warehouse. He remembered Robinson stopping there a while back and wanted to dot all his i's and cross all his t's. He pointed at it. "This is the spot we met up with ol' boy a few months ago, ain't it?"

Rock nodded. "Yeah, but this ma'fucka look empty. I don't think they in here, bro."

"That's what the nigga want us to think. I'm kicking in all doors. I don't give a fuck. He gon' turn up somewhere," Mello scowled, cocking his gun and hopping out. Rock wasn't too far behind him.

Mello didn't even knock. He sent his boot flying against the old wooden door so hard that it immediately slammed open, wood cracking. The stench of dirty pussy and sex wafted through the air. Drugged-out, naked women and their tricks were everywhere. Mello's heart dropped as he stalked through the room, staring at every female's face in the building. If he found Sophie all drugged out and getting fucked, he would lose it.

"Sophie! Sophie, babe, you in here?" he called out to her.

The broads were so high that some continued to turn their tricks while others nodded, rolling from the high dosage of drugs they were fed.

"Sophie!" he continued to call as two big burly men came running down a set of stairs.

"Hey! What'chu doing?" they called out in unison, only to freeze in their tracks as both Mello and Rock pulled their guns from their waists, aiming them at the men's heads.

"Where the fuck is Robinson?" Mello gritted through clenched teeth.

The men threw their hands in the air. The shorter of the two spoke up. "He...He not here, bro. He been stop coming around. We been stopped paying his doped-out ass," the man confirmed.

Mello stared at the man, searching his face for any form of insincerity. He was on a murder spree and wouldn't hesitate to blow the man's brains out for lying to him. After determining he was telling the truth, Mello tapped Rock and nodded for them to leave, disappointed.

"Y'all some nasty motherfuckers," Rock frowned, staring at a trick that was too busy getting his rocks off to care about the underlying danger he was in. He let off one single shot that echoed throughout the warehouse. Gasps and shrieks, followed by scrambling, were heard. If he didn't have everyone's attention before, he sure had it now. "Y'all hoes need to go wash them stankin' cunts, and I hope y'all niggas' dicks fall off." With that, Mello and Rock were back to square one...no clue of where to find Sophie or Robinson, and Mello was about to lose his top.

Several hours later, Mello stood in Graham's hallway, pacing back and forth like a crazed man. It wasn't often that he turned to the old head for advice, but when he did, Graham would give it to him straight up with no chasers. They had developed a relationship outside of Tiffany. She was his baby girl, but he was married to the streets, which gave Mello a slight edge of loyalty.

"You know, everybody pulled back from Robinson long ago. He was into some shady shit. I always wondered why you kept him around."

Mello stopped pacing to stare at Graham. "That's not helping right now, Graham. You could have warned me, and all this could have been avoided."

Graham shook his head. "Nah, that was not for me to do. You had to learn on your own, Young Buck. I peep you. You move how you want, and if you wasn't feeling what I was saying, you was going to keep doing you. Do you know how many people he crossed, using you as his mule?"

"No, I don't. And again, you didn't say shit. So, right now, all that matters is if you know where I can find him. He got my wife, and I'm about to go crazy, my nigga."

Graham frowned. He felt a certain way about the youngster coming to him about another female when he knew that his daughter was in love with him. However, he also knew Mello never loved Tiffany the way she deserved to be loved. He respected Mello for holding her down, despite the obvious.

"You know, you're real brave coming to me with this shit, and I'm Tiffany's father. How do you expect me to feel about that?"

Mello shrugged. "Like any father should. But I also know you're a real nigga. You always knew what was up between me and your daughter. I never faked or fronted, but I kept it respectful because that's just how I rock."

Graham pulled on the hairs of his chin, debating. "Look, Robinson had a little spot ducked off in Grosse Isle. I can't remember the address, but I'm sure you'll find it if you look long enough. Ain't too many Black people out that way. I guarantee you find him and your lady there."

"*His lady*?!" Tiffany's sultry voice boomed. "You got this man coming to you with woe-is-me stories about another girl, Daddy?" She cocked her head, hurt. No one had heard her enter the house. She had listened to it all with tears threatening to escape. She invested a lot into securing Mello. She gave the nigga her mind, body, and soul. Yet, he was about to lose his mind over some random bitch that just waltzed into his life.

"Tiffany," Graham called out to his only baby.

"No, Daddy. This what we doing now? Huh?" She began to walk her petite frame up on Mello. Her chest heaved, and her hair bounced. Rocking a cute racerback dress with matching sandals, Tiffany was gorgeous. Mello never denied that fact. He just never loved her the way she wanted to be loved. He couldn't. Sophie never let go of the grip she had on his heart.

"You love that ho, huh?"

Mello ran his hand through his wavy hair. Now wasn't the time for her antics. He was literally a loose cannon, and what he may have tolerated in the past could be the bomb that sent him clear off the deep end.

"Don't start that shit, Tiff," Mello warned, turning to Graham. "Thanks, OG." He began to walk off, but Tiffany grabbed his arm. She was feeling extra bad with her father standing right in front of her. Mello was going to talk to her.

"Thanks, OG, my ass! *Talk* to me! You think it's cool to play with bitches' feelings?"

"Tiffany, that's enough!" Graham shot, grabbing her up.

Tiffany snatched away. "No! You don't touch me. I always knew that you would choose the streets over me every time. You was never a real father to me. Fuc—"

Graham's hand landed across her face before she could finish her sentence. He pointed an accusing finger. "*That's* your problem. I spoiled your ungrateful ass. Your mouth is why this man or any other hasn't made you an honest woman yet. Get yourself together before we have issues, Tiffany." He shook her before releasing her.

"Mello, have a good day. I pray that you find her in good health. Just do me one favor. Leave Tiffany here in this hallway today and never look back. I respect you as a man, but playing with her feelings will get you and her spoiled ass killed." He grimaced at his daughter, who looked as if she had hell in her.

"Why are you doing this to meeeeeee? Mellloo. Oh God, Mello! Please, don't go."

He heard her calling after him, and under different circumstances, her desperate cries may have affected him. However, nothing and no one mattered other than finding Sophie. Tiffany would be a distant memory after he crossed the threshold and sped out of the driveway.

CHAPTER THIRTY-TWO

ANGEL HAD NEVER been a heavy smoker, yet she had smoked so many blunts in the past twenty-four hours that she felt as if she were on Mars. She couldn't sleep, and she barely ate. The guilt was gnawing at her soul. What if Robinson killed Sophie? That blood would be on her hands, and after everything that had transpired back in Miami, that burden would be too heavy to carry.

It was damn near three o'clock in the morning, and she completely disregarded the time, dialing Mello's number. He answered on the second ring. "What's up, Angel? You heard from your girl?" he asked anxiously.

She shook her head sadly as if he could see her. "No, I was hoping you did. She didn't call you or nothing? Have you got in touch with Robinson?"

Mello turned down the music. "Not yet, ma. I been in these streets all day and night, and I still can't fucking find her. Yo, when I get a hold—"

"Just handle your business. Promise me that you're going to do that." Angel stopped him midsentence. She didn't want him to say too much over the phone.

"No doubt, ma. I'm sorry I got y'all into this bullshit. This on me, and I'm going to take care of it," he promised.

"You love my girl, don't you?" Angel wanted to smile, but she couldn't muster one even if she tried.

"I never stopped. It's just intensified now," he admitted, and Angel knew he was sincere.

"Well, thank you for loving her as much as I do. Find my friend, Mello."

"I am. In the meantime, go to bed, ma. Get you some rest." He paused. "And for the record, I really thought you was one of them other chicks, but for real, you solid as fuck, and any nigga that pull you got them a rider."

Angel finally smiled. "Thanks, bro. Now go find my sister."

She hung up, feeling just an inkling of relief, knowing that somebody was out there doing something about Sophie being missing. She knew that he would find her. She felt it in her soul. Angel just prayed that it wasn't too late when he did.

Angel tried to remember the last time she pulled into her mother's driveway. She hadn't spoken to the lady in nearly eight years or seen her little brother. She swallowed the lump forming in her throat. That little boy looked just like his father. It hurt Angel to her core.

Tammy, Angel's mother, never apologized. She never even explained why her son was the spitting image of Angel's man. In return, Angel didn't explain why she mopped the floors with her mother's head. She had whipped the lady so severely that she had to be hospitalized.

Angel blew out a breath of air to calm her nerves. With Sophie going missing and running into Gamble, she felt it was finally time to release the anguish that had tormented her for years. She didn't know what to expect when she knocked on the door. But she was ready to at least address it.

The door swung open before she could even knock. Her little brother nearly broke the door down, trying to get to her. "Angel!

It's you! I knew you was coming back." Ray wrapped his ten-year-old arms around her so tightly that she almost forgot he was still a child. He began to cry. "I missed you so much, Angel. Why did you leave me?" he sobbed, making her cry too.

She was the best big sister for the first couple of years. Then... he started coming into *his* features. The betrayal began to cut more. Jealousy and hatred crept in like a thief in the night. Angel cried harder, realizing how much her decisions affected the innocent child.

"You...You remember me, Raylon?" she questioned through sniffles.

"You're my sister. I knew you would come back one day. Please, don't ever leave me again. Please. She's mean."

Angel stared into his big brown eyes. They were so innocent. He was so handsome. It was like she was staring right at Gamble, just reincarnated. "She doesn't let anyone touch you where they not supposed to, does she?"

"No!" Raylon screamed incredulously.

"Good, I was just asking. Where's your mother?" Angel asked, looking into the worn-down house. From what she could see, her mother was still a trifling bitch. The place looked filthy.

Ray shrugged. "I don't know. She always gone somewhere with one of my uncles."

"Your uncle who?" Angel shrieked, already knowing the game. She too had a million uncles growing up. Every time the lady got a new man, she had a new uncle. "And who's here with you, Ray?"

"Nobody. Mama told me not to open the door, but I saw you. You came back. Can I just go with you? I hate it here."

Angel swallowed the lump in her throat. He was her little brother. Despite ill feelings toward how he was conceived, the little boy was still her flesh and blood. She plastered on a smile. "Come on, baby. You rolling with big sis."

Ray's face lit up. "Yesss. I got to wash up and call Momma. Can you wait for me?"

Angel shook her head. "How about I take you shopping for all new clothes, and we don't tell Momma. She should have been here."

"OK," Ray reluctantly agreed.

Angel and Ray had visited nearly every store in the mall, purchasing shoes, clothes, and whatever else Angel thought her little brother needed. She knew she couldn't make up for lost time with money, but how his face lit up made it all worth the dent he was putting in her pockets.

"Are you rich or something?" Ray asked, grabbing the bag with his new shoes off the counter.

Angel chuckled. "No, little boy. I just want you to have nice things like I have nice things." She smiled at him, thinking about how much he reminded her of Sophie's son, Ricky Jr. Her chest tightened, remembering that her sister was still missing. A twinge of guilt flowed through her. She enjoyed her little brother so much that she forgot about her homegirl.

"This was the best da—" Ray paused, wrinkling his little nose. "Why that man staring at us like that?" He flinched at the man, poking his underdeveloped chest out. "What's up, man?" he challenged.

He was too much. Angel followed her brother's gaze, shaking her head with a smile. Her smile instantly dropped. Gamble? He was the last person she expected to see, especially since she wasn't strapped and had her little brother with her.

"Shit," she muttered under her breath. "Come on, Ray. Let's go," she ordered, grabbing his arm and turning to leave Foot Locker.

"Nah, don't run, ma'fucka." His baritone was deep and crisp. "Little nigga looking just like me, wit'cho sheisty ass," Gamble called after her, too close for comfort.

Ray snatched away from her grip before Angel knew what was happening. "Don't talk to my Angel like that!" he puffed at Gamble, brave and fearless...just like his father.

Gamble chuckled, loving the little nigga's heart...*his* little nigga. There was no denying him. It was almost like staring into the mirror. A mix of emotions flowed through the man. Yeah, he got caught fucking Angel's mother, but she didn't have to get a nigga back like that. Not only did she rob him and cause him to do a ten-year bid, but she hid a whole kid? She was foul as fuck.

"Come on, let's go, Ray," Angel urged.

"Nah, ma'fucka. Go where? A seed, bro? You standing here with my whole seed?" Gamble cocked his head to the side.

"Yep, and your point?" Angel pretended to be unbothered, but she was bothered as fuck.

"I should kill your dumb ass. Keeping a whole kid from me."

"And I'ma kill you!" Ray shot protectively, causing Gamble to chuckle.

"It's okay, Ray." She ruffled his curly hair, then focused on Gamble. "Since he's my little brother and not my son, I think you woofin' at the wrong bitch! Let's go, Raylon." She grabbed her little brother's hand, leaving Gamble standing there stuck on stupid. Boy, did it feel good.

CHAPTER THIRTY-THREE

ROBINSON CIRCLED THE block three times to ensure that no one followed him before pulling into the driveway he used to share with his wife and two sons. The memories sent a chill to the bottom of his stomach. Sarah, his wife, had utterly washed her hands of him, and it just wasn't sitting right. Of course, he may have dabbled in his guilty pleasure a little too much these days. However, she didn't understand. Being high was his only way to cope with the whirlwind of bullshit he'd gotten himself into.

The Russians, the streets, his job, his family...Every fucking connection he had turned their backs on him, and he was going to make them pay slowly but surely. Just the thought of his sweet revenge caused him to smile.

Pouring a small hit into the crease of his index and thumb fingers, he sucked it up with his left nostril before rubbing his nose and holding his head back for a second. Damn, the drugs made him feel invincible.

He climbed out of the car with a confident stagger. He was so high that he was delusional. Yet, he was so confident in his delusion that he was convinced his wife and children all betrayed him, and they had to pay.

He tried his key, only to become frustrated when he realized the locks had been changed. Oh, that really pissed him off. "Sarah! Sarahhhh! Open this fucking door, you backstabbing bitch," he yelled, not giving a damn about the neighbors or the trouble he could cause himself if Troy police came out. He was an ex-cop that should have known better, and he was a Black man harassing a poor, innocent white woman. The fact that she was his wife didn't even matter.

The front door came flying open. Robinson was greeted by the fiery look in his youngest son's eyes. "Why are you here, Gerome?" Joshua, his eighteen-year-old son, asked, calling his father by his government name. "I'm sick of you harassing my mother. Just leave us alone!" he yelled, pure hatred oozing from his body.

Robinson let out a cynical laugh. "Oh, you're tough now, Joshie?" He leaned his face against the screen. "Are you *really* challenging dear old dad?"

"Just leave. Nobody wants you here." Joshua began to close the door...only to be met by the loud boom of Robinson's Glock, barely missing his head by an inch.

"Open the door, Joshie. Your dad just wants to talk to you and your mother." Robinson began to crack up with laughter. Joshua shot off so fast that he almost disappeared. The tough guy act was gone, replaced by pure fear.

Robinson slammed his body into the door frame, forcing the screen door open. "Sarah! Josh! Daddy's home. Come talk to Daddy!" he yelled in a mocking singsong voice. He had his gun waving, fully prepared to kill every one of them before he allowed them to live happily ever after without him. His delusion...the drugs.

"Gerome, please, just go! I called the police," Sarah called out from somewhere behind him. He stopped in his tracks, whipping around to follow the voice.

"You think I give a damn about the police, Sarah? I *am* the police!" he yelled, beating his chest.

As Robinson got closer to the living room, the whimpering stopped. She was near. He just didn't know where. "Come out and face me like the bitch you are! No, wait. You like to do niggas dirty. Fuck them, take their money, and leave them broke. You took all my money, Sarah? Did you rob me?" He pulled the closet door open so hard that the knob tore a hole through the drywall. She wasn't in there.

"Sarahhhhhh!" He began to yell like a crazed maniac. "You never loved me, did you, Sarah? What happened to 'for better or for worse'? Oh, the poor nigger boy can't buy me Gucci anymore, so I suppose I's got to go." He mocked her in slave slang, becoming more enraged. Everyone told him not to marry her.

"Sar—" his rant was cut short by the sirens in the distance. He was delusional...However, he wasn't that crazy. Robinson knew that he needed to get the hell on before he was taken to jail...or killed in a blaze of glory. He wasn't going out that easily.

"I'll be back, sweetheart," he sang before turning and dashing for the door. Little did he know, his wife and children would be a score he'd never settle because as soon as he left, they planned to disappear and never see the likes of Michigan again.

"I'm going to enjoy watching your pretty ass die," Robinson chuckled sinisterly, feeding off the high that Sophie's fear was giving him. He may have missed the mark with his wife and son, but he had her tied up and open to whatever abuse he saw fit. Mello had ruined everything for him. The motherfucker caused him to lose his job, wife, and money.

Smack!

Sophie's body almost gave out on her as another blow to the left side of her face caused her vision to blur. He wanted to take away something just as dear as the things he had lost. A blind man could see how much Mello loved Sophie, and it would give him great pleasure to see the hurt in Mello's eyes when he delivered her corpse to his doorstep.

Sophie knew she would die, and nothing could prepare her for such a fate. In that instant, she began to pray. That was the only thing she could do as she fought to stay conscious. There was no fighting off Robinson, no escape route, and no mercy in his heartless eyes. A tear slid down her cheek at the thought.

"You sorry motherfuckers thought you could get away with crossing me? Oh, I'm going to love every second of destroying every one of you bitches. Then I'm going to kill your man. Oh, that's going to be the grand finale. Karma is a grimy bitch, and my revenge will be slow, sweet...and gruesome."

With her mouth gagged by a dirty cloth and her arms tied to a chair, Sophie couldn't talk, run, tell him to kiss her ass—nothing. She was helpless, and Robinson had free rein to do whatever he pleased.

He struck her repeatedly until her eyes closed, and her body went numb. He was going to kill her. Her son was going to be motherless, and Mello was going to live happily ever after with some other bitch. She couldn't even cry for herself anymore. The tears ran dry. All Sophie saw was darkness.

Sophie struggled to keep her eyes open when the beating finally stopped. Through swollen, low eyes, she watched as he eagerly walked over to the raggedy coffee table and poured a line of coke, sniffing it. His head tilted, and his eyes rolled to the back of his head. That was his sixth line, and the effects made him feel like he was floating. Maybe he'd overdone it because his head was spinning.

Falling into the swivel chair, Robinson sat there, stuck on stupid. Sophie was the least of his worries. She was tied down and barely hanging on to life. She wasn't going anywhere. He just needed a break to enjoy his high before he finished what he had started.

As soon as Robinson's head slumped, Sophie used what little strength she could muster to try to wiggle herself free from the tape. Her fight was weak, but she was determined to return to her son, Mello, and her sisters. Her head was spinning, and it hurt to breathe. Tears of frustration slid down her eyes as she rocked back and forth until her chair fell over, somehow loosening the grip of the tape by just a bit.

She wiggled frantically, letting off a relieved squeak when her right hand slid loose. "Thank you, Jesus," Sophie cried out, nearly breaking her wrist as she snatched her other hand free. She was almost there. All she had to do was find the strength to drag her battered body up the stairs and away from the house. She didn't give a fuck about her phone, her purse, or nothing as long as she got far away from Robinson.

Pulling herself from the ground, she took off for the stairs—only to be yanked back by her hair. It felt as if her scalp were being ripped off. "And just where do you think you're going, bitch?" Robinson slurred, throwing her, causing her rib to collide with the bar.

Come on. Keep it together, Sophie. Think. You must make it back to your baby, she silently coached herself, spotting a long Grey Goose bottle inches away. She mustered every last drop of strength she had to grab and sent it crashing into Robinson's head as hard as she could. His judgment was off due to the lines of coke, which leveled the playing field. Now, *she* had the upper hand and took full advantage of it, repeatedly slamming the bottle into Robinson's head.

She had blacked out and didn't come to until his bloody body was passed out on the ground. She was free. Adrenaline had her body in overdrive. Limping up the stairs and out of the house, Sophie took off into the streets of whatever city she was in. She had nothing but the clothes on her back and her beaten and bruised body. She didn't even know where she was. All she knew was that she had to get as far away as possible. Only then would she be able to relax.

"Are you okay, ma'am? Should I call the police?" a young Arabic clerk asked, staring at a battered Sophie with sympathetic eyes. She looked horrible. Dried up blood was caked on her face, and her eyes were barely open.

"No!" she squeaked. "Please don't do that. Can I just use your phone? Please. If I can just use your phone, I'll be on my way." Sophie panicked. She didn't know who Robinson knew or his connections within the police department. She needed to call Mello. She needed her man more than she ever needed anyone in her life. She just wanted to go home. She wanted her baby. She wanted all of this to be a nightmare and go back to life as it was before linking with Mello.

The man walked over, opening the door to the back counter. "Come back here. Sit until you figure things out. There's a bathroom to clean up, and no one can see you. I'll let you use the phone, but you really need to call an ambulance."

Sophie followed him to the back. Hell, she didn't have any other options. She was grateful for his kindness. "Thank you so much. Thank you," she said, looking back for the thousandth time to make sure that Robinson hadn't followed her.

His limp body flashed through her head, and her heart raced. What if she killed him? Sophie didn't know if the man was dead or alive, and the fear of the unknown had her beyond terrified.

"Here you go, ma'am." The clerk handed her a face mask, then pointed toward a door a few feet away. "Go clean yourself up and put this on. Just want to keep everyone safe. COVID, you know?"

She hobbled to the bathroom. The sight that stared back at Sophie caused her to break down. Why would someone do a human being the way Robinson had done her? Her eyes were turning purple, the gash on the top right side of her face was ugly, her lip was cut and puffy, and her body was on fire from the beating it had endured. Sophie didn't even recognize herself.

She cleaned up the best she could through tear-streaked eyes. Taking a deep breath, she put on the mask, halfway covering the results of her kidnapping. It took everything in her not to break down. She had to get back to the people who loved her. Then she could fully release.

Jolts of nervous energy flowed through her body as her shaky fingers dialed Mello's number. When his deep baritone sounded into the phone, the adrenaline rush that kept her moving completely dissolved. Words failed her. She broke down.

"Sophie?" She heard scrambling. "Sophie, baby, is that you? Answer me. Baby, where you at?"

"I don't knowwww. Come get meeeee," she cried.

Sophie heard the car door slam and the seat belt alarm going off before she finished her sentence. "Where you at?"

"I don't knowwww."

"Listen to me, sweetheart. Calm down and breathe...You breathing?"

"Yes."

"OK, whose phone you using? Ask them where you at."

Sophie turned to the clerk. He was helping other customers, but his eyes were on her. "Can you tell me where I'm at?"

"Marathon Gas Station on Thirteen Mile and Mound."

"He said I'm on Thirteen and Mound. Please hurry up. I just want to come home."

"I'm on my way, sweetheart. Are you safe?"

"Yes, I'm sitting on the phone behind the counter. No one sees me."

"OK. Stay put until I get there. I don't want to say too much over the phone. Robinson?" he questioned, and Sophie knew exactly what he was asking.

"Yesss."

"OK, don't say anything else. I'll be there in ten minutes, ma. Call me back if anything happens."

Mello reluctantly hung up. He didn't want the wrong things to be said and needed to concentrate on the road. He was running red lights, speeding, switching lanes, the whole nine. The nigga was breaking every driving law possible to get to her.

As promised, ten minutes later, Mello's Range Rover screeched to a stop in front of the gas station. He practically ran into the building, startling the old Caucasian lady paying for her gas.

"Sophie!" he called out.

The sound of Mello's voice caused Sophie's heart to race. She hopped up and shot from behind the counter right into Mello's comforting arms. The past three days had been the worst in her life. She held on to him as if her life depended on it.

Mello pulled her face from his chest, staring into it. His heart dropped. Robinson had really fucked her up. Rage filled his chest. Blood was about to be shed. He could taste the bittersweet nectar of revenge.

"Come on, beautiful. You're good now. Let's go home."

"Don't call me that." Sophie's voice was just above a whisper. "I'm not beautiful. I'm ugly." Silent tears continued to fall.

"You could have a bald head and be seven hundred pounds, and you still gon' be the finest ma'fucka in the world to me."

Sophie's lips curled into a half smile for the first time in three days. "You're a seven-hundred-pound, bald-headed lie."

They both shared a much-needed laugh as they made it to Mello's Range, him helping her into the truck and closing the door before jogging over to the other side and pulling off.

The ride was silent for what seemed like an eternity before Mello finally spoke up. "Sophie, man, what the fuck happened?"

She shrugged. "I don't know. One minute, I was leaving to run a few errands, and the next, I was tied up being beaten by that crazy bastard. Something is wrong with him. He's crazy."

"He didn't...You know. He didn't go there, did he?"

Sophie shook her head. "No, he was too busy snorting lines and beating on me. I thought I was going to die, Kenneth. All I could think about was Jr., you, and my girls. I can't do this anymore. I know that was my Karma, and I got a second chance. I can't do this to my baby." She began to break down again for the thousandth time.

"Shhhh, ma. You don't ever have to do anything you don't want to do again. I got you. Where is Robinson? Can you tell me that?"

Sophie stared out the window, watching the passing trees and buildings. "I think I killed him. He attacked me, and I got a hold of a liquor bottle. I just kept hitting him and hitting him. I couldn't stop. Oh my God. What if I killed him?!"

Mello's jaw flexed. "Then he got off easy. Where did you leave him at?"

"Some house. I don't know, Kenneth. My mind wasn't there. I couldn't think. I—"

"Shhh, it's okay. Don't think. I got it from here." Mello calmed Sophie, pulling out his cell phone and dialing Rock.

"Yooo, is everything good, bro? You got Sophie? She good?" Rock questioned, genuinely concerned.

"Yeah, she good. Meet me at the crib and bring the crew." Mello hung up, not wanting to say too much over the phone.

"Are you taking me to my son?"

Mello shook his head. "Nah, li'l man don't need to see you like that. He with your bird. I'm going to drop a few dollars on her to keep him until you heal up a little. Your girls gon' meet you at my crib and sit with you. Them ma'fuckas been worried sick. You got a team of riders by your side."

"And what are you about to do?" Sophie bit down on her bottom lip, nervously awaiting an answer.

"Don't ask questions you really don't want to know the answer to."

Sophie took his advice. Deep down, she knew what had to happen. She relaxed, closed her eyes for the first time in days, and sucked in her freedom. She had survived…That's all that mattered.

CHAPTER THIRTY-FOUR

"**Y**OU LOOKING REAL stressed, friend. You good?" Brittany had been watching Diamond throughout the entire shift at the salon. The day breezed by. Clients had come and gone. The night sky was only lit by a piece of the moon and the streetlights.

Diamond shrugged. "I don't know how to answer that. On the one hand, life is great. I got the crazy-ass man of my dreams, I'm not struggling, and I'm at peace. But on the other, this shit with Sophie has me on edge, and I just pray my sister is okay."

"Yeah, me too." Brittany spun back and forth in the swivel stylist chair. "But you know I've been around, from your mom opening the shop, her death, and now. You're like family to me. So I have to keep it a buck." She paused, biting into her cheek as if carefully debating her words. "The streets are saying you and your homegirls were out here wilding with Mello. Like, he fell off and had y'all robbing people to come back up."

Diamond's brows furrowed as her heart began to pump faster. Her emotions were all over the place. "And you believe that?"

"I don't know. I have been noticing the changes, Diamond, and I want you to be careful. Your mom wouldn't want—"

"She wouldn't want *what*?" Diamond asked defensively. The mention of her mother triggered emotions that were impossible to ignore. "My mom sold pussy, got down on niggas, and left me here to get harassed by a washed-up pimp. Please don't bring her into this conversation."

Brittany threw up her hands in surrender. "And that was her business. All I was trying to say was that she loved you. Anybody with eyes knew that. She tried to protect you from what she had to go through." She sighed. "That's it, and that's all. Sophie is going to be okay. I'm not putting nothing negative in the atmosphere. I just don't know about Mello's homeboy. Rob, Rod, Rock, or whatever his name is. I liked Manny's married ass better for you."

"Manny? I definitely deserved better than him. He was just a distraction and a good fuck. The fact that he still calls and tries to meet up with me while his ugly-ass wife is posting all types of trips and family photos tells me I dodged a bullet." Diamond rolled her eyes.

"I like how you conveniently skipped over the robbing and Mello falling off part."

"I don't know that man's business. Whoever is giving you that false information should shut up because I know they wouldn't say it to his face."

"You know that," Brittany giggled. "Anyways, I just wanted to check up on you because you look worried. Sophie is going to be fine, boo. I'm about to head out. Lock up and be safe."

"I will." Diamond stood. "I'm coming out right behind you. Rock should be here any minute." She followed Brittany to the door, watching her to the car as her phone rang.

Diamond sauntered over to the receptionist counter to grab her phone, knowing that the person on the other end was Rock. He had been meeting her to make sure she safely locked up the shop and got home every night. Ever since everything popped off with Sophie, they had become extra cautious.

"What's up, babe?" she answered, cheering up at the sight of his name dancing across her screen.

"I'm not gon' be able to make it to you, sweetheart. I just wanted to let you know Mello found your homegirl, and we got to handle some shit."

"Oh my God!" Diamond squealed with relief. "Is she okay? Where she at? I'm about to lock up and go see her." She was filled with joy, knowing that her girl was safe.

"Nah, ma. Give her some time. Mello got the doctors tending to her right now. You got your strap with you?" Rock quizzed.

"Of course."

"Make sure you have your hand on the trigger when you walk out and watch your surroundings. I'll be by your crib as soon as we handle our shit."

"OK, daddy," Diamond cooed into the phone with her lip poked out. "Be safe, and whatever you're about to do, I hope you do it," she said, knowing that it most likely had to do with Robinson and finally silencing the crazy motherfucker.

After hanging up with Rock, Diamond grabbed her things to leave. She had been so paranoid lately that carrying her pistol was a given. Rock didn't have to remind her to do so. Hooking up with Mello was a gift and a curse. It seemed as if, for every good that came out of it, something worse happened.

Diamond sighed, making her way out of the salon. The cool breeze of the night's air kissed her cheeks as soon as she hit the street, as cars zoomed past. She scanned the empty parking lot before making her way to her car.

"Ms. Diamond, I see life has been treating you well." The familiar voice called from behind, causing her to whip around, startling her. She wasn't so much scared of the man. It was more so him sneaking up on her.

"Carlos? What do you want? I paid you," Diamond frowned.

"You did. But I've been peeping you making moves, and I got to thinking. I did a lot of time because of your ho-ass momma. Fifty thousand wasn't enough."

"Wasn't enough?" she screeched. "It was more than enough, considering I didn't have nothing to do with that. Why are you making my life hell? What did I ever do to you?" She felt her emotions on the verge of spilling out. Carlos had terrorized, exploited, belittled, and downright tortured her for the past year. She was tired of it.

"You was born. Your mother was a good ho before she had you. She thought I was going to give a fuck that she got pregnant. I didn't give a damn if you was mine or not. When you turned eighteen, you was gon' be on the corner too. Bitch fucked up everything trying to keep yo' rotten pussy ass safe from the boogeyman." He chuckled sinisterly. "Ain't protect you from shit. That's why she in a grave, and yo' dumb ass may not be on a corner, but you still getting me my money."

Diamond reached onto her waistline and pulled out her gun before she could process what had happened. She pointed it at his head, squeezing the handle so tightly that her fingers threatened to cramp. Her trigger finger was itching, mouth dry with hatred.

"Oh shit, li'l Diamond done grew some balls." Carlos chuckled, taking a step toward her. "What are you going to do with that? You ain't no killer, bitch."

Carlos lunged at Diamond, catching her completely off guard. She squeezed the trigger before she even knew what happened. She didn't stop there. She let off two more rounds that had Carlos's old bones fleeing for his life.

Once she was sure he was gone, she raced to her car and sped off, hearing sirens in the distance. Diamond's heart never stopped racing, the sting of Carlos's words never let up, and the hurt and confusion of her mother's absence were gnawing at her soul.

"Ma, what the hell is going on? I need you so bad right now," she whispered as tears flowed down her cheeks. She was just simply tired.

CHAPTER THIRTY-FIVE

"Y'ALL FOUND HER?! Oh my God, thank you, Jesus!" Angel squealed into the phone, hopping up to grab her keys and purse. She didn't think twice. She needed to lay eyes on her sister.

Sophie going missing was a heavy weight on her soul. She was the one who brought her girl into the game, so she couldn't help but feel responsible. Angel hadn't slept the whole three days Sophie was gone.

"Yeah, but she needs to rest. He did her dirty. Mannn," Mello's voice trailed off as he spoke. Angel could hear and feel the emotion surging through it. "Yeah, man. Let her rest, and you and Diamond can come see her tomorrow."

Angel's face went sour. "First of all, you have me all the way fucked up. You can't tell me I can't come see my sister. She may be your so-called girlfriend, but that's been my sister basically my whole life."

"Yo, who you talkin' to?"

"I'm talking to *you*, nigga! You want to be all big and bad, but where was you when your weak-ass cop friend snatched her up? That was complete bullshit. You don't got your people in check?" Angel didn't mean to go off. Her emotions were surging too.

"Look, I ain't about to argue with you. Yeah, I should have been there to protect her. But remember, we ain't all innocent here, my baby. You the one that introduced her to the game. If you cared so fucking much, you would have kept her and her seed away from this bullshit."

Angel started to go completely off, but Mello had ended the call before she could respond. The truth cut. She felt her chest tighten as she breathed heavily. What if things had turned out differently? She couldn't fathom the thought of someone actually killing Sophie. That was a guilt that would drive her to her own grave.

"You good, bitch? You look like you seen a ghost." Shanell's voice startled her. Angel had forgotten that the girl had stopped by to visit.

"Ye...Yeah, I'm fine."

Shanell plopped down on the couch across from Angel. She tossed her long fire-engine-red weave over her shoulder. "You sure you good? I thought I heard something about your homegirl. Somebody snatched her up? Was it because of Domo?"

"Fuck Domo."

"I know that's right. My cousin said they had him all over the news down there in Atlanta. You remember, I told you somebody killed him execution style. I thought it was y'all. What happened to your girl? We used to be close."

"It isn't none of your business, and I'm not going to discuss it now," Angel shot.

"Humph," Shanell smirked. "Niggas get to a little bag and get to talking crazy. It actually *was* my business...until you decided to go off and work with a group of inexperienced bitches. We ain't never had no real issues when we was running together, hitting our licks. So I'm just trying to figure out why you so secretive now and treating me like I'm the opps. Am I your opp or something? You not fucking with me like that, are you?"

Angel's head cocked. "Are you *really* about to make this about you right now? Let's be totally clear. You're big mad because I cut you out of the licks...not because I wanted to but because Mello didn't want to involve anyone else from the club. However, let's not pretend like I haven't been throwing you something here and there just off the strength."

Shanell sighed, calming down. "You have. I can't even front, and I appreciate it. My bad. I'm tripping. I guess I feel some type of way because we was struggling together, bitch. Whatever I came up on, I was cutting you in. How I'm supposed to feel when I see you whipping foreigns, going on shopping sprees, and leaving the little people behind? Bitch, you don't even come to the club anymore. Our whole operation just stopped."

Angel looked over at Shanell in disbelief. "Are you fucking *serious*? My sister was missing and beat the fuck up. You *really* think I'm worried about some money?" Angel reached into her purse, pulling out a stack of bills and tossing them at Shanell. "This what you worried about? Huh? This what you wanted?" She threw more bills before standing to her feet. "You need to leave. I'm not feeling you. Me and any bitch I rock with don't do jealous, and you hating real hard...*friend*."

Shanell's mouth hung open. "That was so disrespectful." She wanted to go upside Angel's head, but she was no fool. Angel was going to get hers. She'd hit the bitch where it hurt when she least expected it, and until that happened, Shanell would enjoy the free ride.

"No, you're disrespectful, and you got to bounce. Bye, Shanell." Angel pointed to the door.

Shanell didn't bother picking up any of the money Angel had thrown. She still had a little dignity. "I'm going to leave and let you make it. I know you're not yourself with your homegirl getting kidnapped because of you and all." She bit down on her bottom lip, subtly throwing shade. "But let that be the last time you disrespect me, ho. You might think you that bitch, but I'm an even bigger bitch that ain't scared to dog walk a ho." Shanell didn't wait for her to respond. She gladly left after checking the shit out of Angel.

CHAPTER THIRTY-SIX

MELLO'S EYES SLOWLY crept open as the rays from the sun beamed in his face from the crack in the curtains. He looked over to the clock on the nightstand. It was just after nine o'clock, and he knew that Sophie was dying to see her baby. It had been an entire week since she returned home. She needed time to mentally prepare to enter the world and be a mother again. Plus, they both knew Ricky Jr. didn't need to see her like that.

He had paid Sophie's mother five thousand dollars to keep him for another week. Supposedly, Ricardo Sr. was out of town on tour, which had become a common excuse ever since Mello checked his sorry ass. Mello didn't give a damn one way or another because as long as he was fucking with Sophie, Ricky Jr. was good. He couldn't love Sophie without loving her son.

The scars had begun to heal, and the swelling was almost unnoticeable. However, she still woke up in a cold sweat some nights or randomly burst into tears. Robinson traumatized Sophie, and Mello wished he could go back and take him out properly. In his opinion, Robinson's death was too easy. He deserved to be tortured until he used his last breath to beg for mercy.

Mello's gaze turned to Sophie as she peacefully slept curled in a ball, with her ass pressed against his chest. Bruised and all, she was still fine as fuck to him. Her body was soft, and his little man knew exactly what awaited him between the heavens of her thighs. He wasn't in a rush to go there with her, though. Sophie needed tender love and care...not to be fucked senseless. They had forever for that.

Easing out of bed, Mello got himself together before heading to Sophie's mother's house to get Jr. Then he went to the grocery store to grab what he needed to make breakfast. He wasn't anybody's top chef, but he knew how to make a few items.

"Uncle Kenny, we going to see my momma?" Ricky Jr. asked as they walked the aisles of Wholefoods Grocery Store.

Mello smiled down at the snaggletoothed child. Adorned in a Nike short set with matching Jordans and a fresh Mohawk cut, Ricky Jr. had swag. He was going to be a heartbreaker when he grew up. Mello liked that. He wondered what his own child would look like.

"Yeah, she still asleep, li'l man. You gon' help me cook breakfast for her?"

Ricky Jr.'s face turned into a playful frown. "I don't know how to cook, mannnn."

Mello chuckled, grabbing a loaf of wheat bread. "Well, you can learn how to cook, *mannnn*." He mimicked Ricky Jr.

"My daddy said that mens don't cook. Girls supposed to cook." Jr. shrugged.

"Yo' daddy a cl—" Mello caught himself. He wasn't lame enough to down-talk the next man in front of his seed. "Your daddy wrong, li'l man. How you gon' eat if you don't got no woman?"

Jr. looked at Mello as if he had asked the craziest question ever. "My momma, duh."

Mello burst into laughter. "What'chu mean yo' momma? She not gon' be around forever. You got to learn how to cook and take care of yourself, man. That way, you don't need nobody for nothing. Yeah, you can get a girl to help you, but you supposed to always know how to survive."

"Well, my daddy have a hundred thousand and thousand girls. I'm gon' have a hundred million thousand girlfriends too. They gon' cook for me."

"That's sad. You not gon' get that far thinking like that."

Ricky Jr. didn't respond. In his little mind, Mello just didn't know the game. His dad had set the tone for how he saw women and life. He hadn't seen any other formula until Mello came along, and their time together had only been brief. Sophie was skeptical about bringing just anyone around her son.

Mello joked around with Ricky Jr., and, surprisingly, they had fun making breakfast together. He didn't have any children of his own. Ricky Jr. was very opinionated, but he was a cool kid to kick it with and mentor.

"Mommmmmmmyyy, wake uppppp," the baby squealed, pretending to creep into the room with Mello close behind him, holding a tray. He jumped on the bed, shaking Sophie. "Maaaaaaaaa."

Sophie's eyes flew open. She couldn't contain the smile that danced on her face. Lord knows she missed her baby. She began to rain kisses all over his little face, squeezing him so tight that he felt as if he were suffocating.

"Mommmmmmmmaaa, stoppp. I can't breathe," he whined, using his hand to push her face away.

Mello chuckled. "Yeah, he made this big old breakfast for you, and he not going to be alive to watch you eat it if you don't let him go."

Sophie finally looked up at Mello and the tray in his hand. Her heart melted. "Awwww, you cooked for Mommy?"

"Uh-huh," Jr. nodded. "Uncle Kenny said I got to learn how to be a man and take care of myself 'cause you not gon' want to do it one day."

"What?" Mello laughed, amused. "I didn't say that. I said a man supposed to know how to hold himself down, with or without a woman."

"That's right, baby. You need to learn how to survive. But as long as Mommy has air in her lungs, she got you. Okay?"

"OK, but can I go play the game? I'm tired from all that working." Jr. sighed dramatically, running his little hand over his forehead.

Both Mello and Sophie burst into laughter. "Go ahead, boy. You are something else."

Ricky Jr. ran off before she could even get the words out good. "Thank you, Momma. Bye."

"Ricky Jr.," The little boy stopped in his tracks. "I love you," Sophie called out to him.

"I love you too. Bye."

Mello shook his head as he placed the tray of food down in front of Sophie. "I love that little nigga. He something else."

"Tell me about it," Sophie agreed, stuffing a forkful of pancake in her mouth. "Thank you too. You've been a blessing to me and Jr., and I'm so glad you came back into my life."

"No thanks needed." Mello leaned in and pecked her lips. "You got away from me before. I'm playing for keeps this time. You just make sure you play your cards right."

"Well, come play in these cards." Sophie seductively bit into the bacon, causing Mello to burst into laughter.

"That wasn't even sexy with yo' fat ass."

"Fuck you, nigga. I didn't want your little Vienna sausage anyway."

Mello smirked. "Picture that. Look, though, ma. I got to make a run, and I'll be right back."

"Do you have to go?" Sophie pouted.

"Yeah, I'll be back, though. Maybe we can take li'l man to the carnival out in Taylor; have a family day or some shit."

Sophie perked up. "That sounds good. I love you, Kenneth Davis."

"I love you too, Sophie Daniels." He really did. She had become his new addiction.

"Get the fuck off my ass. Damn." Mello frowned, looking into his rearview mirror as a black Tahoe rode his bumper. He pressed down on his brakes, causing the truck to slam on its brakes as well, almost causing an accident. "Yeah, ma'fucka, slow the fuck down."

Hooking a left onto Greenfield, his car came jerking to a stop with a loud screech, almost colliding with another black Tahoe. When the slick-haired Russian hopped out of the truck, Mello's hand immediately went to the pistol under his seat.

Mello's adrenaline was at an all-time high. His eyes scanned the area, searching for an exit plan. The Russians were some ruthless motherfuckers, and although they had resolved their issues, he didn't know which way they were coming, especially with how they rode down on him, boxing him in.

"Fuck," Mello pulled his phone from his pocket, never taking his eye from the man approaching his car. "Aye, Siri, call Rock."

The phone dialed his right-hand's number. Rock answered on the first ring. "What up, bro."

"Some Russian ma'fuckas ran down on me on the corner of Seven Mile and Greenfield. Where you at?"

"What?!" Rock shot. "Say less. I'm around the corner on St. Mary's." Mello could hear scrambling in the background as the phone went dead. If he didn't know anything else, he knew his boy was down to ride. He also knew that if the Russians wanted him dead, his car would be riddled with bullets already. That's why he slid his pistol onto his waist before rolling the window down to see what the man wanted.

"Kenneth, Mr. Ivanov would like to have a word with you." He spoke in a thick Eastern accent.

"So y'all just gon' ride down on a nigga like that? Let's say I ain't got shit to talk about."

The man shrugged. "Then I'd inform you that it's in your best interest to have a conversation with the Don. I cannot be held accountable for what may happen if you don't."

A brow raised. "Is that a threat?"

"No threats; just being informal."

"I'm saying y'all ma'fuckas couldn't just call and pick a time and place? If I got to bustin', I would have been wrong, huh?" Mello complained.

The Russian let out a small laugh. "We aren't concerned about that. Follow me, Kenneth."

Mello sighed before pulling open the door and stepping out of his truck. Just as he closed the door, Rock and an army of his men came hitting the corner; tires screeching, doors opening, and guns cocking.

In the middle of Greenfield, in broad daylight and high traffic, the two crews were engaged in a standoff like they were in an old Western movie. Rock came through with an army, which was why Mello treated him like blood.

"Yo, Mello. You good, my nigga?" Rock called out, throwing his opps the stare of death.

Mello didn't speak. He just held up a hand, signaling for Rock and his crew to stand down as he coolly made his way to the black Tahoe to talk to Ivanov. He knew there was shit in the game if the Don dada himself requested his presence.

Climbing into the truck, Mello looked back at his crew. His chest swelled. They were ready for whatever.

"The package that I requested you deliver to Gerome was never delivered, Kenneth," Ivanov started before Mello could get in the seat good. "There was something specifically for him in that bag, and now I'm wondering what happened to my package."

"I still got it," Mello retorted.

"But you were supposed to deliver it, and now you have caused an issue since Gerome hasn't contacted anyone in a week."

Mello frowned. "Look, I wasn't trying to keep whatever you got in that bag. I ain't even open the ma'fucka. Furthermore, you ain't gon' ever hear from that nigga again. He floatin' in the Detroit River."

"You stupid boy!" Ivanov yelled, catching Mello off guard when he drew his pistol and placed it to Mello's temple. "Do you *know* what you've done?"

Mello swallowed hard, his Adam's apple bobbing. "With all due respect, if you don't plan on using that ma'fucking heater, you better get it the fuck outta my face," he gritted, snatching away. "Any furthermore, that crooked bitch kidnapped and beat my old lady. I don't give a fuck what he had going on. The nigga had to go."

"Fuck! Fuck! Fuck!" Ivanov went off in a rant. He looked up at his driver. "Have everyone prepare to return to Russia. Burn everything that can't come with us." He looked over at Mello. "A man protects his family. I will not hold that against you. However, I will advise you to take your family and disappear. You do not know the chaos that Gerome has caused and the consequences that will follow in his absence. You are dismissed."

The door to the Tahoe swung open, and Mello stepped out. Shit had just gotten real.

"*Breaking News, Nikolay Ivanov, who is said to be the ringleader of a Russian crime cartel, was just picked up at the DTW airport, along with seven members of his enterprise. No further details have been given yet, but we'll keep you posted as the story unfolds...*" the news reported, causing Mello's antennas to go up. The meeting with Ivanov was only hours earlier, and already, he was apprehended.

"Fuck!" Mello stood pacing the floor as his crew stared at him. Things had spiraled so far out of control that it hurt his brain to think about a resolution. That's why he needed to prepare his soldiers for the worst and get lawyered up. He didn't know how much the Feds knew or what type of shit Robinson had stirred up. Now, he would never know since his corpse was chopped up and floating in the Detroit River.

"Yo, what do this shit mean for us, boss man? Niggas out here starving. We got whole families to feed," Durk asked respectfully. He didn't have any beef with Mello or Rock. He just wanted to be able to feed his daughter. Formula was close to fifty dollars a can these days. The cost of everything has jumped since the pandemic.

Mello stopped pacing to look at every one of his men. It wasn't their fault that business with Robinson went south. Nor was it their fault that he and the girls got a little too greedy, causing them to be in too deep with Robinson. Mello's rainy day fund had tripled, and he still had the club and his real estate endeavors. He was good. He didn't expect them to wait around with their livelihood in limbo.

"Anyone that wants to leave is free to go," he shrugged.

Durk frowned. "Free to go? Big bro, I fucked with you the long way. You said go, and I was letting my little bitch sing. Free to go? Go where? All of us been ten toes down. I mean, I get we going through a storm, but come on, boss man. You can do us better than 'free to go.'"

"Yeah, Mello. Man, we fuck with you. It's time to show us you fuck with us too."

Mello took his junior lieutenant in. RJ was a short, stout cat with a lot of heart. He never had to question his loyalty. Even at the moment, he didn't. However, the streets were hot as fish grease. What more did they want from him?

Mello rubbed the hairs on his chin. "OK, so the Feds watching us like hawks. We just got the Russians off our backs. We lost our connect on the inside. What more do you propose I do?" He crossed his arms over his chest, awaiting a realistic response.

RJ rubbed his hands together. "I know a few cats out in North Carolina. You be the plug and get us the work out there, and me and the crew will hold you down until the heat cool off. You ain't getting rid of us that easy, nigga. Put us to work."

Rock took a sip from his drink, listening. That was something he had learned to do over the past year. For so long, he acted first and dealt with the consequences later. But shitttt, life had a way of humbling a motherfucker, and he was truly humbled.

"I'm listening," Mello shot.

"OK, it's like this. The same way we ran our shit here in the D, we can do that in Carolina. Dante got people in Indiana, and Durk got people in New York. We recruit our little crews, and, just like that, we getting more paper than before, off the Feds' radar, and you expanding. It's a win-win, my nigga," RJ proposed.

"Sounds good." Mello continued to pull on the hairs of his beard. "Or, if you go set up shop, I'll hook you up with the supplier. Y'all been under my wing long enough. Whoever want to fly, I ain't trying to clip ya wings."

"Aye, let me holla at you." Rock finally spoke up. He tapped Mello's chest, signaling for him to follow him into the back room.

Rock continued once they made it down the hallway and into the small storage room's solitude. "Yo, I understand you trying to be Captain Planet and shit, but nigggga, do you know how much money you leaving on the floor? Them niggas trying to set it up for us to be the next BMF. You see they down for the team."

"And you see Meech been in the chain gang for twenty years, and they ain't trying to let a nigga out. Fuck trying to be BMF."

"Damn, my nigga. What happened to you? You get a little pussy and—"

Mello grabbed Rock up before he realized what he was doing. "Watch your fucking mouth, my nigga."

Rock snatched away. Neither man was considered soft. They both could hold their own if it ever came down to it. "Bro, I fuck with you the long way. We been fucking with each other since the sandbox, but don't you ever put yo' hands on me again like that, nigga." Rock was respectful with his warning but meant every word he said.

Mello wanted to ask him what the fuck he was going to do if he did. However, reality settled in. Rock was his brother, and beefing wasn't what they did. "Yeah, a'ight. I'm out. Do whatever the fuck you got to do since you want to be Big Meech so bad. Just count me out of that shit."

"So, this really where we at wit' it?" Rock threw his hands in the air.

Mello didn't respond. There was too much going on in his head to even process their disagreement. So he decided to remove himself. He'd holler at Rock when he had a clear mind.

"Babe, what's wrong? Are you okay?" Sophie's soft hands began to caress his shoulders, and Mello's eyes closed as he rested his head back.

"Yeah, I'm good. Ain't nothing I can't figure out," he retorted, not bothering to open his eyes. Sophie was the peace he never knew he needed until that very moment. He placed his hands on top of hers and pulled her onto his lap, holding her tightly.

She let out a soft giggle before leaning in to peck his lips. "I see the stress all in your eyes. Is everything okay, babe? Did they find Robinson or something?"

Mello shook his head. "Not that I know of."

Sophie bit down on her bottom lip. "Did Durk and 'nem find my cell phone and purse?"

Mello shook his head. "Nah, they didn't. We got bigger problems, though. We got to get the fuck on."

"Why, Kenneth? The Russians are in jail, and Robinson is dead. We're free. Between the two of us, we have plenty of money saved. You have the businesses. We can finally live now."

"I love how innocent you are." Mello stared into her sparkling brown eyes. "But it's not that simple, sweetheart. The Feds could be knocking at our door any minute, the Russians might be feeling some type of way, and we have a dead cop on our hands. We got to get the fuck on."

Sophie let out a deep breath of air. "Fine. I'll go pack our important things and schedule a flight out. What about Diamond and Angel?"

"They need to be leaving too."

"Have you talked to them?" Sophie quizzed.

"Yeah, everyone knows. I—"

Before Mello could finish his sentence, a knock at the door jarred his words. He started to grab his pistol. However, he knew that knock. Looking out the picture window, he saw the flashing red and blues, which confirmed his theory. Mello's heart dropped. He had done a lot of dirt in his days. Karma was now strapping up to go to war with him. He just hoped the bitch wasn't ready to come see him just yet.

"Shit, that's the police, Mello!" Sophie squeaked. Everything tingled inside her being. She could feel her breathing go ragged.

Mello grabbed Sophie up as another hard knock shook the door frame. "Police! Open up!" they yelled. He grabbed her face, planting a deep, passionate kiss on her lips. He held her tightly as if it would be their last time embracing each other.

"I love you, ma." He pecked her lips again. "I love the fuck out of you. I want you always to know that. And right now, I need you to stay calm. They probably about to take me in. You got the code to the safe. It's in a black notebook in there with my lawyer's number and money to pay him. Call him as soon as they take me out."

"Take you out? Mello, baby, I can't do this. What if they try to keep you forever?"

Bam! Bam! Bam!

"Open up!" The knocks grew louder.

Mello smiled, wiping the tears from her eyes. "Calm down. They can't keep me forever," he tried assuring her. However, he didn't know what life would throw at him.

Suddenly, the door came flying off its hinges, causing Mello and Sophie to jump, startled. Agents swarmed the place with guns drawn, ripping them apart. They pushed Mello to the side, beaming their guns at Sophie.

"Sophie Daniels, you're under arrest for the murder of Commander Gerome Robinson. Anything you say..." The officer's words trailed off as Mello's brain went dead. It wasn't his own freedom he'd be fighting for. They were there for Sophie?

Damn.

Guilt began to chip away at his soul. Mello dragged her and her girls into the chaos of street life. He had to make things right. Sophie wasn't built for a prison cell, and he wasn't built to live without her.

CHAPTER THIRTY-SEVEN

"OK, FRIEND. I see you comin', big spender today. Let me hold something," Shanell slyly remarked as she watched Angel pull out a thick stack of hundred-dollar bills to pay for the new Gucci purse and three pairs of shoes inside Nordstrom's for herself, her little brother, and Ricky Jr. With Sophie being locked up, Angel had stepped up in the role of being Ricky Jr.'s godmother. It didn't hurt that she had been spending time with Ray more often. He and Ricky Jr. got along like long lost brothers.

Angel ignored the shade. She began to wonder why she even hung with the girl anymore. Instead of being happy for her friend's new come-up, jealousy oozed all through Shanell's pores. "Do you want a pair too?" Angel asked, stunting harder. Maybe that was the reason she kept Shanell around...to stunt.

Shanell's lips curled into a grin. "Hell yeah. If you buying, I want all parts. Oh, and I need you to ride with me somewhere. My homeboy got some cash for me before we go out tonight."

Angel's eyes slanted toward Shanell. "Go out where? I told you I was going to visit Sophie in the morning. So I need to pick up my little brother and nephew."

Surprisingly, having Ray and Ricky Jr. to look after had really matured Angel. A dollar wasn't on her mind every second of the day anymore. She still loved her designer fashions and stunting hard, but her head was on a totally different cloud. Over the months working for Mello, she'd saved up a decent amount and had been dibbling and dabbling in real estate. She was in the process of opening two Airbnbs and a group home to keep the cash flow coming.

Mello had really become a brother to Angel, giving her the game and helping her to get to where she needed to be. He fucked with her because of the way that she loved Sophie and her son. They were both holding Sophie down to the fullest, along with Diamond too.

Shanell rolled her eyes. "Ewww, yo' ass ain't no fun no more. You didn't even ask whose party it was."

"Because I really don't care. I ain't thinking about these niggas or these bitches."

"Fine then, you don't have to party with li'l ol' me. But I still need you to swing me by ol' boy house before we get back to the hood."

Angel let out a sigh, giving Shanell the side-eye. "OK, heffa."

An hour later, Angel's Benz was pulling into the driveway of a subpar three-bedroom ranch on the Eastside of Detroit. She turned her nose up at how poorly the landscaping was kept and the sheets covering the windows serving as curtains.

"Damn, heffa. Where you got me coming to? Is this a spot?" she frowned. "I'm not getting out. So hurry up."

"Act brand new if you want to." Shanell slung her long braids over her shoulder. "Get yo' ass out and stop acting so damned uppity. It may be a few dollars in it for your rich ass too," she smiled reassuringly.

Against her better judgment, Angel dragged herself from the car. Rocking Nike biker shorts and a matching sports bra set with Nike slides, she kept it simple, sexy, and cute. Her curves were outrageous, so she knew whatever nigga Shanell was tricking with had a bunch of thirsty friends, and they would be on her. She rolled her eyes.

Once inside, rap music and heavy weed instantly attacked their senses. Angel counted five niggas and two females in the living room. She had no clue who else was in the house. She held her purse close. She'd blow anybody's head off that tried her. The events of the past few months had her on a shoot-first-and-ask-questions-later basis.

"Damn, who is that, Nelly?" one peon called out.

Shanell giggled. "My homegirl, Angel. The one I was telling y'all about."

Angel frowned. "Bitch, don't be telling them my name. And what you speaking on me for?"

"Because I can," Shanell shot with attitude.

The change in Shanell's demeanor threw off Angel. She cocked her head, staring as if trying to analyze the girl. "Oh, you getting cute because you with your people. Let me remove myself."

Angel started toward the door but was stopped when one of the girls stood up, blocking her path. "Nah, you not about to go nowhere, boo." She smiled curtly as two more men came from the back room.

Angel's heart pounded. She had done too much dirt and robbed too many unsuspecting men not to know what was happening. Shanell set her up. She wanted to be shocked, but deep down, she knew that the bitch was a jealous hater. So she couldn't even be surprised.

"Grab the bitch purse. She keep a heater on her," Shanell called out.

If looks could kill, she would be dead. Angel's fiery eyes were dead set on Shanell. "Bitch, so this how we playing it?"

Shanell shrugged. "Nothing personal. You know the game, boo." She pointed at a chubby dude sitting on the couch, puffing on an L. "Go get D. Tell him the lick here."

"The *lick*?" Angel shook her head. "Bitch, if you don't kill me today, I'm sending you under the grave. Snake-ass ho."

"Shut up," Shanell sent a sharp left hook, popping Angel in the mouth. Without a second thought, Angel charged at her, knocking her to the ground. The two wrestled, rolling around, while the men laughed. One of the ladies stood to help when Angel began to get the best of Shanell, but someone stopped her.

"Nah, ma. Let them fight."

They were going at it like wildcats. Well, it was more so Angel throwing blow after blow. She had never been a slouch when it came to throwing hands.

Finally, someone pulled them apart, pinning Angel down. Shanell's nose was bleeding, and her eye was swollen. "What the fuck was that, D?" Shanell yelled.

"Bitch, I *fed* you! I looked out when I didn't have to, and *this* is what you do to me?" Angel growled.

"You always thought you was better than me. Too good to dance. Too good to fuck. Why I'm the one always getting my ass beat when shit go left, but you come up, and suddenly, I ain't shit? Fuck you!" Shanell lunged at Angel, but D pushed her back so hard that she fell to her ass.

D began to crack up with laughter. "You was trying to hit a lick on *her*?" he quizzed, pointing to Angel with a raised brow. "This my baby right here. Ain't shit shaking this way." Durk turned to Angel. "You good, ma? I ain't even know it was you. I'on even fuck with girlie like that. What you want me to do with her?"

Durk was one of Mello's soldiers, and he'd been on several licks with them. He and Angel had developed a friendship on top of the fact that Mello was fucking with her best friend heavily. The only reason Durk even agreed to see what they lick was about was because the streets were dry since the drug operation shut down, and Durk knew Shanell was known for setting up ballers.

Shanell's mouth dropped open. She looked to her girls for backup, but they had turned away. When Angel cut her out, she formed her own crew of get-money bitches. Angel wasn't the only one getting dough. She was just on another level, and it burned Shanell's soul. She swore that she was going to get the uppity ho. She had plotted for months. Now, her whole plan was falling apart.

She hadn't counted on Durk being close to Angel. She knew that he rolled with Mello occasionally as the flunky, but she hadn't counted on the fact that he was more than a flunky, and Angel was family.

"I don't need you to do nothing, boo. She gon' get this good ass whooping for even thinking about crossing me. These bitches gon' watch, and if anybody jump in, lay they asses the fuck out," Angel ordered.

Just as she said, Angel wore Shanell's ass out and didn't stop beating the girl until she pissed on herself, passing out. Angel was glad that she never let Shanell in too close. She was a wolf in sheep's clothing, and there wasn't any room for jealous, hate-hearted bitches in her circle. She knew Shanell would think a hundred times before crossing her again.

Angel took one last look at Shanell's beaten body on the ground before snatching her purse from the flunky that snatched it from her. Just off principle, she hauled off and smacked the cowboy shit out of the girl.

Angel knew that Karma had a funny way of sneaking up on you. Disgust had her stomach bubbling. She'd never in a million years think that she would almost be robbed by someone she considered an...associate.

The following day, Angel found herself in the passenger seat of Mello's Range Rover, heading to the women's prison to visit Sophie. Ricky Jr. was in the backseat watching something on his tablet while Mello bobbed his head to Tupac.

It had become a routine every Wednesday and Saturday, which were Sophie's visiting days. Usually, Angel would be picking the wild mazes of Mello's brain. He was smart and deep. When he spoke, he dropped jewels. However, today was different. Angel didn't have the energy to retain knowledge.

Life had been on her mind heavy. Although she was building a solid relationship with her little brother, she still hadn't said two words to her mother and didn't plan to. It was crazy. Half the time, her mother didn't even know that Ray was with Angel. The ten-year-old was home alone more than any child should have ever been. Then there was Sophie. Angel couldn't help but feel guilty about her being locked up. She prayed her girl was released and made it home to her man and her son. Jail wasn't for Sophie. Finally, there was Gamble. He was the cause of some of her trauma, and with him popping back up, Angel was forced to face her demons head-on without an apology, explanation, or even a kiss my ass. The rapes, betrayal, and constant disappointment flooded her thoughts, and she was trying her damnedest to dismiss it all. That took a lot of strength. After ten whole years, Angel was finally releasing him, and it felt damned good.

"How did you get mixed up with a scheming ho like Shanell?" Mello asked, interrupting Angel's train of thought.

Angel looked over at Mello and shrugged. "We both needed money, and we both was down to get it however. Shit happens."

"Yeah, I can dig it. I would have had to body that broad if we included her in our shit—"

"What's a broad?" Ricky Jr. leaned forward and asked with a raised brow.

Angel chuckled. "None of your business, little boy. Why ain't you looking at your tablet? What did Auntie tell you about being in grown-folks conversations?"

Jr.'s lip poked out. "That a kid not supposed to."

"That's right. Now watch your tablet and be a kid, little boy."

"OK," he murmured, grabbing the tablet again and pulling on his headphones.

"Dang, meanie. Stall li'l man out," Mello teased.

"Nope, he gon' learn today."

"Yeah, I feel you. Maybe that's what I needed growing up because my momma didn't give a fuc—" he caught himself before he cursed. "My fault. I shouldn't be talking crazy in front of little man. But yeah, my mom was the worst."

"Mine too," Angel agreed. "Try having a little brother by your first love and your virginity being sold to a trick for a couple of dollars."

Mello frowned. "Yoooo, that's wild. Hate you had to go through that. I see you been holding li'l bro down, though. What she say about that?"

"Absolutely nothing, and I had bottled-up hatred and trust issues for a long time. I did a lot of fucked-up shit and blamed it on me being hurt by the one person that was supposed to protect me. Finally, I realized that I was just on some bullshit."

"Knowing is half the battle," Mello chuckled.

"Forget you, Negro. You ain't a saint yourself, but I'll give you a pass because of the way you see about my sister and her son. I'm rooting for y'all. I really hope y'all get your happily ever after."

"Me too," Mello agreed, pulling into the prison's parking lot.

The trio made their way inside, fighting through the crowd, metal detectors, and guards. It took almost an hour for them to finally sit with Sophie for the visit.

"Mommmy." Jr. ran to Sophie, jumping into her arms as soon as he saw her.

Sophie was so overwhelmed with joy that tears slid down her cheeks. She held her baby tightly, wishing she could go home with him. Being in jail was like hell on earth.

"No touching, Daniels," a female guard warned before passing their table.

Sophie ignored her. Nobody was going to tell her she couldn't hold her baby. She missed him like hell. Shit, she missed her girls, she missed Mello, and most importantly, she missed her home and freedom.

"How you been, pretty girl?" Mello asked as they sat. His stare was so intense.

"OK, considering." Sophie gave him a weak smile, bouncing Jr. "I'm just happy to see you, my sister, and my baby. Y'all are the highlight of my week. I love y'all."

"I love you too, Momma, but what happened to your hair?" Jr. tried smoothing out her frizzy ponytail.

"Ricky! That wasn't nice," Angel hissed.

Sophie cracked a smile. "It's OK. I know I'm looking rough."

"No, you not, girl. You a bad bish, even on your worst day," Angel hyped her girl up.

"What's a bish?" Jr. asked.

"Huhhhhh, let me take this little boy and get some chips or something before I have to rough *him* up." Angel pretended to be frustrated, grabbing Jr. from his mother's lap and carrying him to the vending machines to give her and Mello a little privacy.

Once Mello and Angel were alone, he reached over and grabbed her hand. Damn, he wished he could do more than just touch her hands. He missed Sophie like crazy, and she missed him just as much.

"They been treating you right?"

Angel shook her head. "No, the food is nasty. My roommate keep farting, and it smell like somebody done crawled up in her and died. Her pussy stank, they got roaches, and do I need to go on? You got to get me out of here, Kenneth. I'll end up strangling one of these hoes."

"It's coming, pretty girl. The lawyer said it's looking good. We not claiming nothing else."

"I hope so. I'm not strong enough for this. If I have to do life, I'm killing myself."

Mello's face turned sour. "Don't let me hear no weak shit like that again. Do you hear me?" He checked her as tears slid from the creases of her eyes.

"You don't understand. I know if I get life, you'll just go on about your life with the next bitch. My son gon' forget about me. My girls gon' forget about me." She got to rambling.

Mello smirked. "Would you shut up? Damn. I ain't going nowhere, and you coming home. We ain't about to put all that negative energy in the air, a'ight?"

Sophie didn't respond. She poked her lip out, tempting the hell out of Mello. He leaned in fast and pecked her lips, then sat back down. The sensation of their mouths touching lingered, causing Sophie's entire being to tingle...to growl. Fuck. She *needed* to come home.

CHAPTER THIRTY-EIGHT

"Yo' PHAT ASS always want to eat," Rock teased, noticing that Diamond was getting thicker in all the right places.

They had officially become an item before either of them knew what was happening. They did everything together, and for the first time since he could remember, Rock actually cared for a female. Diamond was his baby.

She was probably one of the finest broads he had ever had on his arm. Yeah, her face was cute, but her personality put her on the next level. She wasn't one of those scheming hoes he was used to. Her mind was elevated, and she had him doing and thinking about shit that had never previously crossed his mind. Every moment of his free time was either spent between her legs, out somewhere chilling, or building on a deeper level.

"Shut up, nigga. I must not be too fat because you stay trying to hit something," Diamond teased, swaying her hips as they waited for their food at Sloppy Chops.

Rock reached out to grab her, but she jumped out of the way with a giggle. "Movvve, boy."

"Nah, nigga. Keep fucking with me, and I'm gon' bend yo' ass over right here in front of everybody."

Diamond half-believed his crazy ass. "I bet your freaky ass would."

"You damn right. You know I don't give no fucks," Rock retorted as the cashier called out their number, announcing that their order was ready.

They grabbed their food and hopped in Rock's Camaro, speeding in and out of traffic. Diamond felt like Beyoncé, and he was her Jay-Z. They were the 2022 version of Bonnie and Clyde.

Diamond's phone ringing snapped her out of her zone. She frowned, seeing the foreign number dance across the screen. Rock looked over at her. "Answer that, my baby. Ain't no ducking calls this way."

Diamond rolled her eyes, connecting the call. "Don't nobody got to duck nothing. Hello?"

"I hope you got insurance on that shop, bitch." That was all the caller said before hanging up.

"Who was that?" Rock asked, seeing how all the color flushed from Diamond's face.

"You have to take me to the shop," she muttered just above a whisper.

"What's going on, ma?"

"I don't know. Something's wrong with the shop. If that nigga did anything to my mother's salon, I'm going to kill him."

"Calm down. Everything good. Whatever it is, I got you. I'll get you another shop."

"Another shop? It ain't another shop. That's the only thing I have left of my mother. No pictures, no nothing, just that building that I walk into every day." A tear slid down her cheek. "I don't get it. I never did anything to that man, I paid him what he asked for, and when everything is going right, he just wants to fuck with me."

"He who?" Rock frowned. "I know you not talking about that bitch nigga, Manny."

Diamond rolled her eyes. "Hell no. Him and his wife probably somewhere in Jamaica. He went back to his ho as soon as I stopped fucking with him."

"Why you sounding bitter?" Rock's jaw flexed. "You still care about that nigga?"

"I don't think I ever really loved that man. After kicking it with your ugly ass, it's safe to say Manny was just infatuation."

"Damn, ma. So, you trying to say you love a nigga?" Rock smiled.

"I think I do," she answered shyly.

"Nah, nigga. Say that shit with your chest, like all the other shit you be talking about. You love me, Diamond?"

"Do you love me?" she countered.

"I ain't asked you that. Answer my question. You love me, Diamond?"

She let out a sigh. "Yes, nigga, I do. I love that you keep me on my toes. I love how safe I feel with your ig'nant ass, and I love—"

"This dick," Rock cut her off with a smirk as he turned down Seven Mile.

Fire trucks and smoke plagued the streets. Diamond's heart instantly dropped. Carlos had set her mother's shop on fire. She was so hurt that she was numb. Diamond couldn't speak, she couldn't move, and when Rock's car pulled up to the scene with screeching tires, she couldn't even get out to talk to the fire department. It was almost as if a piece of her was burning in that fire. She cried for her mother's soul and all she had to endure without her. Diamond hated Carlos. She hated his fucking guts.

After finally getting Diamond home, calm, and in bed, Rock paced the floors with fire in his eyes. He was a natural protector, and there was no way in hell he would watch his girl be that broken and not do anything about it.

She refused to tell him who had set the shop on fire, and that pissed him off too. The girls had come to comfort Diamond, and Rock used that as his opportunity to handle things his way. Grabbing her phone off the counter and easing out of the house, he went to her call log to check the number that called her right before the chaos began. He called it, and when Carlos picked up, Rock's brows instantly creased. He knew that voice from anywhere. He'd never forget the man's voice that tortured his mother until she took her last breath. He was weak and helpless as a child. However, Rock was grown now. His revenge was going to be sweet as pie. There would be no mercy on the heartless pimp's soul. Karma was coming in the form of Rakim Jackson for all the chaos Carlos had caused countless women.

CHAPTER THIRTY-NINE

Three months later...

"MOOOOVVEE. YOU'RE GOING to make me late for my sister's court thing," Diamond whined, making a poor attempt to push him away.

Rock gripped her thighs so she couldn't move, playfully grinding into her backside. "You got a whole three hours, nigga. You feel that? Ya man trying to get nasty nasty," he teased, leaning in, sucking on her neck.

Diamond rolled her eyes. "That's all you want to do. Hump on me. That's why my belly full of baby right now. I know he tired of your little dick poking him in the forehead."

Rock chuckled. "He better take cover. I'm in that ma'fucka every chance I get." He began to lick nastily on her neck while using his hand to caress her body.

Their relationship had seemingly happened overnight. One minute, she was Manny's unofficial girl, and the next, she was Rock's whole girlfriend. It was crazy how she never fully committed to Manny, especially with as much as she thought she loved him. Yet, after less than ten months, she was pregnant with Rock's first child, and she loved the nigga more than the air she breathed. Their souls had tied so unexpectedly. She would have never guessed that crazy, foul-mouthed Rock was the yin to her yang.

"Li'l nasty. Did you check with the contractors about the shop? I know they said they could salvage what they could and rebuild it. But truthfully, I'm thinking about letting that part of my life go and moving forward. I mean, I always wanted to keep that little piece of my mother alive, but having a salon isn't even what I really want to do."

Rock stopped kissing on her. His dark eyes settled on her innocent face. "If that's the little piece you got connecting to your mother, why let it go?"

Diamond shrugged. "Because there was so much bad Karma behind that building. Carlos robbing Peter to pay Paul. I mean, trying to keep the shop alive is the reason I agreed to start robbing people. That's not me, Rakim. I'm a good person, and I just want to bring my baby into the world with a fresh start, you know?"

Rock leaned in, pecking her cheek. "I can dig it, li'l momma. Whatever you want to do. You rock, and I'm rolling. I love yo' old watermelon-head ass."

Diamond chuckled. "I love ya ugly ass too."

Time wasn't the measure of true love. You could know somebody your whole life, and a total stranger could come around and show you more love within months than you'd ever experienced in that lifetime. Rock was that stranger. Rakim Jackson was her whole heartbeat.

Angel rolled her eyes as she watched Gamble hop out of his Porsche. When he asked to meet her, she was skeptical. Things didn't necessarily end on good terms. That's why she only agreed to meet up with him in the police station's parking lot. Yet and still, she had her pistol attached to her waist. She'd blow his brains out if he tried anything crazy and wait for the police to arrest her.

He had always been a fly nigga, and the years in prison didn't change that. His dreads were freshly twisted and styled in two-strand twists, his outfit was crisp, and his body was sculpted by the heavens. The nigga was fine as fuck.

Angel knew that he hopped right back into the game after being released. You could tell...or maybe Taj had put him on. She wouldn't know either way. After running into Gamble at the party, she blocked him. A part of her wanted to fuck his cousin to get back at him. However, she had learned her lesson about walking on the wild side.

After eyeing her surroundings, Angel finally stepped out of the car to face Gamble. She knew the man well and knew that if he really wanted to kill her, she'd be dead already. She folded her hands over her chest, trying her best to ignore all the years of buried hatred and pain he had caused.

Angel thought that his prison sentence was enough to heal her wounds. However, she was now seeing that it was just a Band-Aid. He scared her. Gamble was the reason she was so coldhearted and vindictive.

"Damn, Angie Ang, I see you still as fine as I remember you." He licked his lips. "Maybe even finer."

Angel rolled her eyes. "Cut the shit, nigga. What do you want?" She pulled out her cell phone. It was just after ten, and she had to make it to the courthouse for Sophie in an hour and fifteen minutes. "If you trying to kill me, let the first bullet win."

Gamble chuckled. "With yo' tough ass? Ain't nobody trying to kill you. If so, you would have been dead a long time ago. Stop acting like I ain't always had killers that were down for whatever on my team."

Angel shifted her weight to one leg. She looked off, biting the inside of her jaw. "Why my momma, LaDarrius? Out of all the bitches giving away free pussy, why you have to choose my mother? We was supposed to be better than that." Angel couldn't believe she was still hurting. She didn't want to.

"Shit happens; then life goes on. I fucked yo' momma, and you set me up. I guess it's part of the game. Now, how we gon' move forward?"

"Move forward?" Angel's nose wrinkled. "Ain't no moving forward between us. We both got our Karma. We both can put this—"

"Put what where? I might not be ready to blow yo' head off, but we got work to do, baby girl."

Angel frowned. He was still the arrogant, nonchalant asshole. "I'm not the same person I was ten years ago. You not about to manipulate me. That love I once had for you is dead."

"You a lie. That's why you ain't had a nigga since me."

"Negro, please! I haven't had a nigga because I don't need one. Besides, how would you know what I been doing with my pussy?"

Gamble smirked. "I know everything."

"If you know everything, how you ain't know you had a son?"

Gamble looked off. "Yeah, that's fucked up. Yo, bird didn't even tell me about li'l man." His voice trailed off, and Angel could finally see a little piece of emotion. "Man, that was fucked up. I was young and dumb, thinking I was doing something hitting the momma and the daughter. My bad."

Angel rolled her eyes dramatically. "Just your 'bad,' huh? Nigga, please. Why are we here? What do you want?"

"I know you and your homegirls been on some get-money shit. So why beef when we can get back to this paper? We family now. I got a job for you."

Angel shook her head, knowing her girls weren't going for that. They had suffered enough damage. Sophie almost lost her son and her life. She was fighting an entire murder charge. Diamond was finally free and in love with a baby on the way.

"Nope. We good. I don't know what you're talking about."

"Yes, you do." Gamble ran his hand through his beard. "It's a lot of money involved for y'all. You got my number. I need an answer in five days."

Angel watched as Gamble's colossal frame turned, making his way back to his Porsche. Her mouth was salivating at the mention of money. How could she convince the girls to go on one last lick?

She looked at the time on the screen of her cell. Shit! She had to get going for Sophie's trial.

Sophie's eyes traveled back to her son, contently sitting in the stands behind her. He was oblivious to what was going on, and her heart broke. What if the judge sentenced her to life in prison? What would her baby do without her?

The courtroom was packed, and anticipation was at an all-time high. She was finally about to receive the verdict for the murder of Gerome Robinson, a "beloved cop that served the streets of Detroit..." At least, that was the picture the prosecutors were trying to portray before her lawyer revealed the real nitty-gritty. They had a field day with her case. Some of the things she heard were simply ludicrous...and some were true. Her case had even been featured on CNN News. The scandal of the dirty cop and the single mother kidnapped at his hands was in the headlines everywhere.

"Hi, Mommy!" Ricky Jr. shouted, excitedly waving to her. Damn, it was hard. The nightmare started precisely three months ago. She'd been locked in a dirty prison cell for eighty-three days, away from her son, her girls, and her man.

Of course, Mello had gotten her the best lawyer that money could buy. Fargo had fought tooth and nail. He found every loophole, every mistake, and every flaw. She just hoped it was enough to send her home in self-defense. The accounts of her gruesome, short-lived abduction garnered the sympathy of America. They had pictures of the bruises and cuts, a detailed description of her three days with the monster, and a beautiful, teary-eyed single mother with no prior record telling the story. She was the victim. At least, that was the picture that was painted.

Sophie blew her baby a kiss, offering him a quick smile before turning back to the judge. He wore an indifferent look on his face. He was a middle-aged African American with salt-and-pepper hair. During the entire trial, he was hot and cold. He kept his game face on, and the fact that Sophie didn't know where he stood scared her.

"Jury, have we reached a verdict?" The judge looked at the jurors, causing the beat of Sophie's heart to go into overdrive.

Small chatter erupted in the courtroom. Sophie ignored the whispers, closing her eyes and mouthing a silent prayer. Surprisingly, she had done a lot of that since the federal agents kicked down her doors three months ago.

The head juror stood. She was a frail, gray-haired lady with a cheap black ruffled dress. She cleared her throat before speaking. "Your Honor, we have." Sophie's entire body went numb. "We, the jury, find the defendant Sophie Daniels *not guilty* of first-degree murder."

Tears instantly slid down Sophie's face. She was finally free— no more nights without her son and her man. No more having to deal with the different attitudes and rules and regulations that came with prison. Sophie didn't hear the eruption of cheers and sighs. Her hands cuffed her mouth, and she sobbed deeply rooted tears of joy and relief.

"Congratulations, kiddo. You're going home," Fargo said, rubbing her back. Sophie leaned in and hugged him so tight that he felt his circulation would be cut off. He chuckled. "Dammit, Ms. Daniels, you better let me go. I'm not trying to have your husband kill me. Then who's going to defend him?"

Sophie smiled genuinely for the first time in months as she released her attorney. "You're right. Nobody has time for crazy-ass Kenneth Davis. Thank you, Mr. Fargo. I really appreciate you."

"Anytime. It's my job. I just pray we don't have to cross paths under these circumstances again. Be safe, Sophie. You're a smart girl. Get Kenny and your son and go live," he advised, placing files into his briefcase and closing it.

"Mommmyy," Ricky Jr. came running to her as soon as she turned around. Sophie scooped him up into a big bear hug. She missed her baby like crazy. Her heart went out to him. It was almost as if he had lost two parents simultaneously. She couldn't believe Ricardo would abandon their child when she needed him most. Forget their differences. Her son needed a father. Sophie was so thankful for her girls. Diamond and Angel had really come through. Then there was Mello. The man was heaven-sent. He was the true definition of ten toes down.

After having her moment with her son, Sophie placed him back on his feet. Her gaze settled on Mello. She slowly sauntered over to him, letting out a shriek when he lifted her from her feet and spun her around. His arms felt like home, and his lips pressed passionately against hers, which tingled every sensor inside her body.

"Damn, I missed you," Mello whispered into her mouth.

"I missed you too, daddy. I love you, Kenneth Davis." She pecked his lips again. It was almost as if they were the only ones in the room. Time had stood still.

"I love you too, Sophie Davis," he declared, giving her his last name instead of hers.

She smiled. "That's not my name, homeboy."

"It can be if you want it to be," he countered. However, she never got a chance to respond. Her homegirls bum-rushed her, tearing her away from Mello's embrace.

"Uh-uh. Just like an old dick-whipped wanch. You just said fuck your homegirls, huh? The bitches that held you down since training bras and K Swiss?" Angel teased, wrapping her arms around her sister. Diamond joined in too.

All three ladies burst into tears. They had gone through so much together. Their friendship had been put to the ultimate test and had proven to be Ford tough...unbreakable!

"I'm so fucking glad you're home, girl," Diamond sniveled.

"I'm happy to be coming home. I love y'all bald-headed whores."

"We love you too. Time to get back to the *moneyyy*," Angel teased.

Sophie looked around in panic before shaking her head. "Oh, hell no, it ain't. I retired. I'm an honest woman. I read my Bible. Oh no, no."

The trio burst into laughter. "I know that's right. This ho tripping." Diamond chuckled, rubbing her protruding belly.

Angel placed her hands on her hip. "Scary heffas. I was just teasing anyway. I love you bitches. Y'all my sisters for life. Now, let's put this behind us and live it up."

Diamond and Sophie agreed to that. "Sisters for life," they chirped in unison, embracing again.

Too bad no one ever noticed the man sitting in the back of the courtroom with a pair of Gucci shades covering his brown eyes. He had been to every court date since the trial began. He watched Diamond close her shop every other night, and Angel drive Ricky Jr. to school every morning. He had even witnessed Mello's big retirement from the streets and rise into the legal world. His clubs were making motion and he'd acquired a decent amount of real estate. It wasn't over. Just when the crew got good and comfortable...He was going to shake up a few tables.

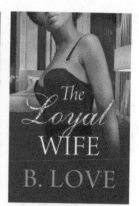

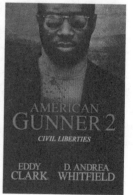